BLACK
GIRLS
MUST
HAVE IT
ALL

ALSO BY JAYNE ALLEN

Black Girls Must Die Exhausted
Black Girls Must Be Magic

BLACK
GIRLS
MUST
HAVE IT
ALL

A Novel

JAYNE ALLEN

HARPER PERENNIAL

NEW YORK • LONDON • TORONTO • SYDNEY • NEW DELHI • AUCKLAND

HARPER ● PERENNIAL

BLACK GIRLS MUST HAVE IT ALL. Copyright © 2023 by Jaunique
Sealey. All rights reserved. Printed in the United States of America.
No part of this book may be used or reproduced in any manner
whatsoever without written permission except in the case of brief
quotations embodied in critical articles and reviews. For information, address HarperCollins Publishers, 195 Broadway, New York,
NY 10007.

HarperCollins books may be purchased for educational, business,
or sales promotional use. For information, please email the Special
Markets Department at SPsales@harpercollins.com.

FIRST EDITION

Designed by Jamie Lynn Kerner

Library of Congress Cataloging-in-Publication Data has been
applied for.

ISBN 978-0-06-313794-3 (pbk.)

23 24 25 26 27 LBC 5 4 3 2 1

For our mothers.
For my mother.
For you.
For me.

PROLOGUE

I LOVE YOU. I LOVE YOU SO SO MUCH. A BROWN CHERUBIC FACE stares back at me with intense curiosity. Dark glistening eyes are fixed upon me with fascination, as if I hold the secrets to the entire world. I love these moments. I adore them, breathe for them. The skin crinkles a bit at the outer corners where her eyelids and whispery lashes meet, and then my baby opens her mouth with a fleeting gummy smile. I stroke the apple of her silky-smooth cheek and she does it again.

When my daughter, Evie, was born, only twenty-two days ago, my mother promised to stay three weeks. Yesterday she left. And today is my first day alone. A little petrified, I retreat to the immaculately set up nursery. I sit quietly in the soft, comfortable chair, perfect for moments like these, to hold her close, wrapped like a squirming football in my arms. The peace and stillness make it easy to just be present, to forget—especially the things I'd rather not remember. Mistakes I'll pay for, but not yet, not today.

Shortly after her birth, in the middle of the night, embraced by the cushions of this same chair for a feeding,

I silently promised my daughter I'd tell her the truth about life's biggest secrets. The realities I'd found hidden between the lines of what everyone said was true. What I learned from my mistakes. *I love you* is my greatest truth to her now. But there is much more that I'll have to say.

1

THREE SHORT WEEKS AND TWO DAYS AGO, I STARTED A NEW JOB
with absolutely no experience. The job of motherhood. Someone should fire me—I've already made a mess of it. I often
call it a hot gloppy mess, both figuratively and literally, for
me to clean up. Although the irony is, as I understand it, I
can't get fired. I'll have this job for life. Strangely enough, it
does not pay well, but the benefits are enormous. Good thing
I have paying employment. I *can* actually get fired from that
position, and I just might be. I made a mess there too. Unfor-
tunately, that cleanup is not as easy as dealing with a bunch
of soiled diapers, or even this Rorschach blot of baby barf
on the third shirt I've changed into since sunrise. A sunrise
I was awake to witness, by the way, as happens often when
there's no chance to sleep.

It's important to know that this job as a mother was one
that I very much wanted. *Very much*. Possibly too much. I'm
very good at wanting things—and then I go after them as if
there aren't any consequences. It's not that I'm not afraid—
it's just that when I really want something, my desire wins
out. Maybe someone else would call it ambition. But raw

ambition runs over some people, ruins things for others. I only ruin things for myself.

With my new job, it's hard to ruin things, because it's the same thing every day. Evie has her schedule—eat, play, cry, sleep—every three hours. It just repeats. And my schedule has become: feed, entertain, panic, scramble to pump, clean, do laundry, and maybe eat or bathe (but not both) while the baby is sleeping. As soon as she's hungry, it starts all over again.

Like right now, I'm in the comfy chair in the lilac-colored nursery listening to the airy *pfwhoosh pfwhoosh* of the breast pump rhythmically coaxing a trickle of milk from my mammaries. I do this for twenty minutes, even though I'm not very good at it, or even that successful. I am a terrible cow. As it turns out, my breasts don't really like to produce large quantities of milk, even after supplements and water, and prayer. It just hasn't been working for me. But I pump anyway, because whatever little bit I can manage is evidently good.

"You don't have to be good at everything," I whisper to sleeping Evie. "Just be good at the things that matter most." I'm sure she'll need that advice just as much as I do. When she wakes up, she will have a bottle of formula waiting for her, at just the right temperature, in the perfect number of ounces. Thankfully, these days, they make machines for that—kind of like the coffee maker at work.

Tabitha Evelyn Walker Brown, my new boss. I call her "Ladybug" sometimes, "Cutie," "Cuddles," or "Baby Love," but mostly Evie. Like E-V. Evie is the name we decided to put on the wall of her nursery, floating cursive on top of a big rectangle of faux peonies and soft pink roses. When I was a little girl, I had a pink room and hated it. I promised I would never, but an accent color isn't terrible. Plus, she'll never know.

In about an hour, my new boss will scream for me, like bloody murder. It will be so loud, I'll think the neighbors will hear and call the authorities. But it's just her way of saying, *Hello, I'm hungry.* If I could imagine a job description, I think it would be: *Loveable but demanding boss seeks food source, comfort, and a human cushion (with ample neck cuddle space), for long-term employment. Please note, punctuality is a plus. Employer expects needs to be anticipated. Working from home is not only preferred, but required.*

Right now, Evie's whole life, and consequently mine too, is set to the pace of hunger. Hunger is easy to satisfy. My other job, my paid employment, is governed by ratings—making sure complete strangers like me so much they tune in to watch every day. That's been a challenge. Until recently, my main focus and title was Tabitha Abigail Walker, weekend news anchor at Los Angeles–based KVTV news. Around this same time in the morning, I'd be walking into the KVTV office, through the glass doors, composed and pristine, ready to do battle. I'd be dressed immaculately, caramel skin glowing, hair flowing, and more recently, curls poppin' in my twist-out. I wanted to succeed at KVTV, and I did—but not without sacrifices. Some of them big. Still, in a short time, I had won an Emmy and been promoted twice to my current position as weekend anchor.

My journey has been one of upward movement. A career with some amount of ambition and an increasing amount of risk. I've been taking big swings lately, playing it a little fast and loose with the rules. It hasn't been whimsical though.

It's been back-against-the wall calculations. If you really want to move forward in battle, sometimes you have to burn the ships. Well, when I went on maternity leave, all the ships were ablaze and the port too. One big tanker fire set in the office of my boss—Chris Perkins, KVTV's news director. In two months, what will I return to? I have no idea, but all I know is there's no turning back. "It's okay to burn the ships, Ladybug," I whisper to Evie. "But make sure you take the map with you."

Can I say I love what I do? Maybe I do love it. It's the career I chose and built, and I need it. Well, I need to have a job, a generously paying one. But this is the work that fulfills me. It's my responsibility to see and make seen and heard the voices and stories that are often forgotten in my city of Los Angeles. I know all too well what it's like to be left behind.

My work is my freedom, my mortgage payment, my backup plan, and my "yes" to the happy hours I used to go to with my best friends, Alexis and Laila. It is Evie's diapers and that expensive-assed formula I have to buy because as it turns out, again, I am not a very good cow. Even so, I *am* determined to be an excellent mother. And just maybe, if I can manage it, I'd really *really* like to be happy—not my mother's kind of happy, or my grandmother's even. What I want is life's very best.

My career is all the more important because I'm not just a mother—I'm also a single mother. Well, maybe *not exactly single*.

Just about two and a half years ago, I was told that if I didn't do something quick, I'd lose the chance to have biological children. As an only child, that was something I'd always wanted. But I didn't have much time, and that means desperation, realizing this dream by any means necessary. I'd run out of options, all but one.

My sweet Evie, she's so precious, I'd love to take full credit. But while I may be a single mother, I am by no means a solo parent. That's where Evie's father, Marc, comes in. He'll be over later, part of the parenting evening shift. Our schedule is well defined—it's just our relationship that isn't. After the devastation of my infertility diagnosis, Marc and I were on the verge of ending things. We wouldn't even be here without my hasty decision-making, and Evie wouldn't be here either if I hadn't been willing to break the rules. But now is not the time to dwell on mistakes, or regrets. Pumping is done. And it's time to make formula. In less than an hour, Evie will be awake and hungry. As I've learned, the sooner the bottle touches her lips, the better—for both of us.

Can you have it all? I thought about it at the kitchen sink while washing pump parts, bottles, and the backup supply of pacifiers. While on maternity leave, there was no way to know what would become of the other parts of my life. When I'd left KVTV, I'd angered Chris with a rogue interview conducted by my friend Lisa Sinclair, our primetime anchor. I'd been dealing with viewer complaints about my natural hair, which I supposed they either weren't used to seeing, or didn't like, or both. But it wasn't my job to hide. My job was to see and also to be seen. To be authentic was crucial.

After a women's issues meeting where I voiced my concerns, Lisa decided that we'd do an interview during her anchor block that evening. I was appreciative of the support, and thought it was what needed to be done.

"In my office," was all that Chris had to say when the broadcast was over.

Lisa and I sat in uncomfortable under-stuffed chairs facing his desk. I was too pregnant to fight. Lisa fought on my behalf. But if I hadn't done it, if I hadn't stood up for myself, who would have? I can't go back into KVTV hiding behind that same old mask. And now my most important viewer will be Evie.

"It isn't all about ratings, Chris," Lisa had said.

"It is to me," Chris replied.

And that was the last thing I heard before I was out the door. The next time I step foot through the KVTV entrance, I'll have been away for three months, like taking a season break in a championship game. I have no idea what I'll be returning to, or even who the players will be.

At least while I'm on maternity leave, things have been predictable and my circle is small. Just a few close friends and family who are all in my corner, like Alexis. Alexis was there on the night of Evie's birth, and a much-appreciated presence these first weeks of her life, especially since I wasn't totally prepared. Not only was the baby born early, but she made her way into the world in a spectacular show that no one would forget, especially not me. And how could I?

My water broke on the dance floor of Alexis and Rob's vows renewal while the spotlight still shone on them from the thank-you speeches. The sudden commotion of my best friends scrambling around in heels and fancy dresses, and Alexis leaving her own party to come with me to the hospital had been no part of my carefully laid birth plans. Evie came so early and with such insistence that we had to head straight for the nearest hospital with a small army in tow.

In the heat of the moment, everything changed. In the delivery room, I screamed for an epidural, even though I never planned for one. And it turned out to be too late in the progress of my labor to have it. Andouele, my doula, held my hand and gave me reassurances that I struggled to believe. "You're stronger than you think," she spoke to me above the shrillness of my own voice.

Somehow, the pain isn't what I remember most. It's the exact second they put Evie on my chest, and I could see her face. My own little Ladybug. Right then, time stopped for me and there was only silence. The room became so still I could hear my breath. Evie opened her eyes and looked up at me for the very first time and I was instantly locked in love. Still, as a new parent, I had a lot to learn, too much. By the end of the first week at home, I found myself barely holding on to sanity.

Nobody tells you this, but as a mother, the sound of my own baby crying is like a primal trigger tuned precisely to my ears. Strangely, it doesn't seem to affect anyone else the same way, not even Marc. Perhaps to others it's a familiar sound, maybe not so different from a dog barking. But to a new mother, that cry from my child? It's nothing less than a wailing siren that activates every cell in my body, dragging my psyche to the brink. Nothing can get in the way of stopping that cry. Nothing. And maybe this is where it starts, the slippery slope of forgetting about your own needs. Maybe it's biological programming.

TODAY, AT ONLY 9:50 IN THE MORNING, A FULL TEN MINUTES early, the crying started again. "Ssshh, it's okay, Sweetpea," I offered, swooping Evie into my arms and swaying her with calm gestures. Thankfully the bottle would be ready quickly and we could return to some semblance of peace. Feeding time came, and I couldn't wait for Alexis to arrive with reinforcements.

An hour and two spit-ups later, finally, she texted her arrival.

At the front door.

I'd been "reading" a book to Evie, *Guess How Much I Love You*, with her little fingers fidgeting toward her face as we flipped through the pages.

It was only as I headed to the front door that I'd given any thought to what I looked like for the day. It couldn't have been good—over a week since I'd styled my hair, and I hadn't yet changed from the latest round of post-feeding dribble stains. There weren't many people I'd let witness me like this.

If only the KVTV audience could see me now, I thought as I pulled the door open.

Alexis Carter looked amazing, as always. She filled out her tailored slacks in a way that only "Sexy Lexi" could, with a flowing blouse and a fresh silk press accentuating her still girlish features. She gestured to me to ask if the baby was sleeping.

"Girl, not yet," I said aloud, opening the door wider and ushering Lexi inside my living room. "We just did a feeding. And I'm starting to think the movie *Poltergeist* was inspired by a newborn." I was only half joking and suddenly self-conscious of the dried baby goo that accessorized my hair and clothes.

Alexis gave me a knowing look. "Girl," she laughingly called out in a cascade of clinking bracelets and heel clacks as she entered my living room. "Be glad you don't have a sprinkler fountain like when we had Rob junior. That extra shower during diaper changes will make you reconsider your entire life!"

I smiled from the memory. The first time Rob junior peed on her, Lexi called me in shock. Now, with a baby of my own, there were much greater traumas to share. "The diaper blowouts, though!" I said through laughter. "Lex, where does it all come from? And with such force?" My arms held the tiny culprit, who squirmed a bit against me, seeming to smile briefly. "Like a little human torpedo. I'm sure you find this hilarious." I tried to give her a serious look.

Alexis laughed again. "Tab, I have to say—it kinda is!" She smiled widely, wending her way toward the kitchen holding the handles of two paper bags stuffed to the brim with food containers. I closed the front door behind her, imagining what a disaster I must have looked like. Disheveled—in dirty, baggy sweats, my face a pimply mess of dark circles and bloodshot eyes—I headed to join Alexis in the kitchen. She was already unloading the stockpile of food that I couldn't dissuade her from bringing.

"Lex!" I said as I walked into the kitchen, "I told you that you didn't have to do meal delivery. I can—"

Alexis shot me a look that stopped me midsentence. Unloading the delicious-smelling food onto my kitchen island, she raised an eyebrow at me. "Mmmm??" she said.

When Alexis told me that she'd help fill in once my mother left, I had no idea that she'd be bringing over an entire restaurant buffet. My mother arrived the day after Evie's birth, on the first commercial flight she could get to Los Angeles from the DC area. And for three weeks, together with

Marc on evening duty, we braved the whirlwind. Finally satisfied that Evie and I would survive without her, she headed back home. I thought I had it under control. Clearly, I was wrong.

"Well . . . maybe I can't," I admitted. "It's only day two alone. I tried to make toast this morning and thought I ran out of butter . . . until an hour later I found the stick from yesterday in the utility drawer when I was looking for a pair of scissors." I shook my head as Alexis chuckled.

"Girl, there is no way you're going to be able to do this on your own. Even as much as you want to. Tabitha Walker, you've been my best friend since forever and you're the same overachiever you've always been. I *know* you. But this time, believe me, you're in over your head." Alexis crossed the kitchen to put her arm around me. When she pulled back, she earnestly looked me up and down. "You look like you could use some sleep . . . and a shower. When's the last time you took one?"

Even with my best friend, I felt self-conscious. "Oh, that's ridiculous," I said, attempting to mount a quick defense. "I just took a shower . . ." But I couldn't remember. "Yesterday? Or, maybe it was the day before," I said weakly.

Alexis didn't react. Instead, she looked down at my arms holding a groggy Evie. "Look at this precious," Alexis cooed at Evie, reaching for her. "Come to your auntie Lex," she said in a soft baby speak, gently scooping my squirming baby into a football. "Yesss," she cooed again. "Isn't it almost nap time?" She looked up at me.

I stood there, suspended, holding my breath, waiting for "the cry." But it didn't come. I shook my head. *Yes.* It would

be nap time soon, assuming full cooperation from my unpre-
dictable infant.

"Go," Alexis said. "GO!" With her free arm, she waved
me in the direction of my bathroom, pointing in the way that
only a mother can. Soon enough, I'd learn how to point that
way, and people would obey me too.

I willed my feet to move down the hallway in the direction of my bath.

AS THE WATER WASHED OVER ME, EXHAUSTED AND OPERATING
on sleep-deprived fumes, I remembered the miracle this
whole situation was. Just a short time ago, I thought this part
of my life would never be a reality. Back then, my idea of a
checklist was something like the life I had now—a child, a
partner, friends, family, and a career I could be proud of. But
just when you think you have it all figured out, things change.

So I had to reevaluate anew what I wanted my life to look
like. What is there to want when you're too overwhelmed to
think of anything other than a hot shower and just a few mins
of REM sleep? If I made a new checklist, it would have re-
volved around number of diapers changed (infinite), stained
shirts, loads of laundry, hours of sleep (none), and tears cried,
both Evie's and my own, just from frustration. Frustration
born of love and fear and complete confusion, understanding
that for the first time in my life, I had absolutely no idea what
I was doing.

2

GOOGLE, CAN YOU DIE FROM LACK OF SLEEP?

Ridiculous, of course, but maybe not? As a new mother, at least three times a day, usually more frequently, I found myself typing a combination of words I would never have imagined before into a search bar.

"Projectile vomit newborn."

"Is my baby possessed?"

"Best way to get poop out of your hair."

"Swaddles for sleeping."

"Are newborns supposed to snore?"

Websites and message boards had become the cobbled-together survivalist handbook that I never knew I needed. Deep down, it was absurd, sure, but I searched every manner of notion from the gradations of color of baby poop (who knew it came in green?), to coughing, signs of fever, burps, gas, and how to breastfeed, just to be certain. So many things about the baby the doctor wasn't concerned about. But for me, it was as if someone had dropped a tiny alien into my care—a tiny alien that I loved more than anything I'd ever loved in my entire life.

This was one of the first times it had even occurred to me to be concerned about myself. As it turned out, the day's investigation yielded no evidence that you could die of lack of sleep exactly, but the number of articles on the topic showed that I was far from the first or only person who needed to know.

We spent a lot of time together, Evie and me. With my rapidly dwindling maternity leave, I knew it was special. These were the moments to hold on to, to try my best to remember, and that would be gone far too soon.

Midday in the nursery, just a few days before the four-week benchmark, I started to feel a hint of comfort that I definitely thought impossible at the start. The idea began to bubble that keeping a tiny human alive was within my abilities. In our familiar position, peering into the deep brown of my daughter's bright eyes, the same rich mahogany pools as her father's, I gently touched her cheeks as she looked up at me, my little way of trying to make her smile. This quiet moment, feeling the weight of her in my arms and the calming warmth of her presence, ignited a love so deep within me it could have consumed me completely. Her tiny hands, which I'd learned to cover with drawstring cotton mittens from HotOhioMom225 on my message board, brushed against me as the toothless grin finally emerged. I still believed it was something more than just a reflex. I genuinely believed I could make her happy. And I knew that no matter what, I would always try.

Of course, the perfectly logical type-A new mother extension of this was that all of her life could possibly boil down to any one decision I would make.

Small but consequential decisions had become a constant of my life. And somehow, the smaller the decision, the bigger the stakes seemed to feel. If turning thirty was the start of "everything matters," then motherhood had become the moment of "every decision counts." Decisions like how long I should try to give her breast milk, should she wear only organic cotton, or does it matter what preservatives are in her baby shampoo. These made up the river of constant crises that had invaded my everyday life.

But my life with Evie was not just my own. I wasn't the only parent, or the only decision-maker. As big as the day-to-day choices felt, they were just distractions from the inevitable. While I wanted to continue pretending it wasn't real, there was one question, one decision that outweighed the others. That decision had a name, and a social security number. And at times, like his daughter, he had his own way of taking my breath away and causing sleepless nights: Marc Brown.

Marc was my paper-perfect Prince Charming. Could he make me swoon effortlessly? No question. He had leading-man energy for every type of imagined happy ending. His skin was flawless, a deep brown with a silky, poreless complexion—the perfect backdrop for the dark, thick hair of his neatly shaped eyebrows, his long lashes, and his full, rich beard that was immaculately trimmed and just starting to show a speckling of gray hairs. You could see overwhelming intelligence in his eyes and hear it in the words that came out of his mouth through perfect teeth and full, pillowy lips. You could even smell it on him—in sandalwood, sweet spice, and warm citrus like bergamot, so subtle but lingering just long enough that you knew he'd been there. Oh yes, you'd definitely know. This is what got me every time with Marc, his attention to detail, his knowledge of just the right thing to say or do to excite my mind and, too often, my body.

And if everything had stayed perfect and uncomplicated, like I'd planned it, Marc and I could have remained in orbit, perhaps forever. Only, over the years, my idea of a happy ending started to change. One day, without meaning to, I developed the notion that maybe I didn't need saving. That maybe, in the most important ways, I could save myself. Marc moved from main character to a supporting role in my ever-evolving fairy tale. I no longer needed him to be happy.

That Marc became Evie's father was my best and favorite mistake. It brought us together in ways that neither of us expected. All of a sudden, we were family. Not by choice, but by circumstance. In another few hours, I could only hope, like most days, he'd be here to spend time with our daughter, trying to catch one of her brief periods of pleasant wakefulness before she went down for another slumber.

Once upon a time, my version of a perfect life was being a wife and mother, a version to which Marc originally said no. *I love you*, he told me once, *but I don't know that I'm in love with you . . . I don't know that I can be.* He said that he wasn't sure he could be in love with anyone. That's not something you forget. Not easily. Maybe not ever.

My mother blamed my career for the slow pace of my relationship. She told me, *If you put less focus on your career for a second and more focus on him*, that Marc would have been more inclined to make more of a commitment. But he wasn't.

When I told him about my fertility struggles about a year into our relationship, he told me, *We're still getting to know each other.* When he said he wasn't ready for that big a commitment. I was devastated.

So I went about things on my own. I went to a fertility doctor, found a sperm donor, and went through IVF. Only fate had its own design. What happened was such a freak occurrence, we couldn't have planned it if we wanted to. I thought I was already pregnant, and that I'd done it on my own. But he had that way about him, that magnetism. I couldn't stay away. Maybe it's my same way of holding on to things. Things I should have let go. I thought it was safe to get that close. But with Marc, it's never safe. That spark, it causes fire. And with him, I wasn't ready to burn the ships. I no longer knew where I wanted us to go.

When he became a father, it was almost like the lights came on for him. All of a sudden he wanted to become a husband, even though he was once adamant that marriage wasn't what he envisioned for himself and didn't know if it would ever be. But, a *leopard doesn't change his spots*, my mother always says. Circumstances shift, and people may adjust, but do they ever change? And if they do, can you trust it?

I never imagined I would say no to the idea of a proposal, but I knew all too well what could happen when you don't get it right. *And yet, here we are.* Our relationship became something different than before. Because I became different. And Marc promised me that he'd support that, that we'd figure it out together. But in the silences, even though he never brought it up, I knew he expected me to change my mind.

Once Evie came, my romantic relationship to Marc might still have been undefined, but we were absolutely clear when it came to her. We were teammates by necessity. Allies in a cautious truce to survive the gauntlet of life as new parents. My home was the nest, and Marc would come over to steal what time he could. He was already back to work after his flimsy two-week paternity leave ended.

He could have taken more time off, but he was up for partner at his firm, so he planned instead to take more time off when Evie was a little older. My house, my food, my maternity leave and natural bonding time—without the conventions of a defined role, I could see that it was hard for Marc to find a place to feel necessary.

Still, it spurred the sweetest stirring in my soul to watch him hold Evie, to see him fumble with her diaper, to know that in the middle of the night he'd nestle with her, reading a book and holding her bottle. Could I have done it on my own? Of course. But in these times, Marc made me feel fortunate that I didn't have to.

But our happy fantasy has been just that. Things with Marc have only been working in a fragile equilibrium. An illusion, as temporary as the rainbow reflection on a soap bubble. As beautiful and perfect as it looks, you just know that at some point it's going to pop.

The ping of my phone in my pocket was an unexpected interruption. I fumbled in a rush to silence it, wondering if he was early, why Marc would message me rather than just use his key. Instead, as I pulled the phone into focus, Lisa Sinclair's name was illuminated on the screen along with a short text.

> Sorry to bother, but need to speak with you. Call me back as soon as you can.

It was a strange message from Lisa, concerning even. She would never interrupt me casually during my maternity

leave. It had to be something important. But as I went to reply, the baby in my arms created bigger and more immediate
concerns.

Evie was starting to get fussy, and the sound of the phone
message notification startled her right into a shrill shrieking
cry, my panic button. It wasn't until I'd completed my 177th
lap across the burnished wooden planks of the living room
floor, shushing and soothing, that I heard the turn of Marc's
key in the door and his attempt at a quiet entry. Relief flooded
my body at the sight of his face, and I wasn't sure if it was just
the company of another person who could hold their head
above their shoulders and speak in sounds other than crying,
or if I was just simply glad to see him.

He did handsome so well, and today was no exception.
He dressed in a casual button-down, dark fitted jeans, and
expensive understated sneakers. And that smell was there,
intoxicating as it always was.

"Is she sleeping already?" he called out in a rough whisper. I hated that I wanted her to be. I needed a break from a
long day.

"I wish," I said, heading in his direction, his arms outstretched to greet us.

"I had just these few minutes between meetings and I
was hoping to catch her awake," Marc said softly. "Look at
those eyes." Marc became lost in the cooing and admiration
of his daughter as he lifted her out of my arms and folded her
into the cradle of his own. He stood there just briefly. "I think
I can get her down for a nap," he said. "Bedroom or nursery?"

"Bedroom," I replied. I needed a nap myself. The bedroom bassinet would allow me to sleep along with her.

Marc nodded before turning to head in the direction of the hallway.

This was how we operated, taking turns, flowing, orbiting. I always thought it was working for the both of us.

After a few minutes, I found my way to the back of the house, into the bedroom where Marc was standing over Evie's bassinet. He turned to me quickly with his finger over his lips.

"She's sleeping?" I mouthed to him. He nodded. And turned to usher us out of the room. I had to resist the urge to see for myself.

Back in the living room, Marc held me by my elbow and turned me gently to him. His stare was intense as he searched my eyes.

"Tab, there's something that's been on my mind. Something I wanted to talk about."

"Marc, please don't tell me that—" I didn't want to go there, but he cut me off. Somehow, I knew it was going to happen anyway. It was only a matter of time.

"It has to do with me . . . and you . . . and Evie. I don't know how much longer I can do this like this—I always feel like I'm stealing time. Like everything is passing me by and I'm just a spectator. I should be doing more, and if I was here, like really here, I could be."

This wasn't at all what I wanted, or expected, to hear. It was a threat to the delicate balance we'd achieved. "Marc, you are here." I tried my best to reassure him. "You're here all the time. I'm not complaining at all." I didn't see any effect of those words register on his face.

"No, see, Tab, that's not it." His whisper was intense, full of the tension of frustration. I could hear it in his voice. "You're not complaining because we're doing *everything* just the way *you* wanted to. But, it's not . . . it's not working for me this way, Tab. Two places, two lives. We should be a stable family, together. This . . . this doesn't even make sense." He was pacing now, tracing the same circle around the living room I had.

"But, Marc, I thought we'd agreed that we'd do this . . ." Marc had no patience for this reminder.

"You agreed, Tabby, but . . ." He turned to face me and gently placed both hands on my arms. I felt my face flush. "Sometimes plans need to change."

"What does that mean?" My chest felt tighter. The room, hotter. But I knew the temperature was the same. It was panic. The heat I felt was within. The heat you feel when things are starting to burn, when options start to disappear. The flicker of ships aflame flashed briefly in my mind.

"It means that . . . Tabby, we need to think about growing together. About making moves *together*. I'm not asking you today. I don't need a decision right this second, but I want you to think about it."

"Think about what?" There was no hiding the concern in my voice. It was silly delay. I knew what he was asking. We were going to have to choose a path forward—together, or apart.

"Think about getting married." *Oh no. He said it.* "I know you're not ready and you feel like you haven't decided, but I'm going to ask you. I'm going to ask you to marry me, because I know it's the right thing to do. I'm not going to pressure you. I'm not going to ask again. But I need to know that at least I tried."

Shit. This was the record skip. I could feel my eyes widening as my pulse quickened and my breathing picked up. Was I panicking? Yes. The prior three and a half weeks had been such a blur, eventful but uneventful at the same time, and yet, today was the day of no return.

"Marc . . . I . . . I . . ." I couldn't find words to force out. The thing I would have wanted to hear so badly, so earnestly, just a couple of years ago now sounded more like a threat. It was everything I didn't need and nothing I wanted to confront.

"Tabby, there's nothing to say now. Just think about it, okay? That's all I'm asking. I've got to get to work." Marc moved himself past me toward the door. "I'll be back before bedtime."

Even though he let himself out, I followed behind him until he carefully, quietly closed the front door. I turned to lean against it to catch my breath.

I don't remember leaving the door or walking past the kitchen to flop in the chair in the family room or dozing off in front of the television. Once you're past the point of exhaustion, there's very little difference between being asleep and awake. And for this reason, I was able to pretend, even if for a moment, that the entire day had been a dream. Just a dream that wasn't forcing difficult decisions or asking impossible questions. Hadn't Marc just threatened me with a marriage proposal? What would happen if I said no? And what would happen if I said yes?

Once I'd let go of convention, thinking it wasn't an option for me, a whole other world of possibilities had started to open up. A new idea of happiness began to form. But it was fragile, a door held open by thin strings. Wanting is a lot easier when what you want is what you're supposed to.

When it came to the life I'd be creating for Evie, going off script with zeal and blind enthusiasm just wasn't as appealing. For this there was no playbook or search term. Without knowing for sure who I was supposed to be, how was I supposed to know who I wanted to be? Yet, here I was—confronted with the most daunting question that anyone in the world has ever faced: *What do you really want?*

With less than an hour left in Evie's nap and without the usual pumping, I woke up abruptly and restlessly flipped through the channels to take my mind off swirling thoughts I could do nothing about. I couldn't bring myself to see who they'd put in the midday position today at KVTV. I was sure if the ratings dictated, I'd be replaced in a heartbeat. That'd be so much easier for Chris.

Instead, I turned to KTLA, and there was Scott Stone, my former KVTV rival, sitting at the news anchor desk, smiling with an enormous grin that said he'd never lost anything in his entire life. Sure, I'd won the promotion over him at KVTV, years ago now, but what did he lose along the way? Already he'd surpassed me at another station. He would never have to take a maternity leave. He'd never have to change his hair texture; he'd never be told he was too angry, or too political, or too anything. And he'd never be told he wasn't enough either. He'd just keep failing up.

Seeing Scott reminded me of that strange text from Lisa. She needed to speak with me? Was something happening at the station? My job was my lifeline. I'd left things on anything but stable ground. And still, even this concern might as well have been a lullaby. I still had time in Evie's nap to sleep. Fatigue finally lifted me adrift, carrying me away toward a few more minutes of irresistible slumber.

I'd set things in motion, put myself on an inevitable collision course with some sort of drastic consequence. *The port is burning. The ships are gone. Now I have only one choice—to find out what's ahead.*

3

I ALMOST NEVER LEFT THE HOUSE BEFORE MARC WAS THREE months old. The voice of Marc's mother, Yvonne Brown, careered a crash course through my imagination. The woman had an entire baby registry's worth of criticism ready to dispense for nearly every occasion. Meanwhile, I enjoyed the delights of tiny rebellions. Evie and I had started taking walks around the neighborhood. It was a good way to break up the day. Long days staring at the walls of my home made me feel like a prisoner to a never-ending feeding, cleaning, chores schedule, and the walks were a much-needed escape.

"Exercise is for a sound mind in a sound body," I told Evie as I carefully placed her in the stroller for walking. With some water and leave-in conditioner, I managed to wrestle my hair into a low pouf under a baseball cap. It felt good to make a smooth departure. At first, the only place we'd felt comfortable visiting was the doctor's office for Evie's checkups.

As new parents, we were petrified. Each doctor's visit was a complete production worthy of a royal offspring. Marc, usually so put together, was a vision, scrambling with a car seat and then driving miles below the speed limit, stopping feet before every stoplight, just to cover the distance to the doctor's office safely. He gripped the steering wheel so tight, I could see the white shadow of knuckle bone, even through the chocolate tone of his skin. I was no better, with my constant glances in the rearview mirror to watch a sleeping Evie, blissfully unaware of how she'd thrown two otherwise (mostly) sane adults into a frenzy. I turned every few minutes just to get a glimpse of her with my own eyes and to check the latest detail of her blanket, the car seat, and her pacifier.

Evie had been measured at the doctor's office, and the shame of being behind schedule for weight gain was enough to make me feel like an absolute failure. In all the glossy images of motherhood, breast milk was something that just happened effortlessly. Not for me. I could pump and pump every two hours, and still the trickle of milk didn't measure up. "This happens more often than you'd imagine," the doctor told me, trying to be reassuring.

And in spite of the lactation consultant, adjustments, and even a regular pumping schedule, dependency on formula supplement was my other little motherhood dirty secret. One more way I was doing this whole thing wrong—something else to be ashamed about. Let Yvonne Brown tell it, she probably produced enough milk with Marc to feed the entire neighborhood with some left over for coffee.

Several times now, we'd made it safely to the office and back. And still, despite all the fuss, neither one of us felt silly for it. Marc and I felt just like anybody else embarking on something entirely new and unfamiliar that you absolutely, certainly, one hundred percent didn't want to screw up. That you couldn't screw up, because for some things, there are no second chances.

Nearing four weeks into my maternity leave, the walls of my home had me feeling stir crazy. I wasn't used to having nowhere to go. With tiny Evie bundled in her onesie and blanket, I smoothed down the silky halo of her baby curls and made sure to double-check that the stroller nestled her closely. Part of me felt like I was betraying Marc, taking these moments and milestones for myself, but he hadn't chosen a career pit stop. He was still full steam ahead at work.

For now, it was me, day in and day out, who soothed her, struggled to feed her with my own body, and now possibly even sacrificed my career at the most critical juncture, just to have her as a part of our family. And getting into the rhythm of my new identity, day by day, it was up to me to reclaim a few crumbs of life for myself. The walks would be mine. "Never be afraid of the sunshine, beautiful brown girl," I leaned down to whisper to Evie as we set off down my driveway.

As soon as I felt the wheels of the stroller cross over to the pavement in front of our house, I sensed the release of my nervousness. With each thump over the concrete seams, my grip on the cushioned handle loosened a little more. The crunch of the cement against the soles of my sneakers reached a steady rhythm, and my breath got deeper and more refreshing. The crisp breeze that wrapped up the smells of cut grass and faint florals made me feel relaxed in a way that the stagnant inside air never could. When I lifted my face to the sun, the warm rays felt splendid on my skin. I felt golden, lit from the inside. I hoped that Evie would come to know and love this feeling too.

In our neighborhood of View Park, my house, which I managed to purchase just before gentrification drove prices beyond affordability, was in the area closer to the "bottom of

the hill" than the top. The bottom of the hill was still lovely—
sloping streets parsed by lots belonging to single-story homes
with styles ranging from boxy to bungalow, with a smattering of newer contemporary construction. But it was obvious
as we walked up the hill that the lifestyle, and the prices, were
"moving on up" just as the slope of our street was.

The house on the corner, the two-story Spanish-style
home, covered in sparkling white stucco, caught my eye and
my breath when I saw the FOR SALE sign out in front of it.
If Marc and I moved in together, combined, we could afford
something like this. Maybe even this exact home. More space,
more stability, more rooms, maybe even one for my sisters
again. The thought was tempting, but I had other dreams for
Evie and me. I envisioned happiness for us—the kind that
doesn't self-destruct. I'd have loved to be able to afford a home
up the hill on my own, whether Marc was in the picture or
not, or anyone else for that matter. Our little walk made me
feel like my dreams could be mine, that life could be what I
made it, that the pressing internal question of *What do you
want?* had an answer somewhere inside of me. I just had to
find it.

LATER THAT NIGHT, WHEN EVIE'S CRY STARTLED ME OUT OF MY
sleep, I felt a heavy hand against my shoulder, nudging me
back to my pillow.

"Stay in bed, Tab, I can go."

"Marc," I mumbled half into the pillow, "you don't have
to." He was spending the night again as he did most nights.
In the circumstances, we weren't actually sleeping together,
not like a couple would. We were basking in the convenience

of sleeping in the same place. I wondered whether it would be the same if not for Evie, whether I'd still want him in my bed.

"I do, Tab, I wanna help. Let me take this one."

"Okay," I sighed, turning my back to him. I'd memorized the sounds of him picking her up, him shushing her, him shuffling the two of them out of the room, his footsteps heading into the kitchen and the door of the refrigerator opening to rummage for a bottle that I always left in the exact same place on the middle shelf. My body was already wired for disturbance, and even though I'd pumped before bed, my breasts started to ache at the feeding that was happening without them, without me.

"You should let me help with hiring a nanny," he'd offered in the early days as we stood together bewildered in the middle of the kitchen. But my mom was there and was all the help we seemed to need. When she left, he offered again. Even though I needed a shower and would have killed for a block of sleep lasting more than three hours, I said no— because my time with Evie already felt so brief. I'd be back at work soon, sooner than I wanted to, and then there'd be no option but to rely on someone else to look after my daughter.

I'd gotten so much of what I wanted, more even, from that once tightly held checklist for my life. For my partner, my wants were much more streamlined: tall, handsome, smart, successful—all the characteristics of so-called marriage material—someone who valued my ambition and drive. That was supposed to be Marc. It seemed like a world away, a lifetime even, when I thought that what I'd always wanted I couldn't have.

A man that ain't got no plan for you. Ms. Gretchen warned me about this type of person on more than one of the visits I used to make to see my Granny Tab at Crestmire. If she was still here, Granny Tab would know what to do. They say babies come with guardian angels—I wondered if Granny Tab found Evie, like she promised. She believed that somehow, some way, even in spite of infertility, I'd have children. "And I hope I'll get to meet them—either here, or before they get here if I'm up there," she said shortly before she passed. Maybe she knew something I didn't—that our time together here was drawing to an end. I wish I'd known. Instead, I made a mistake. I can't let Marc be another one. I can't afford another regret.

This was all harder than I ever expected. Harder, more consuming, more intense. It was easier than ever to doubt myself. The people who had been the support beams of my life before Evie had become missed calls and, with the exception of Alexis's food deliveries and Marc's daddy duties, interactive video avatars on my phone. Before, when I doubted myself, I'd always had someone to remind me of who I was. To encourage me to hold on to even the thinnest thread of what I wanted, to keep it from slipping away. To keep *me* from slipping away. Now it seemed like all I could do was hang on by a thread and hope I didn't lose myself entirely in the process.

4

I HELD THE PHONE IN MY HAND WITH ANTICIPATION. FINALLY, a full three days after her text, I'd gotten a moment to reply to Lisa. I'd been distracted with Evie and biting my nails right up to her four-week infant checkup the day prior. With the formula supplements, we were back on track, thankfully. But the window of relief always seemed to be so short. Barely after my finger hit the send button on my message, Lisa called. With Evie down for a nap and my constant companion of the breast pump attached, the timing worked to multitask, but I couldn't imagine what was so important.

"I don't even know how to say this." I could hear the sounds of fatigue relaxing Lisa Sinclair's normally crisp and upbeat anchor diction. I held my breath and waited. "My husband . . . got his dream job, finally, and it's a good thing. I mean, a really good thing, Tabby, for us, you know, but that means that I'm going to be leaving KVTV. He's really excited and I . . ."

"Lisa, you what?" I forced a hissed whisper so I didn't wake Evie, even though my body wanted to shout instead. "Why didn't you tell me you were thinking of leaving? When? Why now?" Lisa took a deep breath at the other end of the phone. I imagined her perfectly manicured nails raking through the glossy ultra-blond highlights in her hair, while I waited for an explanation of the unimaginable. Lisa was in the prime of her career at KVTV, the queen bee of the station, dues paid by this point; all she needed to do was continue to show up and collect her very generous pile of coins. She had the best time slot, the easiest hours, the most seniority; it made no sense for her to be leaving, not now. Not even for a spouse's dream job. Plus, she was my friend—my only friend—at the station.

"We made this deal, Tabby, that one of us would always be home with Charlie, and Bill has already sacrificed so much. I've been the one working. Bill wants his chance at a career, and I really can't deny him that. It's my turn. It really is. I've had a great run."

Not only were Lisa's words unbelievable to me, but it sounded like she was still trying to convince herself. A successful woman, well into her career, with as much work as she'd put in? This wasn't what was supposed to come next. Now seemed like the worst time to bench herself. "But, but . . . Lisa, what? Does the GM know? Does Chris? Have you told the station?" I'd heard her words, but still struggled to understand.

"I will, soon, next week, but I wanted to tell you first. I know you're on maternity leave, but, Tabby, you really need to think about what's next. Maybe you could even take my place. Right now, there's time to figure that out. When you come back, there won't be."

The old me, the one with ripe energy and fresh ambition, would have jumped at the idea, even as far-fetched as it seemed. Another promotion so soon? Sure, it would mean more money, a better time slot, and it would get me out from under Chris into a more protected position. But this new me, she was stretched too thin, exhausted and unprepared for another battle.

"Lisa, I don't even know what to say. I'm flattered and I . . . I just can't even think about that right now. Right now my planning for the future consists of being strapped to this suction machine trying to fill up baby bottles. For the next two months, my success is being measured in ounces of breast milk." The *pfwhoosh* of the breast pump beneath me seemed to accentuate my reply.

Lisa groaned. "Believe me, I understand—but, Tabby, there's something else . . ." Of course there was, shoes always drop in pairs. "The other day, I saw Scott Stone at the station. Maybe it was just a lunch, saying hello to old friends." My stomach dropped. "But it's not Scott you need to worry about. No one knows I'm leaving yet. It's the new temp hire, the one pulled in to cover for you. Competition is tough, and it's clear he's maneuvering to stay. I don't want you to get sidelined, Tabby." Lisa's sigh on the other end of the phone was heavy, leaving a pause before she continued. I could hear my own heart thumping in my ears right up until she spoke again. "Maybe we overplayed our hand a bit with Chris. Went a little too far. I'm concerned about it."

I knew it. I'd left things a mess. "Lisa, I . . ." I struggled to find words. Meanwhile, the heat continued to rise in my face; the moisture appearing on my palms made the phone a bit slippery. I had to adjust my grip on it. Lisa continued before I had a chance to find a response.

"It's not fair to ask you to think about it on your maternity leave. But please, just hear me out on this. I want to help you.

It's something I need to do before I leave. If you're on the outs with Chris, it's my fault—that interview was my idea. Tabby, we need a plan. An hour face-to-face to talk this out. Your life and your career are going to continue past motherhood. But trust me, when you come back from leave, your options at KVTV are looking more and more like up or out. Sometimes there are sacrifices—" Lisa's voice caught on her last words before she concluded. "But don't let this be one, not for you. We need to meet. Things are going to be crazy next week, but the week after, can you do it?"

For a moment, the whirring of the pumping machine and the pounding in my ears were the only sounds I could hear. The silence between Lisa and me lasted so long I thought she'd hung up. But she hadn't. And neither had I. There was heavy meaning in the words unspoken.

Losing Lisa was losing a lifeline at work, the shred of hope I had for consistent support. The confidence I needed to take risks, to take my stand for what was right when Chris wouldn't take my side, she'd been there with a hand at my back. Lisa was losing something too. I could hear the strain of it in her voice, the tones of sacrifice—all the ones up to now and all of those ahead. This too was motherhood. And this too, at least for Lisa, was being a wife. A wife and mother, just like I thought I always wanted to be.

"I . . . I don't know," I stammered, trying more to break the silence than to offer anything helpful. "This is all so sudden. But it seems like I don't have a choice. I don't have childcare right now, but I'll figure it out. Yes, of course we can meet. Evie and me, I mean, we can meet you after my doctor's appointment, in two weeks. Will that work? We'll be in West Hollywood around lunchtime."

"Yes, let's do that. We can go for pizza while we plot," Lisa said. She then added she'd message me closer to our meeting to confirm the exact place.

I agreed, inviting reality back into my life. Still new to motherhood, something about Lisa's words rang very true. *Sometimes there are sacrifices.* Without exactly meaning to, I'd already set fire to the port, this conversation confirmed it. Chris *was* pissed. Even for good reason, I'd pushed him too far. The ships were burning. I'd abandoned the map. No choice but to push forward, into the unknown.

5

THE GOOD LORD GIVETH AND THE GOOD LORD TAKETH AWAY.
Lisa's news was so unexpected, and equally difficult to process.
I didn't realize how much I'd come to rely on her presence
and friendship at KVTV. With her support, I felt like I had
enough strength to fight my way forward and up at the station. But that courage wasn't strong enough to stand on its
own, especially not against Chris, or whatever Scott Stone
was planning. *Only a fool would think they'd gotten anywhere
on their own*, Ms. Gretchen would say.

I'd been letting the developments brew in my mind for
three days. All it did was make me more anxious about what
was to come. With my rescue reflex activated, it was easy to
understand why Marc thought he was giving me such a good
option. Clearly, he wanted to be the breadwinner. Maybe I
wouldn't need a job. He'd do my fighting for me, win my
battles. Even in a moment of weakness, the idea was far from
appealing. I could fight my own battles. I wanted to, rather
than be rescued. What seemed so much more desirable was
having a partner, a meaningful relationship of equals. *But
you don't have any other options*, my mind taunted.

Not so. Just as I began to think of Marc as a one-way street, to my complete surprise, two days after I spoke with Lisa, I received a message from Todd. After what I did to his shoes, the only communication I'd expected from him was a cleaning bill. But I paid attention to his outreach; maybe it was a second chance, some kind of divine intervention. The timing was terrible, but I didn't want to waste a second chance. Todd's message read:

Hey Tabby. Been meaning to check on you. When's a good time to catch up?

Unlike the message from Lisa, I reread Todd's words so many times that I memorized them. "When's a good time to catch up?" and "Hey Tabby?" Was that like "Heeeeyyyy, Tabby?" Was there any way in the world he could still be interested? At Alexis's re-wedding, Marc had acted a fool. I think he literally growled at Todd. *Growled.* Even more, I'd probably gotten baby water on his shoes. And didn't he spend my labor with Laila in the parking lot? But the tease of the possibility, of an alternate ending to the life with Marc that was rapidly closing in on me, felt like a beacon. This would be another thing just for me, breathing room I needed.

Hey Todd! I'm fine. Just over here being a mom, you know, squeezing my boobs into a mechanical sucking device. *No, Tabby, that's ridiculous, delete that.*

Hey Todd! I started again. Everything is good, I mean with the baby and all. I hesitated, fingers hovering over the screen before I finally typed the last words. How's next week?

It was no big deal to meet up with Todd, I told myself. He'd practically helped deliver Evie, and I owed it to myself to know what he'd meant when he asked me to dance, and if he still meant it. What if my future could be different? What if somehow I could hold on to myself and my dreams? My maternity leave was starting to feel like a high-stakes game of musical chairs. Each day meant one less option for me. The walls of an inevitable life were closing in. But what if my happy ending was never supposed to be with Marc? What if I made the biggest mistake of my life canceling that second date with Todd? There was only one way to find out before I'd never know at all.

Still, I couldn't bring myself to hit send. *You should leave this alone*, my mind warned. Things were already too complicated, unresolved.

Instead of replying to Todd, I called Alexis. She answered quickly.

"Tabby! How are you? It's the middle of the day—is everything okay with Evie? Do you need anything?" The concern in Lexi's voice poured through the phone.

"Everything is fine, Lex, at least I think it is," I said, attempting to defuse the worry I heard.

"You just usually text in the middle of the day. I saw a call from you and I immediately thought emergency. You *never* call . . . especially lately," she said. I rolled my eyes a bit. Lexi was that way: you'd find out about her expectations of you out of the blue, at the strangest times. I chose to ignore it.

"Lex, Todd just texted me, and I don't know what to do."

"Wait, Todd? Texted what? Please don't say it's about his shoes!" After a shared laugh, I recapped the actual details of his message.

"You don't think it's wrong?" I asked.

"Wrong? Wrong where?" Alexis sang back in motherly

admonition. "Tabby, I told you that you should have gotten with Dr. Todd a looongg time ago, but then we wouldn't have beautiful little Evie, would we?" My mouth opened to protest, but nothing came out. Alexis spoke straight into the heart of my deepest fear—at any given moment, was I somehow, some way, making the wrong decision that would eventually affect everything?

"I tried, but it was so soon." It was hard to admit, even to Alexis. My connection to Marc had been stronger then, my feelings uncontrolled.

"So what, you just fumbled the catch, Tabby!" Alexis said with more cheer than usual. "But now you have another chance! You should take it. So what if Marc wants what Marc wants. You can make your way out to see a friend. What Marc doesn't know—you know what they say. Although that didn't work out so well for Rob . . ." She trailed off.

"Lex, please don't compare me and Rob—not even!" I couldn't imagine how a harmless text from Todd would rise to the level of Rob's indiscretions in his and Alexis's marriage. Plus, Marc and I weren't married. The comparison was curious, and it was my turn to be concerned. "How are things going, by the way, with Rob and everything? Are you two still re-newlyweds?" I smiled at my own weak reference to their recent re-wedding.

"Girl, it's day by day." Alexis sighed heavily. "And he's over here talking about wanting another baby, like he can't sit for a minute and just be glad he's still married. But I'm the one picking up all the slack."

"And what about all the changes you made? The 'new' Alexis?"

"Who? Girl, I need more help for that. And not just from

Rob. He moved back in and it didn't take long . . . clothes everywhere, acting like he can't cook, looking at me like I'm still supposed to do everything I used to."

"Lex, you were supposed to be my hero," I teased. We both shared a true laugh that was interrupted by the familiar sound of crying coming from the nursery. "I don't know if you hear that, but duty calls. Midday nap is officially over. Girl, I've gotta go."

"Believe me, I understand. And, Tabby, do yourself a favor and stop creating what-ifs. Just text Todd back and see what he wants."

As I made my way over to Evie, Alexis and I said our goodbyes through the phone. Then, I pulled up my text to Todd . . . and put it away again, still too afraid to hit send.

"TELL ME, HOW ARE YOU FEELING?" ANDOUELE SAT LIGHTLY perched with perfect posture on my sofa, studying me with sincerity. Her locs hung softly at her shoulders, brushing across her usual brightly colored top. She'd been my doula throughout my pregnancy and continued with me even after Evie's birth, during the critical period she called the "fourth trimester."

It was comforting to have our twice weekly times together, just a place to have questions answered and sometimes to vent frustrations. Even though breastfeeding wasn't going well, postpartum had otherwise been remarkably kind to me. So many big things could have gone wrong, and it wasn't lost on me that I was lucky to have such expert and attentive care.

I was fortunate in so many ways. And still. There's never

been anything as effective as a simple "how are you?" to trigger unexpected tears, no matter how hard you fight to push them back. When Andouele asked me today, the feeling of my face crumpling in response opened a door that the rest of me just seemed to pour through. I looked up at the ceiling, I dabbed at the corners of my eye. I took deep breaths. But I couldn't stop the feeling from overtaking me. Pure, sheer exhaustion. Next thing I knew, I hadn't managed a word, but I was sobbing. Andouele came over to comfort me, arms around me, her warm scent—sweet and woody—centering me. I felt all at once ashamed, bewildered, and still, a sense of safety.

"I have no idea why I'm crying," I sniffled. "Everything seems to be going so well." I didn't feel like I had the right to be crying at all. I had so much that so many other new mothers didn't. Help and resources. My birth had gone smoothly enough to avoid surgery. I had gotten an opportunity to breastfeed. Even if I wasn't making enough milk, I was able to pump and could afford to supplement with formula. Sure, maybe she wasn't sleeping through the night, but I had Marc, who helped. And so what if he . . . Andouele interrupted my cascade of thoughts with an embrace, pausing my effort to verbalize the root of my unhappiness.

"It's normal to cry, Tabby," she said, pulling away from me gently. "And it's okay. Remember I told you about the journey of motherhood. You never know what's going to come up or what you'll have to confront. But don't think your journey should be easy just because you don't have larger problems. How are you sleeping?" My response was an involuntary sniffle. Andouele took my hands in hers and studied my face closely, patience radiating through her demeanor.

"I'm not really . . . not really sleeping, or showering, or doing anything like I normally would," I finally managed to say. "And I feel guilty about going out with Evie, other than to necessary things like the doctor. I worry about everything. And the time is just going by so fast. I have less than two months left of maternity leave and maybe I won't have a job when I go back, so I guess . . . it's a lot."

"Tabby, your hormones are shifting. Your life is completely different. It's so many changes all at once."

"I look different too . . . I don't recognize myself," I pointed out. My usually immaculately styled hair was in shambles. I hadn't made much progress at all in dropping pregnancy weight. I couldn't imagine this version of myself returning to television and had never felt so out of sync with my body.

Andouele smiled at me. "Be gentle with yourself." Her voice was euphonious, soothing, a balsam to my ears. "And patient," she continued. "You and the baby are both figuring this out. This is a new world for her and a different world for you. A different body, a different rhythm. Do you need more support? What about your friends?"

"I've felt guilty, Andouele. I haven't seen them as much, and I don't mean to be distant. I had such a strong connection to the people in my life before, you know?"

"Maybe you need to reach out. Go meet up with friends when you feel up to it. Take Evie. This is the easiest time to do it."

Hearing this, I could feel my eyebrow raise on its own. Either my body was skeptical, or it was exactly what I needed to hear.

"She'll be okay, trust yourself," Andouele continued.

"Taking care of yourself is also taking care of your baby, re-member that."

As Andouele soothed me and my tears dried, first on my cheeks and then in wads of balled-up tissue, I started to feel something other than overwhelm. I was feeling a desire to branch out, to know what could be rather than just drifting in the current of what I'd already created. If Todd wanted to meet, so be it. I'd at least hear what he had to say. Finally, I was ready to hit send.

IN RESPONSE TO MY MESSAGE, TODD SUGGESTED THAT WE MEET a few days later at the same quaint French bistro that'd we'd chosen for our first date. "It should be easy to remember," he said. I wondered if he wasn't laying it on a little thick. Sure, we might both want to explore a second chance, but to pursue a do-over at the place we'd had our first date? Charming, I guess?

I timed our meeting to coincide with the most reliable of Evie's naps. Todd and I would have at most two hours, if we were lucky. Beyond that and Evie's hunger timer would become the alarm that none of us needed. It wasn't quite the scene I was hoping to create at the table. Todd and I had already reached a lifetime quota of dramatic encounters.

Since this was one of our first outings and part of my new-found effort to turn my maternity leave into a "me-ternity" leave, I arrived a full ten minutes early just to get settled and comfortable with a cup of tea, waiting for Todd to walk in the door. It had been years since I'd been to this place. The glossy white subway tiles on the walls with the black iron accents at the bar made it a perfectly set scene of an ideal sidewalk café. One more glance at Evie in her stroller, an adjustment of my top, and a finger fluff of my freshly twisted-out hair, and I was ready to see Todd among the stream of downtowners who flowed in and out the door.

I almost didn't recognize him as he walked in wearing a hat and sunglasses. His slight frame looked sturdier in his trendy casual clothes. This Todd looked much cooler, like he wasn't a doctor *all* the time. This Todd seemed like he might at least have some awareness of the latest happenings in the culture, like he might know what's up. I could feel my palms sweating a bit, as if I were doing something wrong and maybe getting away with it. Maybe. If it all worked out. The last time Todd and I had a moment, there was Marc to interrupt. This time, it seemed that only Evie could get in the way of what we needed to discuss.

He spotted me quickly and headed over to the table. Seeing a sleeping baby, he made a silent gesture—in spite of the ambient noise of our environment—as if he were afraid his voice might startle her.

"It's okay, she's deep into her nap," I told him with a smile. After a faltering step, his open-armed approach signaled me to stand for an awkward hug. The embrace was nice—he smelled fresh and soapy, with the faint trail of dry cleaning. I pulled away with a grin and gestured for him to sit down. "I got here a little early since this is my first time bringing Evie to a restaurant."

Todd's eyes widened with mild surprise.

"I think I've been going a little stir-crazy," I said quickly. Instantly, I realized my mistake.

The sides of Todd's mouth dropped, and I remembered that he was a psychiatrist.

"I mean, you know, cabin feverish, imprisoned . . . with this newborn," I blurted. With mounting nervousness, I continued, although wishing I could stop. "I'm totally sane—I think. I guess, well unless you think otherwise . . . and I probably shouldn't say 'crazy' . . ." I brought my hand to my mouth to stop myself from saying another word.

Todd gave a thin-lipped smile. "Yes, we don't consider 'crazy' a technical term," he said with a chuckle. "But I understand what you mean." I was grateful for the release of tension between us. "It's really good to see you, Tabby." Todd's smile broadened.

My voice caught in my throat. *It was good to see me? Really? Like this?* I'd never felt less desirable and couldn't for the life of me remember having feelings for Todd, but maybe I hadn't been making any space for them. I gave him another smile. Bigger this time.

"It's good to see you too, Todd. I was really happy that you reached out. It's been a blur since Alexis's party. Wild turn of events, right?" Todd smiled and looked over at a still peacefully sleeping Evie.

"Absolutely unbelievable," he said slowly, shaking his head. My heart rose into my throat. "But turned out so beautifully. Congratulations, Tabby, really." *Whew.*

"I guess I should be thanking you . . ." I started, and then paused, realizing that I was about to give a detailed description of one of the most embarrassing moments of my life.

"Yes, things got a little exciting just before the little one came." I studied Todd's face as he spoke. Smiling, and still it gave nothing away. *Why are we here, Todd?* is what I wanted to ask, but instead I took a deep breath and continued the dance of extended silences. Todd interrupted the lull, asking, "So, how's your friend . . . Laila?"

"Oh? Um, Laila? Well, I don't get to see her as much, but she's starting a business, so I know how busy that can be. You were with her at the hospital, right? Have . . . you talked to her?"

"Me?" Todd looked genuinely surprised. "Oh no. I mean, I'd *like* to. I'd definitely like to." My heart sank—not only at his words, but moreso at the excitement in his tone—pierced by a pang of jealousy. I tried not to show it as Todd continued. "She and I had a great conversation while we were waiting to hear about your delivery. I stayed there with her pretty much until we got the good news."

"I think I was out of it, probably. I had no idea you stayed." My voice had already dropped its buoyancy. I hoped my confusion didn't register in my face.

If Todd noticed, he didn't show it. "By the end we were all so tired, I didn't even think to get her number so that we could keep in touch," he said without an ounce of discomfort. I tried with all of my professional training to keep Todd from reading the shock. This was nothing that Laila had ever mentioned, not that I'd thought to ask. Somewhere in this situation was a fringe case of the "girlfriend rule," and I didn't know on what side it fell. Sure, Todd and I had never formally dated, but wasn't it clear that he was in the reserve option category? And if he was asking about Laila in the first few minutes of seeing me, how interested was he, really? Then again, when he first reached out, he only asked to "catch up." Maybe it had been me who suggested meeting? And then read all the rest into an innocent and simple desire to just check in on the woman who basically broke water all over his shoes. Amid all of this and the growing realization of my likely misinterpretation, I struggled to find words.

"I, um." I shifted in my seat and lifted my teacup to my lips, trying again. "I, uh . . ." Words still caught in my throat. My face started to feel warm, a burn building in my cheeks. I brought my hands to my hair for a faux fluff, and offered a faux smile. "Would you like me to connect you two?" I finally managed to chirp the words at him, fully conscious that my smile might have been a little too wide, or my teeth a little too closed to read as genuine.

But even that, Todd didn't seem to notice. "Yeah, actually, that would be great," he said. "I mean, if you don't mind."

"Mind? Todd, no! That's my girl, of course I don't mind." And most of that was true. I didn't mind connecting Laila to anyone. I just hated sitting face-to-face with another of my mistakes. Once again, the music stopped, leaving one less option than before.

Todd and I had time to order, eat, and talk a bit more, and then Evie started to stir, demanding her portion of me and my attention. That was the signal our time was up. He'd already told me about the end of his psychiatry residency and his thoughts about choosing a fellowship over heading into practice. His father was also a psychiatrist with a hankering to pass on a legacy, but was willing to wait an extra year or two before his son formally joined to take over his office. He'd also gotten a new condo downtown, and no, he hadn't seen or spoken to Alexis and Rob since their party.

I listened to it all, now seeing Laila in the place I'd foolishly imagined for myself. I shared my own updates, of which there were few lately, as I was most concerned these days about milk production and hours of consecutive napping. And the latest sale on diapers, which who knew how expensive they could be when you're using so many a day?

I hadn't expected things to go that way with Todd, and a small part of me felt like I could have spoken up and asked was there anything left of the interest it seemed like he had before Marc had shown up at Alexis's re-wedding. But Marc had shown up, hadn't he? He had claimed me and Evie as his, and maybe he was right. Even in the face of reality, it was hard to let go of the dream of other possibilities, and I wanted to hold on to this a little longer. Connecting him to Laila made it real, closing the door on my imagination. I promised myself I'd talk to her about it, just in my own time.

6

"I'VE GOTTA WORK PRETTY LATE TONIGHT, SO I THINK I'M GO-ing to miss the evening shift." Marc's voice drifted through my phone as I sat in the deep comfy chair in the nursery, lulled by the whirring of the breast pump. It had been a whole day since my encounter with Todd, and fatigue was the only ingredient I needed to put the conversation out of my mind, at least in the short term.

"Um-hmm, okay," I murmured back.

"And there's something else. Something I'm kind of ex-cited about." Hearing the lift in his tone, I perked up slightly, pulled out of my hazy relaxation. "My mom said she wanted to come and help out with the baby," he continued. "She's got a nurse scheduled for my dad, and I just booked her a ticket. She'll be here the day after tomorrow." *Shit.* And I could hear the genuine excitement in Marc's voice. So I managed to sti-fle my groan. I should've just accepted Marc's offer to hire a nanny. Instead, Yvonne Brown *was coming*.

Yvonne Brown? Under normal circumstances, she cer-tainly would have come sooner, at the same time as my own mother, right after the baby was born. As I'd been learning all too well, that was how Yvonne was. But Marc's father's health had taken a turn. Yvonne had been afraid to leave him. I'm sure it took considerable restraint for her to stay back in Florida, because she was absolutely obsessed with her first grandchild. I'd logged innumerable hours of FaceTime as proof.

"Oh? Well, that's . . . a surprise, definitely," I said with an intentional lilt in my voice. Years of practice in the news allowed me to speak in a range of emotions that I didn't feel. And I was thankful for that now. Over the phone, Marc's mother had provided nothing but judgment and pronouncements of everything I should have done or that she would do differently. I could only imagine what her arrival would bring. "Did she say how long she'd be staying?" I added with a careful measure of performed curiosity. This was what I really wanted to know. For how long would I be expected to put up with this woman?

"She said she'd stay as long as she could, Tab. I know you could use the extra support and now you'll have someone to help watch Evie every day. Maybe you can get out a bit sometimes." At Marc's words, a pang of guilt coursed through me. He had no idea that I'd seen Todd, or that I'd ventured out, taking Evie with me into the world of downtown LA. And if I'd known that his thinking of me as homebound would result in his mother showing up, even though it was inevitable at some point, I would have coughed up the facts.

"Wh . . . where." I cleared my throat and my mind to remain as neutral as possible. "Where is she going to stay?"

"Well, we hadn't discussed that, Tab, but she'll stay with me and I'll just bring her over every day, does that work?" Through the phone, Marc's voice sounded so excited, so hopeful. "That means I probably won't be spending the night with you and Evie, if that's what you're worried about, but we'll work it out while she's here."

On my end of the line, I smiled and shook my head lightly. Even as a father now, Marc was still beholden to his mother's watchful expectations. She wasn't even my mother, or mother-in-law, yet her ready critique had seeped into my pores—the judgments of my every move were a presence that I had to work hard to shake. Wasn't it already hard enough on a day-to-day basis amid the crying, spills, diaper change disasters, wet burping, baby goop, weight checks, and everything else that comes along with new motherhood? Now I'd have Yvonne physically present, on a one-way ticket, watching over my shoulder and calling it "help."

"Wow, well, that's some news, Marc," I said and tried again to hide my feelings. If I could sound even slightly less than perturbed, it would be a victory.

"I know, right?" he added, his excitement seemingly expanding. "I never thought she'd be able to leave my dad anytime soon, but now look."

A few more words of a thin exchange and Marc had to go. The evening was left to me and Evie in what seemed to be one of my few remaining days of peace. No one wants to be judged in their own home, but especially not a brand-new mother just trying to make sense of it all. In different circumstances, I'd be willing to tolerate Marc's mother because I loved him, and the burden would feel lighter. But in reality, obligations and love had spun together so tightly that one was indistinguishable from the other. And there was the other ingredient of family, which we were, even if the only formal document stating so was Evie's birth certificate.

Todd turned out to be wistful thinking. And that much

I could live with. But the idea of him wanting Laila, that killed the dream I'd crafted in my mind. The one of escape. I couldn't dream my way out of my circumstances with Marc, or be rescued from them either. No matter what, Marc was in my future, and now, as I'd become very aware, his mother was as well. To be happy on my own terms, if I still had options, I'd have to find another way.

7

THE FIRST DAY OF YVONNE BROWN'S VISIT FELT LIKE A JOB IN-
terview. And for this interview, I'd also had to contend with a
fussy, crying newborn, virtually no sleep, and a shower that
was shorter than the time that it took for the water to fully
heat up. But this was what I had to work with.

As things go, the one day that I was hoping Evie would
stick to her regular schedule, she refused to shut her eyes or
go down for a nap and wouldn't soothe until I put her in the
newborn baby rocker as a last resort. Normally, I never let her
sleep in there, but I didn't dare move her to her bassinet right
away, lest we find ourselves back where we started. It wasn't
perfect, but she was safe for a few minutes. I was watching
her like a hawk. On this day, one woman with a questionable attitude was more than enough for my fragile and frayed
nerves.

Marc let me know earlier, when he was heading to pick
Yvonne up from the airport, that the only thing his mother
said she wanted to do that morning was to see her granddaughter. She didn't want to drop her belongings at Marc's

place, nor did she want to stop for her favorite meal of chicken and waffles at the world-famous Roscoe's near the airport.

When she arrived, I'd plastered on my practiced smile before I pulled open the front door, seemingly heavier for my lack of will to pry it open. On my porch was Yvonne Brown, front and center, looking like she was headed to church. Marc stood behind her carrying a small bag and looking rather small himself. As I recalled, he usually seemed to shrink in his mom's presence.

"Tabby," she said curtly, "very nice to see you again." And having raised not a single arm for a hug, she looked me from top to bottom and then craned her neck to see past me. I nearly gasped. "Well, are you going to let us in? I've been waiting to see my grandbaby, finally in the flesh!" And without waiting for a response from me, as the whole exchange had taken only seconds, she headed past me before I could offer her entrance.

"Please," I said to the back of her head, waving my arms wide open. "Come in. She's down for her nap." I managed to scurry alongside her in the direction of my sleeping infant in her rocker seat. Yvonne's eyes zeroed in on Evie, and for the first time, her arms reached above her waist.

"Well, that's unusual, this contraption, you just leave her in it as a newborn? Would seem to me that babies like to be held, or better for her to sleep in a bassinet, you know . . . flat on her back?" With pursed lips she turned to Marc and then to me, progressively moving in the direction of Evie. I quickly moved to step in between, blocking her reach with my body.

"I'm planning to move her in a bit," I said, on the breath of a sigh I couldn't contain. "We've actually been pretty lucky that she's taken to the rocker, I heard that it was a fifty-fifty chance of whether she'd love it or hate it." Although I wasn't sure if she would, Yvonne stopped short of what seemed to be an attempted but unnecessary rescue.

"Hmph," she said, looking around me at Evie. "Well, generally, babies like to be held. That thing must have cost a fortune." I let my eyelids drop to hide my eye roll and took a deep breath. *She's not wrong*, my thoughts taunted.

"Shall we have a seat in the kitchen?" I offered. "Would you like some tea or coffee?"

"Well, since the baby's sleeping, some breakfast might be nice. *After* you move her to the bassinet." Yvonne looked at me and then it occurred to me that she wasn't offering, she was expecting me to also be her breakfast service. This led us into a deafening impasse.

"Let me know what you want, Mom." Marc's voice broke into the silence. "I'll run out to pick up something. Let me guess, you want Roscoe's, right? The Obama Special?" Marc rushed over to put his hands on his mother's shoulders, giving them a squeeze. It seemed that he'd also given me a wink. The silence from a yet-unmoved Yvonne continued. "Whatchu think, huh, Ma? Some delicious fried chicken . . . a fluffy waffle . . . some butter? Yeaaaah, you put that butter on top of that waffle and let it melt a little bit, you know what I mean?" he coaxed. When I saw the corners of her mouth fighting their way upward, I knew that he had won.

I couldn't remember the last time I had a meal that I truly wanted when I wanted it or had time to eat it, and so I happily ordered as well, hoping that Marc would be back quickly. It wasn't lost on me that there was a time when I would have been nervous for this woman's approval, her so-called "green light" for her son to want to marry me. And now, after breakups and makeups and babies and maybes, we were in some other place. Neither of our current roles or positions could be changed by the other. And it wouldn't matter if we wanted it to, not now, not ever.

I already knew it was going to be a long day, a long week, or weeks even. As I headed over to Evie, to dutifully move her to the bassinet, I realized that only one of the three of us would get to eat our fill. I'd never seen Yvonne move as fast as she did when she realized I was heading over to the baby. I managed to grab ahold of my phone on the way to Evie, trailing her church lady trot as she retraced her steps to the baby soother, finding her way directly to my daughter with the focus of a bloodhound. As she reached her arms out with her "now let me see my grandbaby," I managed to pull up a quick message and send my first 911 text in the longest time to the outstretched arms that always comforted me. Alexis and Laila.

AFTER TWO DAYS OF UNCOMFORTABLE AND VERY FOCUSED preparation, I came up with a shopping excuse to break free of Yvonne Brown and give her what she wanted most, full rein over her granddaughter. Midday, I headed for downtown brunch at Poppy + Rose to get what could be my first undisturbed meal in a month, but mainly to see Alexis and Laila.

Poppy + Rose was a new Black-owned café that served both alcohol and tea, making it the perfect meeting spot. After two full days with the constant assault of Yvonne's let-me-second-guess-you style of grandparenting, I was ready for a drink. On the upside, I knew that she could be trusted with my child. Downside, she was the one driving me out of my own home. Given her views on newborns' need to stay indoors for "at least the first three months," she was more than happy to let me out for a "shopping trip" to spare Evie the insult of public air.

When I arrived, I was surprised to see Laila already seated, squinting at her open laptop screen at a casual picnic-style table on the back patio. With her new business, I hadn't seen as much of her, and the new baby didn't allow me to keep to our regular schedule of at least one activity a week together, like the yoga classes we'd enjoyed. It made me a little happier than usual to know that she'd made it and that our 911 calls still meant something to each other, no matter what else was happening in life. I'd be there for her and she'd be there for me, even when it wasn't convenient. That also meant that I'd need tell her about Todd—he never belonged to me anyway and I already felt foolish waiting so long.

"Hey, girl!" I said, sliding into the seat across from Laila, startling her intentionally. She looked up with genuine surprise, the bright sunshine of the day glinting in the layered brown of her eyes.

"Oh my god! Tab! I didn't even see you!" With the creaking of the wood beneath her, she made a maneuver off her bench and came over to my side, embracing me. I never took for granted the opportunity to hold her and feel her solidly in my arms. She was still thinner than she'd ever been, but she looked well and healthy. Her hair was down, grown out in ringlets almost at her shoulders. Her golden skin highlighted her freckles, and she looked beautiful.

"Girl, you just let me creep up on you like that?" I pushed her shoulder gently. She smiled.

"Tab, if you only knew. Shit, if I had only known! Starting

this business was one thing, but now that it's started to grow, it's a whole ass undertaking. Harder and more work than I ever imagined. I'm trying to raise some money to—"

"Heyyy, you two!" Alexis's voice cut Laila off as she jingled her way to the table, her oversize designer bag thumping against her hip in time with her brisk pace. She breezed over in a cloud of floral-tinged air, first hugging Laila, then me, adding a single cheek kiss and an extra squeeze. We all settled into places at the table, quickly bridging the time that had passed since we were last together. In short order, months ago felt like yesterday. So much had happened between us in just the last few years. Life-changing things. Alexis, who'd lived for so long in her identity as a wife and mother, had almost gotten divorced. Laila, who would forever be the strongest person I knew, had reached her breaking point. And me, after my whole world had fallen apart, I became a mother. Where I'd once dreamed of becoming a wife, the idea now felt stifling, and I had no idea if that was because I had the wrong person, or just a changing vision of what I wanted for my life.

"Hey, Alexis! Let me just close this . . ." Laila quickly became distracted, wrapped up again in her laptop, rather than completing her earlier thought. Fluttering keystrokes clicked in the background of my and Alexis's chatter.

"Girl, what is going on?" Alexis exclaimed. "Marc's mother has taken over your house? I thought she wasn't able to leave Florida!"

"I guess Marc was sensing I needed a break. And his mother seemed like she really wanted to see Evie, if only to make sure I didn't break her since I'm such a terrible mom." I squinted to look across at Alexis sitting against the bright midday Southern California sun.

"Tab, no!" Alexis reached over put her hand on my arm. "You are not a terrible mother! You are a *fantastic* mother. You have almost singlehandedly kept a small, helpless human alive for nearly five whole weeks! That is something!"

"Just one more sec . . ." Laila murmured. I turned back to Alexis.

"Lex, I don't even know what to do. I just needed to get out. I already feel like I have no idea what I'm doing. It's great to have another set of hands, but to have everything I do feel like someone's going to be lifting up scorecards at the judging table, I just can't take it."

"Trust me, Tab, there are no trophies for good parenting. The only reward you get is more. More work, more stress. Less time for yourself." Alexis looked over at Laila who was still hunched over her computer. "Laila, you seem bored with us."

"Um, hum, just a little," Laila said absentmindedly. "But one sec, I need to finish this and—"

"Are you serious?" Alexis squealed at her. "Our friend is having a minor crisis and—"

Cutting Alexis off, Laila flipped the top of the computer down with a thud that made me wonder if she might have broken something. Then she snapped. "Alexis, honestly, can you just lay off for one second? One second? You and Tabby, all you talk about are Marc and Rob and the boys and kids and all your shit. And I'm sorry, I'm here, but I have my own stuff going on too."

"Hey, why you gotta bring me into this?" I asked.

Laila just looked at me and then turned back to Alexis. "I'm trying to be here, but that's not my life, okay? I'm starting a business and it sucks and it's hard and I'm trying to raise money and keep a staff going. All that means I can't really focus on what you're talking about right now like *you*, Alexis, might want me to. But I'm still here. I'm here, okay? And that might need to be enough right now."

My mouth dropped open and the pang of fear started to well that Laila was going to storm off again, or that Alexis was going to say something that we'd all regret. As Laila stood up, my breath caught in a suspended inhale.

"I'm going to get something to drink," she said. "I'll be back."

Alexis and I looked at each other, the unspoken feeling between us the same as when we were kids and had done something we knew we'd be caught for. Somehow, again and without meaning to, we'd done something wrong.

"I don't know what I said *this* time." Alexis raked her fingers through her silky pressed hair. "She's just always so busy or distracted." Alexis let out a deep sigh. "Tab, sometimes I just feel like I don't know how to be her friend." Alexis's words ricocheted through my mind. It was true that Laila was complex. She didn't always say what needed to be said until it was an eruption, which felt too late. But knowing her, this small outburst was a warning, something to pay attention to. And even though I'd come for some support from my girls, it was easy to see that life was beating on them too. That they even showed up was its own small miracle. We dragged ourselves together, wounded and ragged, hoping that united we'd cleave in the weakest places and be stronger together in our haphazard unity.

"Before you came, she said she was raising money," I said to Alexis. "I've just been trying to give her some space. But knowing Lah, maybe we should ask. Seems like there's something going on that she's not talking about."

"Oh? Well, if she's trying to raise money, then that's enough of a problem. And as a Black woman? I hear about it all the time from clients, people coming to LA to work in tech, hoping that somehow real estate can help fund their business ideas because they don't have the same access to capital as their non-Black colleagues." Alexis stopped abruptly. "She's coming back . . ." We both looked up in time to see Laila walking toward us, squinting from the sun in her eyes, carrying three glasses of water.

"Sorry," she said, setting the glasses down. "I didn't mean to make it seem like I don't care about what's going on in your lives or that I feel like you don't care what's going on in mine." Laila walked back over to her side of the table and slid into her seat. "It's just that sometimes lately I feel invisible. No, I didn't have a baby. No, I'm not married. I started a business. But that doesn't mean that what I'm doing isn't hard, or consuming, or goddamn frightening. It is." Laila seemed to catch herself and shook her head. "I'm not looking for sympathy or anything . . . Maybe I'm just venting."

"Laila," I said, reaching across the table to her. "Girl, maybe we don't know what to ask, or how to ask. I thought I was helping by just giving you space. I know how busy you are."

"Tab." Laila laughed a bit, which gave me the slightest relief. "You just had a baby. And it bothers me to know that I can't be there like I want to. It's like I have a different kind of baby. This company. It's just not something we celebrate in the same way, and half the time I don't know what the hell I'm doing. The other half of the time I actually don't want to talk about the shit, honestly." We all broke into laughter at Laila's last words.

"Well, Laila, I *definitely* know how hard it is to get a business off the ground," Alexis said. "It was a real struggle for me in real estate and I'm just getting to the point where I can expand my own team. I guess we used to spend a lot more time talking about this kind of stuff." Alexis adjusted her arm bracelets and continued in a murmur so low that I wasn't even sure if Laila heard it. "Back before Rob lost his damn mind." I tried to stifle a laugh, but Laila didn't. And thankfully, just like that, whatever tension was building between us began to dissipate.

"Alexis," I added, "didn't you say you were adding to your real estate team?

"I am!" Alexis brightened. "I just hired a young guy, Andre . . ." I could have sworn I saw her blush. Laila must have seen it too.

"Andre? Who is Andre?" Laila perked up again. Alexis's face went into a full flush and her words came out in a stutter.

"He's, um, well, this young junior agent. He's just joined the office and is starting on my team. He's . . ."

"Cute?" I added, teasing.

"Single?" Laila added on.

"Actually, both," Alexis admitted sheepishly. "But way too young for any of us." Alexis looked from me to Laila and back, and seemed to interpret the incredulous looks on our faces. "Okay! Maybe there's a little harmless flirtation," Alexis uttered flippantly with a casual turn of her wrist, setting anew a cascade of jingles. "*Harmless!* It's nothing."

"Then maybe you could finally hook me up," Laila added casually.

"With him?" asked Alexis, clueless. "Seriously?"

"Never mind, Lex," Laila said, turning away. "I'm sure you have it under control."

Todd, I thought. With the discussion of introductions, I realized that I'd forgotten to tell Laila about Todd. The conversation continued without me.

"Him, I have under control," Alexis said. "The rest of my life, girl, not at all." Alexis and Laila both laughed.

With them both on the same page, I wanted so badly to keep the good vibes going. And thankfully, a brilliant distraction came to mind. One that we could all agree on.

"Hey, Laila," I interjected. Both of my friends looked up in my direction. "I was just thinking about what you said, about your business, and how nobody celebrates entrepreneurship the way we still do for marriage and babies. Well, I was just thinking, why don't we celebrate the birth of your business?" Laila and Alexis both looked puzzled. But at least they weren't focused on land-mine topics. "Aaannnd . . ." I continued, growing more excited by the word, "Alexis, why don't we throw a business shower for Laila?"

"Nice, Tab, if this is your way of saying you think I'll never get married . . ." Laila muttered into her water glass. At her words, I sat briefly frozen in the middle of deciding what would be better for Laila. Was it better to push forward with something that could bring us all together, convincing both her and Alexis there was a way to make her feel seen as a business owner? Or better to pass along Todd's request—a possible romantic opportunity with some baggage. I chose business over baggage.

"Not even!" I replied quickly. "I'm sure, in fact I know, that you'll have every option you're looking for as soon as you're

ready. This is really about supporting you. And you're right—
Alexis has had two or three weddings by now." Teasing, I gave
Alexis a wink and a nudge. "Plus both of the boys, and I've
had . . . a baby shower."

"You know what, Tab," Alexis said, "it would have made
a big difference if someone had done that for me when I first
started in real estate." She started to nod her head. "Um-
hmm, yep. I think we should do it."

"Tab, I love you and all," Laila said, dropping her palm on
the wood slat of the table. "But how is this supposed to go? A
room decorated with balloons, taking pictures for the 'gram?
Am I supposed to send an Amazon wish list? Or how about
just my banking information. Maybe we make it a crowdfunding theme? Girl, *nobody* is going to come. I did a Kick-
starter campaign and *it failed*."

At this point, Alexis animated. I could tell she was in. She
never missed a chance to plan a good party. "No, no, I can see
this," Alexis said. "People will come to a good party. And we
can keep it small, just for the people we know. And yes, you'll
do a registry, and Tab and I will handle the rest." Laila looked
at us, her face still in the scrunch of disbelief. But she didn't
say no. And that was already a victory.

"Well then, it's settled," I said. "We're doing a business
shower for your business baby." Laila opened her mouth and
then closed it again. But still, she didn't say no. And even
though she didn't, I knew it wasn't settled. Because even
when it's your best friends, being cared for is still sometimes
the hardest habit to learn. And caring for others, especially
being able to finally do something for Laila, turned out to be
the best way to forget my troubles and an overbearing Yvonne
Brown waiting at my house. I'd already stayed too long.

8

I'D ALMOST FORGOTTEN THAT TO ESCAPE MARC'S MOTHER, MY lie of convenience was a shopping trip. She had a way of making me forget I was an adult, and that it was *my* house she was perched in. Rushing back, I was already heading down my block before I realized that I couldn't very well return empty-handed. After a thirty-minute detour of a most haphazard grocery store scavenger hunt, I found myself finally walking back in the door of my home. In the living room, Yvonne was sitting like a sentry on the sofa, holding Evie and looking at me like I had just tried to sneak in past curfew.

"All that time and just two bags?" she asked sternly. "I thought you'd have enough for a holiday dinner by now." I started to answer, but she continued with an expression on her face that was as tight as the curls in her roller-set hairstyle. "And the baby was fussy, looking for her mother, I'm sure. I don't know if she likes those bottles you have." She turned to Evie again, and only then did her tone soften. "But Grandma was here, and I got you to eat, didn't I?" When her attention turned to Evie, she sang sweetly to her.

She could have picked so many other places to be, in the

family room with the television, or in the nursery with the most comfortable chair. But instead, she was right here, front and center. She wanted to be the first thing I saw. I headed past her to drop the bags on the counter and then over to her quickly, arms outstretched for my daughter.

Once I'd retrieved Evie, I could tell she was fighting sleep. And I suddenly felt terrible that I hadn't brought her with me to see Alexis and Laila. If Yvonne hadn't been visiting, I wouldn't have needed to pretend at all, and could make my own decisions freely.

"She didn't want to go down for her nap," Yvonne continued. "And when she's fussing like that, I don't know how you manage to get her down on that schedule you say you keep. You might have to hold her a little longer, you know, that's just part of the newborn stage. Of course, my mother wouldn't have dared let me step foot out of the house before Marc was three months old." Although I'd heard it many times over video visits, in person her common refrain was even more needling.

Silently, I counted down the time to when Marc might walk in the door, still hours away. Maybe Yvonne couldn't get Evie to settle because babies can sense people's energy. No wonder Marc had never introduced a woman to his mother before me. She'd have run anyone away. But I couldn't go anywhere. I was stuck.

Within minutes of me holding her, Evie started to snuggle her way into her usual sleeping position against my torso, facing toward my chest. I decided to use the opportunity to head into the bedroom, because I also realized I was fighting back an urge to cry. And I wanted to. But I promised I wouldn't give the satisfaction. "Not everybody deserves your tears," I whispered softly to Evie.

It was so easy to find any one thing to hold on to and criticize. But had Yvonne noticed that I picked Evie the very perfect bassinet? The one that had four thousand five-star reviews and was recommended by Alexis and Andouele and at least four other people? Did she even realize that her grandchild slept in hundreds of hours of web searching and research, books read, and message board scouring? That recommendations and time were reflected in every onesie, diaper, bottle, bottle warmer, blanket, pacifier, breast pump, and accessory in my house?

She counted every minute I'd spent away, but what about the invisible hours of worry behind every decision, every moment of self-doubt, and every instance when I got it right? Nobody thanks you for that. Nobody says, *Congratulations, you kept them alive today, and you're all right too. Not great, not your best self—you could use a much longer shower and a real glass of wine—but you're hanging in there and that's still something.* Even in Evie's nursery, immaculate decorations covered the room that was once designated for my sisters, relationships that I hadn't been able to nurture as fully as I'd wished. But there was not one word for any of the invisible sacrifices. From Yvonne, there was only judgment.

HOURS LATER, FROM MY BEDROOM, I COULD HEAR THE FRONT door close and Marc's voice drifting down the hallway. Pregnancy had tuned my ears to the slightest sound. I didn't remember lying down on my bed and certainly not deciding to take my own nap alongside Evie, now gently stirring in her bedside bassinet. She'd given me three hours of continuous sleep, a first for us. This sensation of extended rest was something I'd forgotten about over these past weeks of frequent feedings.

I couldn't make out the specific words of Marc's exchange with his mother, but I heard his voice, and then hers, a hushed call and response of my extensive list of shortcomings. *What kind of mother stays out almost three hours at the grocery store?* I imagined her saying. *Really, Marc, you should just let me stay here forever.* I could hear it echoing in my mind like a living nightmare. When the voices stopped, the sound of Marc's footsteps drew closer, rubber soles against floorboard, the creaks marking the distance. Soon he'd be at my door, peeking in at me in the still darkness, curled in an S on the bed, facing the bassinet, eyes wide open.

"Hey," I said, looking at him leaning against the doorframe. He moved as if startled to hear my voice.

"I was trying not to make any noise," he whispered. "I thought you two might still be sleeping."

Marc let me know that he'd brought dinner, which lately had been his nightly buffer between his mother's look of expectation and my unwillingness to add yet another task to my own plate. "Are you okay?" he asked. How to answer that question? *Yes? I'm okay because I finally got three consecutive hours of sleep and even though your mother makes me wish I'd never met you, being rested somehow makes that easier to accept. Or, no? I'm not okay because, your mother. And I'm sure that you must know that because you grew up with her. And now I'm stuck with both of you.*

"Long day," I replied to Marc. "I'll be fine." But somehow, even then, I knew that wasn't true.

"I WANT TO TAKE ALL OF MY LADIES TO DINNER TOMORROW night," Marc said later, the three of us sitting at my modest table. "Mom, I know how you feel about Evie being out, but it's a special occasion. So we're all going to go." His firmness surprised me. I hadn't seen Marc push back on his mother in the slightest way before. He hadn't even done it to stand up for me. Or himself, for that matter.

"What's tomorrow night, Marc?" I asked.

"Oh, you'll find out. Trust me, I have something special planned, and it's so much better now that Moms is here too." He rubbed his hands together like he was starting a fire inside his palm. My appetite started to wane. Ever since he told me how seriously he was thinking about marriage, the risk of any particular moment becoming the most awkward of my life loomed. And Marc and I didn't have the best track record at dinners.

As I'd gotten to know him, Marc had always liked to pair big news—usually big bad news—with a dose of fine dining. There was of course the time that he broke up with me at the bar of one of my favorite downtown rooftop brunch destinations. And then there was the time he took me for a breathtaking view and meal so delicious that I almost overlooked the moment, a year and half into our relationship, when he told me he only just realized that he didn't want to have children. And yet, here we were, sitting at a kitchen table with two people I'd never thought I'd get a chance to meet—his mother and *our* daughter. Marc's mother quietly lifted her fork of potato mash to her mouth. She seemed not to register a word of what Marc said, or at least was pretending not to.

"Marc . . . sounds . . . great," I said. But it didn't sound great. It sounded terrifying, a strike of apprehension that the music was about to stop once again in my high-stakes game of musical chairs.

TRUE TO HIS WORD, THE NEXT EVENING MARC FOUND A NICE, but not-so-nice-as-to-be-stuffy restaurant that accommodated both his mother's simpler tastes and the fact that we were walking in with a five-week-old baby.

Prior to becoming a mother, I hadn't registered all the trade-offs that came with parenthood. The thinly hidden stares coming from other diners while walking into the dark wood-paneled lobby, me confronting the exceedingly polite hostess who made her commentary with only her eyes, and not needing to but also compulsively explaining that the baby will just be sleeping and will be quiet in her rocker seat, while hoping, but not really knowing, if that was actually true.

There was also Marc's mother, who sat in a light sulk the entire drive over, who'd reminded us with her frequent refrain that the common wisdom was to wait at least three months, and "who needed to go out with a baby anyway?" But Marc had insisted. So here we were, somehow dining out with a baby on an excursion that required enough coordination and supplies to suffice for a weekend camping trip. On the Evie nap timer schedule, we only had ninety minutes. That was ninety minutes to be seated, to order, eat, announce, and leave before my breasts leaked through my blouse.

After just a short wait, we were seated with drinks that quickly followed, and we had made our dinner orders. Then there was nothing else to do but wait—with our hands placed on the white tablecloth, waiting for the promised news. We were all fidgety, impatient, speaking little, wondering when Marc would let go of the suspense. After a particularly long and awkward lull, Marc seemed to perk up, looking back and forth between me and Yvonne with a humongous grin on his face.

"It finally happened! I made partner," Marc blurted out, slapping the white-linen-covered dinner table. I looked at him blankly and took a sharp breath. Apprehension caused a delay in expressing my genuine happiness for him. It took a second for my brain to catch up to my body.

"So you know what that means . . ." Marc had a sly look in his eye, and reached over first for my hand and then his mother's. I willed a smile to my face, but my heart was beating so fast I was sure he could feel it in my palm. Yvonne was impossible to read, in part, because so far in the evening her mouth had barely uttered more than her dinner order. Which, based on the experience of her visit, was a much better purpose than the usual criticism that she used it for.

"Marc, I . . ." I began, not even knowing what he was going to say, but feeling the need to fill the air.

"Tab, you probably already know." Marc turned to me with a wide smile that made him look as giddy as a kid on Christmas. The moment seemed to be sliding out of control. And in front of his mother? Maybe I could just go along to . . . "Tab, I'm going to do it." My breath caught in my throat. *Do it here?* "I'm finally going to . . . buy a house!" *A house?* I thought. He turned to his mother. "That's right, Ma, no more cramped-up

space when you come to visit, and . . ." Marc turned to me
and took my hand, his thumb caressing the space behind my
thumb. "And it can be the house of your dreams, Tab. Plenty
of space for us, together, Evie and maybe—" Marc's mother
cleared her throat, breaking the spell of the moment. And
then came the first time I'd seen her smile in days.

"Congratulations, baby, you know your daddy would be
so proud . . . if he could be here." The faltering in her voice
took me by surprise. And then I turned to see her quickly
dab at her eye with her napkin. I was just so surprised to
witness any softness or break in her veneer of righteousness,
that I almost forgot to feel relieved about the pivoting of the
moment from the danger zone of a proposal. And what did
Marc mean that it could be the house of *my* dreams? What
about my house? And what life was he describing? I looked
down at still sleeping Evie in her rocker, blissfully unaware
that even right then, her parents were making decisions that
might affect her forever. Ms. Gretchen was right all along.
Men do make plans. But maybe now was the time for me to
make my own.

9

IF I KNEW NOTHING ELSE, IT WAS CLEAR THAT I NEEDED TO LET go of my fantasy of a life with the pre—"I like Laila" Todd or whatever had been holding me back from chasing Laila down to connect them. In fact, guilt was the strongest motivation to take action. After the amount of time that had passed since his request, whether intentional or not, I was now officially being messy.

Marc made it clear at dinner that he was moving forward with his intentions, and I'd done absolutely nothing to stop him. And for a brief moment, while he was describing his vision for us, I found myself floating down the river, on the path of least resistance, caught up in the scenery of a so-called perfect life. *Just maybe*, I thought, *when you become a mother, you give up your right to be all-the-way happy*. Believing that could make everything so much easier. And yet, some part of me still believed in more. More just didn't involve Todd. At least, not for me. Laila still had a chance, though, a big wide-open shot at maybe having it all, whatever that is.

Two days after Marc's "announcement," Alexis and I were set to meet at my place to plan Laila's "Business-Baby Shower," as we'd decided to call it. This was how I made it through my days in captivity with Yvonne, focusing on Evie and then on any excuse to find myself in another room. She'd been in town just under a week, and my house had never felt so small.

Like clockwork, every morning Marc would drop her off, each day with a seemingly fresh list of inadequacies to address. That we'd tolerate each other much longer seemed like an impossibility. And I wondered which one of the scenarios from my imagination would find its way into reality—the scream that I'd been suppressing, or the full unloading of what I really thought over her first steaming-hot cup of tea. Didn't Marc know that his mother was insufferable, and that somehow I'd have to love her to be with him, and that loving her was impossible?

USHERING ALEXIS IN UNDER YVONNE BROWN'S OCCUPATION OF my home felt like the times in our childhood when we'd try to sneak an extra snack past bedtime, or smuggle Rob and his friends into Alexis's parents' house when it was supposed to be a girls-only sleepover. There was a certain thrill to it, a small taste of freedom.

"Where's your 'mother-in-law'?" Alexis whispered to me with air quotes, walking in the door and sneaking a look around the empty living room.

I rolled my eyes. "Girl, she's sitting reading the *Daily Word* in the nursery, and it's Evie's nap."

"If she's reading, it's probably through her eyelids, Tabby. You know that woman is sleeping." I pushed Alexis away from the door across the living room to the hallway that led out to my backyard.

"Ssshh. You know she can probably hear us."

"Right, and see us with the eyes in the back of her head. Come on, Tab, it can't be that bad."

"Okay, yes it can, Alexis. And it is, but that's okay. You don't have to believe me."

I ushered Alexis quickly out the back door that would ensure us some privacy. Here, there were only my lemon tree and the leafy bushes topped with heads of birds of paradise as our witnesses. We settled into seats at the table, allowing the slivers of late-morning sun to warm us through the crisp air.

"Tabby," Alexis said, and leaned forward to place her hand gingerly on my arm, "I love you and I'm saying this as your friend. I'm sure the woman is probably a disaster, but you can be a little dramatic." Alexis shrugged as if that made her words sting any less.

"How can you say I'm being dramatic, Lex? Who comes to another woman's house to supposedly 'help,' but instead offers nothing but criticism and hospitality demands?"

"Sorry to break this to you, girl, but you sound like just about every person who has a problematic mother-in-law. Maybe in her own way she's just testing you, or preparing you for life as part of her family."

"Exactly!" I said, bringing my hands down on the table. "Seriously, Alexis, who does that!" I spoke in a loud whisper. I had to remind myself that Yvonne could always be lurking nearby. "How can I even think about being with her son when she makes the package deal look so unappealing? It's like she wants to drive me away, but it's a little late, lady!" I said, directing my last words back in the direction of the house.

Alexis reached over to touch the top of my hand, looking at me like I was a lost child. "No matter what your relationship becomes with Marc, you're still family," she said softly. "I had to learn that when I was separated from Rob. Believe me, every mother-in-law believes she's acting out of love somehow. You just need to figure what her language is. Some mothers, it's criticism; some, it's sacrifice. Once you know what it is, it's easy, like a lock and key. She'll be like putty in your hands."

I took a deep breath and let the fresh air fill my lungs. Rather than reply right away, I gave a light chew to my bottom lip—a fidget. "I don't know, Lex." I let the words draw out of me slowly. "Maybe she's just thinks it's my fault that Marc and I aren't married."

"Right." Alexis looked at me skeptically. "Tab, pay enough attention, and you'll figure it out. And anyway, what about Todd? Although I don't know how you could even manage to find the time."

"Actually, Lex, I did find the time. It just wasn't what I thought. He asked me to connect him with Laila." As much as I thought I was over it, I felt a warm flush of embarrassment come to my face. I wondered if Alexis could tell I was blushing.

"What? And he knows you two are friends?" Alexis brought her head to her hands. "What is wrong with these guys? I swear, all of Rob's friends . . ." Alexis just shook her head. "I'm sorry, Tab, now I feel like I should never have introduced you to him. And how does he even know Laila, anyway? Just from meeting her at our re-wedding?"

"Actually, they were waiting together at the hospital that night. And I guess Laila did her disappearing thing, and now he's looking for the woman with the glass slipper."

Alexis sighed heavily and slouched back in her seat. "That girl, she is really just in her own world at all times," she said.

Shaking her head slowly, she reached inside her generous, large-handled purse and pulled out a notebook with a pen attached. "And here we are, planning an event for her. Tab, I can't believe you talked me into this. There's all kinds of stuff to still plan for your baby, and you're going back to work in a couple of months . . ."

"See, Alexis? Tell me you realize you're proving Laila's point. Why would we automatically think one thing is more important than the other? Our friend has basically had a whole baby, and we didn't even notice." I watched Alexis's face as her disposition softened.

"I remember getting my business started as a real estate agent. It was definitely hard as hell, and I was also having to deal with Rob and Junior, but that whole time, I was just fumbling my way forward anyway."

"And imagine if you'd just asked me and Laila for help."

"Just imagine," Alexis said in a sigh. "It would be my luck to have you two planning my business shower—back then, neither one of you could coordinate more than 'let's meet for drinks.' It's just not fair." Alexis leaned back again and shook her silky pressed hair to brush against her shoulders. Casually, she added, "You know I've always loved giving a good party." We both laughed. Alexis was so right. She had always been the first to celebrate anything. No matter our differences, it felt special for the two of us to find a way to center Laila.

"Lex, I can see how Laila would feel invisible. Especially since the choices she's made aren't seen as sacrifices."

Alexis sighed. "I don't know," she said, shaking her head. "But I'm game. I'm in. Let's plan this party."

In the surprisingly short time that we had before my next feeding window, we were able to agree on a venue, decorations, and an invite list. We also decided that we'd let Laila make her own registry. At some point along the way, we did come to an agreement that it could be just as expensive to start a business as it is to have a baby, possibly more so. Although maybe we should have factored in the cost of diapers, and all the gadgets you're basically forced to buy via social media ads.

"Tabithaaa!" Yvonne Brown's voice rang out from inside my home. It was impossible not to hear her. She came to the door, looking out at Alexis and me without stepping outside. "Tabitha, Evie's stirring. I was thinking you'd want to feed her?" But I was already planning to. *Like a lock and key?* Alexis's words sounded impossible. And the more Yvonne pushed, the more resistance started to build within me. One thing became clear, Yvonne Brown and I weren't going to make it all the way through this visit on civil terms.

10

FOCUSING ON THE DETAILS OF LAILA'S BUSINESS SHOWER WITH Alexis brought me feelings of giddiness and excitement that I hadn't felt since Todd's text. In spite of what Alexis thought, it was time for me to talk to Laila. Todd was now her possibility. I was ready to hand it over to her, no more delay.

At first, I thought that it was Marc's fault that I'd canceled that date with Todd early on—for stunning me into thinking that resolution with him was better than starting something new. That it was his fault for not knowing what he wanted and then being so sure what he wanted wasn't me. And it was his fault for not wanting to create this life that we'd now somehow stumbled our way into anyhow. But it wasn't Marc's fault. All along, Marc had been showing me who he was, eventually even telling me the truth about his family. I didn't want to believe it because it wasn't what I wanted to hear. Todd had served his purpose, as a reminder that I could feel something for someone else. That maybe what I really wanted was still somewhere out there.

Laila was an inspiration, my fearless friend. My breath of fresh air. She kept asking questions, demanding more from

life. She got laid off; she started a business. I found it fascinating. Lately friendship from my end meant giving her
the space and understanding it seemed she needed. To do
my best to see the incredible courage in her life path and to
celebrate that, even when we couldn't do it together like we
usually did. She'd been pushed to the brink, but came out on
the other side with a fierceness that I could only watch with a
"yassss, sis!" and get out of the way.

When she said she couldn't make it to my baby shower
because she was still healing from loss, it stung. But I ap-
plauded her commitment to self-care. When she'd become
harder and harder to reach, and our weekly get-togethers
paused, I simply blamed new motherhood. Laila just always
seemed to be the one who was unafraid to try, to believe that
anything was possible, and to take the knocks of the lessons
along the way. So many other people I knew were so afraid,
they never tried for anything uncertain.

But time and perseverance had been a powerful combination for her online media company. She started out
writing all her content herself, slowly building traffic and
revenue through advertising and her own freelance writing
on the side. In less than a year, she was able to get her own
place, but business growth was hard. She complained about
needing more money to hire other writers, to improve her
site, to speed up the experience, and to create more exciting
and unique content.

Based on how quickly Laila had developed her company,
coupled with her irresistible energy, I always believed that
she'd have no trouble securing investors. But as she told it,
walking into rooms of people who looked nothing like her,

"no" was a common refrain, delivered under the guise of questions about her experience, her business credentials, or wanting to know what other investors had already committed. So rather than getting the support to scale, she was starved for resources and scrambling to make the most of every moment. But to know Laila was to know her determination to meet her goal, with or without support.

Todd had made his choice, and I thought it was a good one. Laila deserved to know she'd become the one he wanted so she could make choices of her own.

"Hey, Tab." Laila answered my call after several rings, sounding distracted. The screen on my phone showed a tired version of my friend in what looked like the office alcove in her Mid-Wilshire apartment. Her backdrop was characteristic wallpaper, textured black with bold primary-color accents, creatively dotted with framed covers of iconic magazine issues and two floating shelves with potted cacti.

"Hey, Lah, you busy? Because . . . I wanted to talk to you about something." I caught Laila's sigh. It hadn't seemed like she meant to.

"I can talk if I can be hands-free. Do you mind if we turn off video?" Some part of me felt slightly disappointed, as if missing a chance to fully connect with her. It was too easy to become two ships sailing past each other in different life directions. Our friendship wouldn't be that way. Not even if it would be my sacrifice that prevented it. I acquiesced easily with a nod and muttered agreement. "So what's up?" she continued.

"Well, just that I wondered if you remembered Todd? You know, the doctor from Alexis's—"

Laila cut me off. "Of course, you basically went into labor all over his shoes." Her laugh sparkled its way through the phone. I felt my face flush.

"A moment I've been trying to forget, but clearly will never be able to," I mumbled back, mostly to myself. Laila apologized quickly, and I moved past it, not wanting to get distracted. "Well, I saw him the other day, and he asked about you."

"He did? What about me?" Laila sounded genuinely surprised.

"Basically, that he really enjoyed talking to you while you waited together at the hospital and . . . he didn't get a chance to get your number."

"Well, that's not exactly true," Laila said quickly. "He did have a chance to get my number. He asked for it, and I didn't give it to him. I told him I'd see him around."

I was genuinely shocked. "But why?" I implored.

"Because, Tab, the same thing is true now that was true then. The solution to my problems is not a man. Is he 'seeking arrangement'? 'Cuz then we can talk. I need an investor. And I'm just tired of wasting my time and energy on dating when all I've ever gotten out of it is more of the same silly shit. I'm focused—in my bag. Drinking my water and literally minding my business."

"Girl, what happened to having your NBA baby?" I joked.

"Tab, you've got that. My business is my payday." I felt a pang in my stomach, like I'd been cornered. I had no real way to say that wasn't true. The exact thing we'd joked about so long ago was what happened with Marc, just not planned or intentional. And now that the joke was unfolding before my eyes, the reality of living it was nowhere near as funny.

"Damn, tell me how you really feel, Lah." I wondered if I sounded as hurt as I felt.

"Girl, stop. You know I didn't mean anything more than what we used to laugh about."

"You just make it sound like I'm on some hoe shit."

"Tab, please. You couldn't be on hoe shit if you actually tried to be on hoe shit." Laila laughed. And then I did too. Sitting in my nursery, still swollen with unrecognizable breasts, a lumpy figure, and twist-out-turned-puff so old that it had essentially turned into a single dreadlock on my head, my "hoe" options were long over.

"Hoes stay winning," I said with a laugh.

"Hoes definitely stay winning," Laila echoed.

"So I guess that means you don't want me to connect you and Todd?"

"Girl, tell him to find me on AngelList," Laila said flippantly. I understood from there—she really wasn't interested and never had been. And more important than that, the business shower that Alexis and I were planning was maybe more necessary than we originally thought.

11

EVEN THOUGH IT WAS BECOMING A FAMILIAR INTIMACY, I would never tire of nuzzling Evie in my arms during the quiet of just the two of us. I could spend forever in our little cocoon of a world that smelled so delicately of the soft florals of baby powder and sugared milk. She was the reminder of the newness of life, the opportunities in each day to be better than before. She revived me, even while early motherhood had been a constant reminder that I was no longer my own.

While there had been so many visits to the doctor to check on Evie, my own care was less frequent. Finally, the date of my six-week postpartum checkup approached. Even more important, it was finally my chance to meet with Lisa, to find a way forward at work while I still had sure support.

It hadn't even been two full months since I'd walked out of KVTV, flaring with indignation. Taking my leave for maternity, I was protected from that place, or so I believed. Lisa had made it clear that the workplace I'd return to wouldn't be the same one that I'd left. My life might have been on pause, but KVTV kept on going with its own developments. Although I resolved to push work out of my mind, I could imagine going back only to find that Scott Stone had been rehired in Lisa's position. The idea of it seemed surreal, unfair even, but in our industry, it was all too possible. After all, Scott had already made it to midday anchor at our competitor station.

Sure enough, Chris Perkins told me in his office two years ago, when I'd first gotten my promotion to senior reporter, that Scott Stone would likely surpass me with ease. And he also said that he didn't believe that I deserved my position or that I'd fight for it. I'd been fighting ever since. Maybe I had taken it too far.

I could only laugh to myself remembering Chris's beet-red face when Lisa and I scrambled to do the interview about my natural hair experience at work. But if we hadn't taken the moment, it would never have happened. Now I was left in a limbo, paying for the risks I'd taken. I faced the uncertainty that I'd go back and there would be a position waiting for me, but no future. One way or another, for me, the only way forward was up.

ON THE DAY OF MY APPOINTMENT, I WAS HAPPY TO BUNDLE UP a sleeping Evie and take her along as I went to see my gynecologist, Dr. Ellis, a fortysomething black woman, who was considered the go-to obstetrician in Los Angeles. Dr. Ellis was the one who started my journey to motherhood with the infertility diagnosis we stumbled upon a couple of years prior. Her office was in the Beverly Center area, a medical complex off Third Street, on the border of Beverly Hills and near the large in-city mall where I'd spent a lot of my time as a teenager.

It was a little sad that a doctor's appointment was on the short list of things that I did just for myself these days, but it felt like a tiny reminder of who I used to be. Guiltlessly venturing into the great outdoors. And immediately after was lunch with Lisa.

Two weeks earlier was Evie's one-month doctor's visit. Now, with Yvonne in town, I was so thankful it was something done by just Marc and me. I'd already been filled with enough apprehension leading into that appointment—and honestly, embarrassment. It was my fault that Evie was behind in her growth measurements. No matter what I tried, I couldn't produce enough breast milk. There had never been anything in my life that I'd wanted to do so badly, but failed. Of course, I imagined, Marc's mother would have insisted on coming . . . and judging. But some things don't need to be shared experiences, especially the struggles of new parenthood.

When it came time for my own checkup with my OB-GYN, I went alone. As Dr. Ellis came into my room in her monogrammed white coat, I noticed her hair in beautifully textured salt-and-pepper two-strand twists. The warm glow of pride flowed through me, seeing them graze just lightly against her shoulders as she moved. It never got old, the recognition of silent victory witnessing hair like mine in spaces that we'd always been told it didn't belong. I felt a sense of solidarity with her simply knowing how weighty the decision was to wear our natural hair at work. In that moment, I felt seen, even before I was actually examined.

"And how are you feeling?" Dr. Ellis asked me just over a half-hour later. Following such an invasive exam, it seemed like the answer should have been available through observation.

"I feel generally well. Tired, of course," I answered, looking for the correct response.

"Oh yes, you're healing great," Dr. Ellis said, consulting the stack of papers in her arms. She looked up at me and continued, "But I mean *emotionally*, how are you feeling? Like yourself, not like yourself? Any changes you've noticed?" There are some questions that seem so simple, but only by your reaction to them do you realize how deeply they root for an answer. Without quite noticing when it started, I felt the warm trickle down my cheek. I swiped at it quickly, feeling betrayed. Evidently, my eyes knew how to say something my mouth did not.

Dr. Ellis crossed the room to pull a series of tissues for me and handed them over in a bunch. She then stepped back slightly, giving me a moment of distance to compose myself. But instead of composure, the more I fought them, the more the tears intensified, and soon I was sobbing and hiccupping on my words as I tried to explain.

"I . . . I'm fine, I think. I am. Really, just that I'm sorry, I don't know what's wrong with me. Maybe it's just hormonal." I sniffled through my fibbing. None of it was true, and I knew it. I *wasn't* fine, and I did know what was wrong with me.

"It's okay, really, this happens all the time." Dr. Ellis reached out to put a hand on my still-heaving shoulder. I looked up at her.

"You mean, you think I'm depressed?"

She smiled at me, the crinkles at the corners of her eyes conveying her kind wisdom. "Not necessarily, but that's common too. You're going through a lot of changes, some hormones too, but lots outside of that. It's important to check in and make sure your needs are being met. Happy mothers make for happy babies."

I searched for the words to tell her about the experience

of Marc's mother and the strain of being separated from my friends, feeling like I needed to be at home all the time, and the guilt that my stolen excursions brought me. And even though we'd gotten a pediatrician to tell me what I already knew, that Evie was doing great now, I was still grappling with the thought that any decision I made for myself was selfish.

"Sometimes I feel like I don't get to be happy anymore," I admitted.

"Overwhelm is a real concern for new mothers," Dr. Ellis told me as I struggled through my recounting of the last six weeks. "Do you have a strategy to stay connected to the community of people who've previously been your support system?" I realized I didn't. I'd become unmoored from the relationships that had been keeping me grounded. I told her as much.

"The good news is that your recovery is progressing very nicely. Your blood pressure is a little high, which we'll need to watch. So we'll check in on that again in a month and on the rest of you. In the meantime, I'm going to write you a script." Dr. Ellis pulled a small square pad of paper out of her pocket and began to scribble. She ripped off the top layer and handed it to me, looking me straight in the eyes. I looked down at what she'd written.

On the paper, it said in relatively legible handwriting: *Ask for help from your friends and family.* I looked up again at Dr. Ellis and she was smiling.

"Doctor's orders," she said as she left the room.

HAVING MADE USE OF DR. ELLIS'S LOVELY "MOTHER'S ROOM" IN her office to pump and to feed Evie after my appointment, I made my way to meet Lisa with a new sense of purpose.

This was "me time." I appreciated Lisa taking time out of her schedule to try to help me, and I really couldn't imagine what it would be like in the world of KVTV without her there. I'd spent so much time wondering if Chris Perkins was on my side or if he wasn't; meanwhile Lisa had become the one person I didn't have doubts about.

Not far from the doctor's office, a well-fed, contented, and hopefully sleepy Evie and I arrived at Berri's Café. The art deco lettered sign was as familiar as the menu offering, because for as long as I'd been going there, it was my go-to place for their take on lobster pizza. Thankfully, Lisa loved it too—it had been her selection. Walking up, I could see her in sunglasses, sitting at a table on the outside patio waving in my direction.

One of the best things about LA and especially about being on local news in LA is that "everyday celebrities" very rarely garner much more attention than a head nod and perhaps a smile, especially in West Hollywood. So for Lisa, sitting outside alone at a highly trafficked restaurant barely registered a blip, even as the primetime anchor for KVTV.

More noticeable was Lisa's buoyant enthusiasm at seeing Evie in person for the first time, an announcement to our entire surroundings that I was a new mom venturing out with a newborn. I was grateful to reach my seat and place Evie's carrier down between us. Lisa hugged me so tightly I felt like I'd lose my breath. But, somehow, in the very best way. She admired and smiled and cooed over the baby and thought she looked just like me.

"I'm so sorry that it took me so long to make it out to see you," I said. Lisa looked at me with curiosity. "I thought maternity leave was going to be a break, but it's basically been on-the-job training in a position I'm *completely* unqualified for. Seems like there's even less time, and I'm not even working!" I threw my hands above my head.

"I remember those days," Lisa said, smiling at me. "You're more than qualified, Tabby! What're you worried about?" Lisa asked with an incredulous lift to her tone.

"There's so much. Even making it out of the house," I said. "And of course, when you asked me to meet you, I knew it was important, but it's hard not to feel like I'm placing my job over my child's well-being."

"Welcome to my everyday," Lisa said. She smiled at me and reached over to place her flawless French manicure on top of my dowdy and bare clipped-down nails. "Sometimes you kinda have to just make a call, you know? Like, *I need this.* Somehow, some way, it is all gonna work out and everybody's gonna be okay. And don't be afraid to ask for help!" I sighed, feeling deeply that Lisa's words were right, especially after the counsel I'd received from Dr. Ellis.

"I guess I still need someone to tell me that. Like a doctor. Evidently it's so bad, I had to be given a prescription."

"Oh, don't feel bad. We've all been there," Lisa said with a warm smile. "What'd she give you? Prozac? Or Xanax? Lexipro?" I rummaged in my bag for the small square paper to hand to Lisa.

"Not yet," I said to her running list of medications. "She literally wrote me a prescription for this. Basically, this exact moment." Lisa's eyes widened and then narrowed in on the "prescription" I'd handed her. I could see it register on her face as she processed what she'd read.

"Oh, oh! This is amazing." Lisa said, flapping the paper in her hand. She read the text aloud. "Ask for help."

"Doctor's orders, she said."

LISA JUST KEPT STARING AT THE PAPER. "I'M TELLING YOU, I wish I'd had that doctor as a new mom. And look, all I have to offer you is a lobster pizza, so if this doesn't work, you can always go back for the good stuff." Lisa lifted her water glass and took a sip before continuing, casually, as if what she said was an afterthought. "Believe me, I've been through a few rounds of prescription 'help' myself. Nothing at all to be ashamed of." She took another sip of water, leaving her finger marks in the condensation around the glass. "Are you a lobster pizza person?" she asked me, referencing the hallmark menu item at the restaurant.

"Is there anything else? I don't think I've ever looked at a full menu here," I said, laughing. Taking a minute to catch up on all things, we finally got to the news that Lisa had shared weeks ago. She'd made the announcement of her departure at the station.

"I wanted to make sure that you and I had a time set to see each other before I told Chris and Doug. I told Doug first and made my request to have you test for my position *before* I talked to Chris. And, Tabby, you should have seen the look on Chris's face. And as much as he plays that ratings game, he knows there's nothing he can do if the general manager gives the okay, you know?"

I nodded. Lisa was playing strategy that I needed to learn from. I let her continue.

"And I know it's your maternity leave, but I think I can get them to agree to a meeting as a lead-up to a test for my anchor slot. They're going to be testing other candidates, but an internal person already has familiarity in the market. I think you have a good shot, and it's worth taking, especially if you want to stay at KVTV."

"You think one of those people would be Scott Stone?"

"You know, could be. I think it's safe to assume that anyone's fair game. They're going to want to fill the position quickly." I could feel my face fall. Lisa seemed to notice and reached over with a hand to my shoulder. "Don't worry, Tabby. You're going to get your shot, I promise."

Although I knew I needed to ask Marc to send his mother back to Florida, at least while she stayed, I'd have a babysitter for the day if I needed to go in to work, and a doctor's note that covered the rest. How funny was it that a simple piece of paper was somehow the difference between being able to afford myself a moment and staying lost in the overwhelm of new responsibility?

"There's no way I can let Scott Stone steal a spot from me. I'm sure Chris would love that after the stunt we pulled." I stole a glance at Evie, thankfully sleeping soundly, pacifier still in place, moving steadily between her tiny lips. "I have a feeling that I'm not Chris's favorite person, especially not now."

"Tabby, you'll outshine Scott at the anchor desk. We've just got to get you that test spot. Chris? He'll get over it—we'll give him no choice. He wouldn't say it, but I happen to know that segment on your hair got great ratings. Just because he's your boss doesn't mean he knows everything." Lisa turned to thank our waitress, who'd delivered the deliciousness of our lunch. With the quick confirmation that Evie was still sleeping peacefully in the din of the lunchtime conversations around us, I returned my attention to Lisa.

"I was hoping I could just keep my head down for a while."

"This is a cutthroat industry, Tabby. Heads down get the

ax," Lisa quickly replied. "So I'll be with you at the meeting," she added, as we wrapped up our planning. As a follow-up, Lisa said she'd take on the task of getting us on the schedule to meet with both Chris and Doug. All I could do from there on was wait.

Lisa knew what I was only starting to accept. I'd taken risks that placed bets on my future, in order to create one that would allow me to be both successful and true to myself. Now I'd have to take more. I could lose. But this was the reality of the workplace. Speak up, they tell you, but don't say what you really mean. Be yourself, but only if it doesn't make other people uncomfortable. Take risks and be unique, but you better always win. Because if you don't, there's going to be no one from the cheering section to save you—you're on your own.

12

THERE'S NO GOOD WAY TO TELL YOUR SOMETIMES BOYFRIEND, threatened fiancé, and daughter's father that you really, *really* want him to send his mother home. You could thank him first, for his good intentions and for being a dutiful son and father, but at some point, the truth would have to come out. There was no way to soften the hurt of it. Yvonne Brown was driving me crazy. And unless Dr. Ellis was going to prescribe me more than what was on that paper, I just couldn't take it anymore.

I was ready to ask for help. My own mother was dying to be involved, and who better to ask for advice on how to get rid of another grandmother? For once, Jeanie Walker Williams and I could quite possibly be on the same page. On the way home from my lunch with Lisa, I did two things. First, I double-checked on a seemingly calm baby, secured in the back seat. "When the going gets tough, Ladybug," I said to her in the rearview, "the tough get going." I smiled to myself, thinking that Evie brought out of me an expression I could easily imagine said by my Granny Tab. I allowed myself to bask for just a moment in the comfort of remembering her at her best. Then it was time for reinforcements. I instructed my car system to "Call Mom."

"Tabby Cat! Is that you and my grandbaby?!" My mother picked up right away, her voice singing to me a little too loudly through the car speakers. She'd always sounded happy to hear from me, but never had I heard her so happy as lately. In the three-week blur of Evie's first weeks home from the hospital, it had been my mother supporting me, even though I was too exhausted to fully remember exactly how. Marc tried his best to help, but it was me and my mother doing the feedings, changing the diapers, cleaning up, and mainly my mother, in the midst of all the chaos, reassuring me that it was all going to be okay—that Evie would survive and I would too. I told her about the doctor's appointment, as she'd already checked in many times since Evie's one-month, and it was a relief to know that I was also doing fine.

"Well, everything is *almost* fine," I said, gripping the wheel and easing into a stop at a red light.

"I knew something was wrong, Tabby, I could hear it in your voice," my mother scolded back at me.

"It's Marc's mother. She's been here a full week, and I don't think I can take it much longer. I need to figure out how to ask Marc to *please* get her back home."

"Well, you only let me stay three weeks!" my mother said.

"Mom," I replied, already exasperated, "I never asked you to leave, you said it was time to head back. And with Yvonne, there is *no way* that we're going to make it that long. Marc's father is sick, so I thought that she'd have to go back quickly. But nope, every day, she's just . . . here . . . and so are her . . . opinions."

"Well, can you say something to Marc?" she finally replied after a pause.

"What could I say?" The exchange made me wonder what the early dynamic was like between my mother and Granny Tab in the days after I was born.

"That's a tough one, Tab." The sound of my mom's heavy sigh whirled its way through my car. "You know how men are about their mothers."

"Yeah, and Marc can't seem to say no to his about anything."

"Well . . ." My mom drew out the one word long enough to form a sentence of its own. "How about you tell him that I'm coming and that you need a break."

"But he'll know when you don't show up that I made it up."

"So then, I guess we'll have to make it true!" she said brightly. "I'll come back to LA and that will really be the end of whatever reason she feels she needs to be there."

If you'd put a million dollars in neat stacks on a table in front of me before this call and given me three chances to predict what would happen next, I'd have lost the money on this outcome. But the more I thought about it, the more it started to make perfect sense. Maybe she had me on the ropes, but Yvonne Brown was no match for Jeanie Walker Williams.

Having my mother feel like an accomplice was unexpectedly exhilarating. The last time we'd been so purely aligned I was eight years old, and she'd helped me make a cake for my dad as a surprise for his birthday. The cake was chocolate layers, with chocolate icing. And it fell. A lopsided disaster. But in the end, my mom fixed it so you could hardly tell. Keeping that secret with her was fun. And I loved the feeling that my mom knew just what to do, even if I couldn't quite follow all the instructions. Just maybe, the arrival of Evie was our opportunity for a second chance.

By the time I made it home, Marc had already sent me a text that he'd picked up his mother while I was at my appointment and taken her for a meal and some sightseeing. The relief I felt walking into my empty living room was exhilarating. "Grandma Yvonne is going h-ooo-ome!" I sang to Evie, who clearly understood none of what I said, but whose scrunchy babyface smile attempts made me believe she was entertained by her mother's elation. We'd only known each other on the same side of my belly for a month and a couple of weeks, but she'd already started to change me in ways that I hadn't expected, forcing me to expand the limits of my heart and mind. "A single mother by courage," is what Andouele told me when I was pregnant. She told me to expect to find the truth of myself, and that my baby would require that of me. Today wasn't so much about unearthing the truth of how I'd been feeling, but the perfect storm of what I needed to finally take action.

My text to Marc was a simple request. I needed to talk . . . alone. That seemed like a huge win given that we'd all been essentially connected as one giant three-pronged entity since his mother had arrived. Marc and I had had no time to ourselves, not as new parents and certainly not as adults. The latter I was probably thankful for. No opportunity to blur the lines. Not that he'd inspired any sense of romance recently anyway. It seemed nearly impossible to remember that there'd been a time when Marc felt like a fantasy come to life—that there'd been a quickening of my breath when he touched me, and a float of hope in my heart each time he looked at me. I used to yearn for a future together. Now that future was a certainty, whether I still wanted it or not.

Marc messaged me back saying that he understood and would come over just as soon as he dropped his mother off at his place after dinner.

Do you want me to bring anything?

Anything or anyone but Yvonne, I wanted to answer.

No, just you.

I messaged in reply. Now there was no turning back.

A FEW HOURS LATER, I'D PUT EVIE DOWN FOR WHAT WOULD either be a long nap or the magic of sleeping through at least part of the night. Marc breezed in the door, trailing his usual mix of expensive-smelling wood, spice, and citrus greenery in the air behind him. I told him he smelled nice and invited him in for a seat. His grin looked mischievous, like a young boy had taken over his body. I took an awkward seat next to him on the sofa and tried to face him squarely. The intensity of his eyes beneath his long dark lashes made me squirm a bit. I took his hand in mine.

"Marc," I began, tentatively searching for words, "I really appreciate that your mother took all this time to spend with us. And I know she left your father at home ill . . . and I, um, my mother has offered to come and help . . . you know, to give her a chance . . . *to go back.*" The last words poured out of my mouth. A mix of truth, half-truth, and downright complete untruth had made a thick soup of the air between us. I took a sharp breath and held it, waiting for his reply, studying his face all the while. Marc leaned back some and I watched his shoulders drop. He let out a deep breath, and his head hung a bit. And then he turned to me.

"Well, that's a relief," he said, shaking his head slowly. "My dad's been calling her to come back almost every day this past week, and she's insisted on staying because she said she knew you needed help. And she didn't know when she'd get a chance to spend the same amount of time with Evie." I tried to keep my mouth from dropping wide. "Plus, I think she was enjoying getting to know you."

"What? Wait, are you kidding?" I asked Marc, not sure if he'd been watching something completely different than what had actually been happening between his mother and me.

"No, no, not at all. She was just saying today that she thinks you're nice. When's your mother coming?" I couldn't believe it. Somehow, Marc's mother had turned me into the bad guy, and she wasn't even in the room. I felt terrible, confused, and wary of pushing further, testing my luck.

"A few days from now, or a week. When do you think your mom would be ready to leave?" I hesitated, not ready to address his mother's behavior. I was too tired to start a fight, especially when it seemed like I'd won.

"Let me talk to her tonight. I'm sure she'll feel much better about heading back now that she knows you'll have your mother here."

I thanked him sincerely. And in the moment when our eyes met, I could feel the energy of his focused observation. He moved closer, and then a bit closer, to the point I could feel the heat of him near my face. He hovered, drawing his hand up to curve his fingers softly behind my neck, and then in the next moment, his lips were on mine. Briefly, I lost touch with who I'd become or the fact that I'd just pumped or that baby slobber was still on my shoulder even though I'd clumsily wiped at it earlier. I lingered in that escape as long as I could, which was just a second. Because the realities of my body came back in a wave. I wasn't ready to get back to the woman I used to be; I'd become used to being someone else.

"Are you okay?" he asked as I pulled away from him, my restless hand rising to fumble with my hair reflexively.

"I am, I just . . . I'm not . . ." The words to follow I couldn't find. *I'm not myself? I'm not feeling the same? I'm not feeling the same about you?* Somewhere within me, these were all true and also untrue, equally. My body still felt alien to me in its current form, the functions having turned to comfort and sustenance, and a slow healing, more gradual than I'd ever anticipated. Marc studied me. His eyes moved across my face, crossing my cheeks, so deliberately as to almost be sensed physically, like a caress.

Concern flooded the space between us, and I could see his effort not to bring his glance lower. We both knew my body had changed, but he wasn't aware that my mind had also. At some point, I forgot about the part of myself who'd indulged herself physically so carefree and confidently. And then without her, I stopped looking for that person in Marc.

I needed Marc to be something different, someone who could protect me and not consume me, or subsume me either. But it was like casting for a new role that wasn't in any script. And so, while he was ignoring my physical changes, or at least pretending not to notice, probably thinking of it as a kindness, he had no idea that my mind had made the biggest transformation of all.

"Tab," Marc said finally, "I know a lot of women feel self-conscious after . . . everything, but I want you to know that I feel the same way . . . I see you the same way." His hand came up to stroke my cheek, sincerity pooled in his eyes. "You're still beautiful . . ."

"Marc." I paused, looking for the right words. "I appreciate . . . I mean . . . It's not that. Or maybe it is that. I think I just need some space, okay? And some more time. That too, I need time." And then, it was my turn to study him. We'd entered the scariest place in the world. We were in the silence after you've finally found the words and the courage to speak your truth. That was my truth—I needed space, and time, and also support, acceptance, patience, and love. Just then, I realized how much of an ask that was.

I watched Marc lean back, sinking slightly into the cushions of the sofa. A deep exhale deflated his chest. And then, very slowly, a sly smile teased at the sides of his mouth. "Tab, I thought that maybe you wanted . . . I mean, after you said 'alone' and . . ." He started to laugh. "I just thought you wanted some *adult* attention," he said, with a look in his eyes, partially obscured by still-lowered lashes, that made me briefly question my thinking. And then I started to laugh too. It was confusing, and messy, and I was fumbling. But so was Marc, and somehow, that was exactly what I needed to know. I gave him a playful push in his shoulder, his muscles pushed back against my hand.

"Not even at all!"

Marc winked at me. "Not even a little bit?"

"Marc Brown, not a chance." But I was still smiling, and so was Marc.

13

"I'M GLAD YOU CALLED ME," ANDOUELE SAID, AS WE WALKED the paved loop of the Reuben Ingold Park in my neighborhood. A tracksuit-clad couple passed us, the delicate lines in their brown faces revealing a maturity belied by their walking pace. The community park served as a green space and gathering place for health and exercise, and also for catching up with friends in motion. My time with Andouele seemed to be a perfect continuation of Dr. Ellis's prescription and my ongoing effort to find support in the midst of my constantly moving life.

It did feel strange meeting with Andouele outside of my home and away from Evie, but until Yvonne's departure, promised by Marc to be within the week, my only privacy was outdoors. I still felt thankful, knowing that plenty of other mothers didn't have even a fraction of the options that I did. As much as Yvonne's constant critique and correction was overbearing, I could appreciate that I had the ability to leave comfortably for a few hours at a time with Evie in her expense-free care. I needed Andouele to help me. To be a soft transition, and to help unpack the weight of whatever caused me to break down in unexpected tears in my doctor's office.

I told her about that incident and the feelings I'd been sure about, the anxiety from Yvonne's criticism and fears of being a new mom overall. My elevated blood pressure that we needed to watch, and the sense of being alone all the time, except that I was never, ever by myself. She listened patiently, and then around lap three, when I'd finished pouring out my insides, pulled us onto a gravel patch on the inside of the track.

"Let's come up with a plan," she said.

"To not feel alone?" I said, entirely confused.

"Overwhelm can become a practice, Tabby. Before you know it, especially as a new mom, you've taken on too much. So you need a new practice. Friendship is a practice too, and even if you get out of practice you can always just start again." To those walking by, it probably looked like the two of us were having some kind of quarrel. My hands were on top of my head as I paced in small circles. Andouele was standing still, as patient and steady as ever. Was I practicing overwhelm? There was so much to do, I didn't even have time to sleep. Who else would do it? It was hard to process what she was saying.

"It's very simple, but a big challenge," she continued. "You're going to have to learn how to ask for help. Asking for help is self-care." Her words stopped my movements. The concept was so uncomfortable, I felt the urge to physically remove it, like an itchy sweater or a shirt that was too tight.

"I ask for help," I protested. "I asked you today, and my mom, she's coming and—" Andouele put her hand up for me to pause.

"Accepting an offer of help isn't the same thing, Tabby.

My job as a doula is to be an offer of help. Your mother offered to help. But when are you asking? Who are you asking? A cry for help isn't the same thing as asking. Sorry." She smiled sheepishly before continuing. "No pun intended."

I had no answer. I thought back to all the moments before, and what I had actually asked for. Honestly, it wasn't much. Maybe I'd pushed my needs so far to the side that I'd hidden them from myself and from everyone else. *Are you asking for what you need?* Was I? Wasn't I already silently asking? And not just asking, begging. Couldn't everyone see?

Maybe my version of begging was hoping that everyone would notice how hard I'd been trying—with every inch and fiber of my being—and that my greatest prayer was that somebody would offer some assistance without me having to burden anyone with a request. And that was it. After everything, I still didn't want to encumber anyone else with what I could carry myself. If I was drowning, I'd just sink, dragged down by the weight of my good intentions.

"Come on, let's keep walking." Andouele cut through my thoughts with a gentle tug at my elbow. "It's surprising how far so many of us get pretending like we don't need anyone. A great illusion that's perfectly understandable. If you don't ask, you don't give anyone a chance to say no. But imagine how much further we'd get if we knew there were people we could depend on."

The silence that followed was filled with the muffled sounds of other people's conversations as they passed, the scuffling of sneaker bottoms against the pavement, and the jostling of fabric layers rubbing together in the brisk rhythm of walking.

I knew Andouele's words were meant for me, but they

made me think most immediately of Laila. Laila, who almost never asked anyone for anything. Who'd suffered her way to a breakdown, who fought her way back, and who just barely said to Alexis and me that she felt left out in our obsessing over men and children. Alexis and I had to fight to understand her. She was the kind of friend who'd be there for you, but withdraw in her own time of need, intent on fixing it herself. My version of asking for help was the low-stakes kind. The way that never required me to risk myself, because maybe Andouele was right—I was too afraid to find out who'd be there and who wouldn't.

I realized then I'd paused us again in our walking. I turned my eyes up to the blue sky and fixated on the scattered clouds above. Andouele observed me, but gave the grace of saying nothing, just standing still with me while I tried to hold it all together.

I was past the time of having a doula. My mother was coming; Marc's mother was still here and was able to give me enough of a physical break to at least take a shower each day and escape for air. I had my own doctor and a pediatrician and friends who would show up if I could get over myself to ask. And I had Marc, who was trying to be what he thought I needed, even if he had no clue what that actually was. And so I felt guilty needing this one more thing. Maybe it was just the perspective that Andouele brought, or simply the indulgence of her calm. Maybe it was the permission she gave me to need and ask. Maybe it was just knowing that this was one person who I could count on not to say no. "Can we do this again next week?" I heard myself say. She smiled back at me. I already knew the answer. Maybe I'd call it practice, but either way, it was a start.

MY "VILLAGE" WASN'T QUITE WHAT I'D ENVISIONED WHEN I first started on the journey to motherhood. I thought Alexis and Laila would be ever present and unavoidable. I thought my Granny Tab would be living with me, and I thought Marc would be someone who stopped by once in a while out of curiosity and a loose connection of friendship. Instead, Laila was launching her own "business baby" that was growing with demands of its own; Ms. Gretchen was on the injured reserve list and stuck at Crestmire doing rehab; and Marc had become the baby daddy teaching me the meaning of "good idea in theory." And while I'd wondered why it took so long to meet Marc's mother when we were dating, I'd learned the answer firsthand, and wished it had taken even longer.

I had just one more day until my mother arrived, and three before Yvonne departed, so in the name of giving her a little bit more time with her granddaughter and me another sliver of sanity, I decided to make my own trip to see Ms. Gretchen. According to her, our video calls, however infrequent, were keeping her sane. She'd been so disappointed that an evening of line dancing in kitten heels resulted in a calamity with Ms. Cora, who she said could barely see. The collision left her with an infirmity and kept her bound to Crestmire. She'd told the story enough times that we had both reached a point where we could laugh about it, knowing that it was something she'd heal from given enough time, ice cream, and attention from a particularly good-looking rehabilitation therapist named Justin. "Justin's coming today" was a new refrain that had begun to replace the frustration in her voice about not being able to come and spend time with me and Evie.

When I pulled into the familiar parking lot of the Crest-mire building, I expected I would walk in to find the residents just finishing lunch and settling into a round of either games or naps. Entering, I passed the reception desk to find Ms. Gretchen plunked in her favorite chair in the middle of the recreation space, a slow frenzy of her fellow residents orbiting around her. She waved at me, which brought an instant smile to my face as I walked over.

I handed her a small bunch of flowers I'd picked up on my way.

"They're gorgeous!" she said, giving the reaction I'd been hoping for. She beamed more brightly at me and tucked them into the chair next to her. "Now see, if that woman hadn't stepped on my foot, I'd be putting them into water right away," she said with a rare flare of anger.

"I'm sure they'll be fine for a bit. I can't stay long. And plus, there's flower food just inside the plastic wrapping. I heard it makes them last longer." I rubbed her arm gently and then positioned myself in the chair next to hers.

Anchored by her propped-up foot, she adjusted to face me. Her expression had the vigor of a preteen girl, as if we were going to dish the hottest of gossip in the middle of the night at a sleepover.

"So, tell me everything. How is Evie? And what about Yvonne? You kick her out yet? And Marc, he still threatening you with marriage?"

When I managed to stop laughing, I told Ms. Gretchen about Evie, who was doing wonderfully in the midst of hundreds of dirty diapers and baby spit-up and soiled garments and several onesies that I just decided to throw away rather than try to salvage. And then there were the few fevers that didn't last long, but generally I felt lucky and only worried that she was growing and changing so much every day that if I blinked, I would miss something.

The look on her face dropped, and I could see a hint of sadness, probably because she knew she was missing these moments. I quickly changed the subject.

"And you know Marc's been saying he wants to get married. He's been trying to sell me on the idea of this perfect life, you know. And that feels so strange to me because there was a time when that was all I wanted. Now I just don't know what I want."

Ms. Gretchen leaned farther into me, as if she had a big secret to tell. "No woman with a full life like you have wouldn't be scared to death marrying somebody. Once you fall in love with yourself, you can always be the woman you fell in love with, but who he becomes . . . well, you have no control over that. I had to learn that two times," she said, holding up two thin fingers with hot pink nails at the tips.

"Ms. Gretchen, how are you still getting your nails done? You're not supposed to leave Crestmire," I scolded.

"Honey, I called the salon, and they made a special exception to come to me. Even with a hurt foot, you know I can't just let *everything* go." As she shook her head for emphasis, I could see that she'd even managed to maintain the color and bounce of her blond curls. I just assumed that she'd finagled that visit as well. "Self is wealth, honey," she continued. "Self is wealth."

"Self is wealth," I repeated. "I like that, Ms. Gretchen," I gave her a teasing smile.

"Oh yes, honey. And, like I said, no rich woman in her

right mind wouldn't be scared to death when a man wanted to marry her. Whether or not she planned on saying yes. These days, that's a lot to give up." Ms. Gretchen shifted again in her chair, seeming like she was searching for a more comfortable position. "Good on you for at least putting some thought into it," she continued. "I'm far from his biggest fan, but I can see plenty well. I know a lot of women would get all twisted up inside if a Marc came calling for them and feel the pressure all the same because of the child."

"That's the thing, Ms. Gretchen, I feel like I'm saying no to everything I'm supposed to want. We used to talk about Marc not wanting to commit, and now that he does . . . I'm not sure I want it anymore."

"Honey, women have been asking themselves these same kinda questions for a long time, but not too many would say it out loud. We leave it to the artists and the poets to say it for us. The fearless women who venture to the other side of what we're all afraid to do and come back with perfect words for it. So then some of us don't have to be so afraid anymore.

"Back before you were even born, Ms. Nikki Giovanni said after having her son that she didn't get married because she didn't want to, and not only did she not want to, she could afford not to get married. Can you imagine a black single mother saying that in the seventies? People didn't understand it then, but I did. Of course, I was married and ready to not be married to that first husband of mine. And what she said made me realize, as long as I had myself and could support myself, I could do whatever I damn well wanted to. And so I did. And then I tried it again, and said 'nope, not for me,' and undid it again." She finished with a smile, as she swept her palms together, flashes of bright pink seeming to emphasize her sentiment.

"I've been told it's being a single mother by courage, Ms. Gretchen. And it's taking a lot to say no."

"Well, who're you drawing inspiration from?" Ms. Gretchen said with a very playful wink. "Honey, mistakes can be like magnets. Each one attracts another if you don't slow down and think. Seems like you're trying to make some important decisions."

"I just don't want to regret anything," I confessed. "What if I'm being selfish and Marc gets fed up and finds someone else? What will I be dealing with? Another woman, a bunch of confusion? And I had the chance to create a stable home for Evie?"

"Bridges are crossed when you reach them, honey, not before. Do you still love him?"

"I do love him, Ms. Gretchen, but not in the same way I did before." It was hard to admit that truth, but I needed to say it aloud. "It seems like forever ago, when everything was perfect on paper. Real life is so different from what I imagined. I couldn't be happier in so many ways, and it couldn't be harder in so many others. But right now? Love is just not enough for me. There's more that I want." Ms. Gretchen raised a eyebrow at me, leaning forward a bit for the reveal of my next words. "Love looks like the life I want for Evie—to make sure that she's always able to see the best version of me, even if I'm still finding that person."

Ms. Gretchen smiled at me with such kindness, it was almost a hug. "That person, that woman you want to be," she said. "She's right there, Tabby. Look in the mirror, and you'll see she's been with you all the while."

I stayed as long as I could with Ms. Gretchen, watching her shift, adjust, missing just a little of her spark. I wish I could have spent more time with her that day. But time wasn't on my side.

14

IN THE CAR ON THE WAY TO THE AIRPORT TO PICK UP MY mother, I wondered if Evie and I would be enough of a welcome. Since she'd only just left, her return was unplanned, but I wondered if Jeanie Walker Williams had just been waiting for any kind of invitation to come back. There'd only be one day of overlap with Yvonne, and then my mother and I would be on our own.

After my dad left, even the nine-year-old version of me noticed that my mother became a different person. The same person who would delight in the girlish gathering of snipped marigolds and bright pink zinnias turned into the person who would let fresh fruit sit in our kitchen until rotten and would often forget to raise lowered blinds for days at a time. After she'd met "the general," for the first time in a long time, I saw the glint of a sparkle return to her eyes. A sense of the whimsical part of her sprit broke its way back into our home. Just for brief moments. After I'd gone to live with Granny Tab and we established our own new normal, my visits with my mother had become awkward at best, grueling at worst; it seemed like she tried to cram a life's worth of parenting into every spare moment. No longer could we just be and laugh or enjoy simple times. Everything was an opportunity for correction or critique, the *Impossible Standard to Live By* became our constant companion, even on the vacation we took together to New York City that was supposed to be my high school graduation present.

The New York Trip, as I was sure we both remembered it but never spoke of, was our last time traveling together, intentionally, just the two of us. And during that trip we'd fought. And I almost said the unspeakable—*You left me*—in the heat of our worst argument. On that night, she'd planned for us to see *Hairspray* on Broadway, and we were all dressed up for dinner and a show. When we ran a little late and I switched up my outfit, we hit the moment where we'd both had enough. "Why can't you just cooperate?" she asked me. And all I could think of was the fact that this person didn't know me at all. She didn't know that back then, I preferred Converse to kitten heels, and that in a huge bustling city so far from everything I knew on the West Coast, I just wanted to feel comfortable, like myself. With no words other than the explosive truth between us, all I could do was switch my outfit and sulk—late to a dinner I barely ate, followed by a show I could hardly watch and scarcely recall.

In the time since, we, or mainly I, felt the pins and needles of our interactions, even now. A delicate orchestration of mainly my conformity made our time tolerable. I told myself this was the price to pay for a relationship. The changes were only temporary—it was the smoother way to go. In many ways still, even as a mother, even with my own home and my own life decisions in front of me, I felt like that little girl, lost in a big city, who just wanted to wear her Chucks.

"Hello, Tabby Cat! And is that my little Evie?" my immaculately dressed mother gushed through the rolled-down passenger side window as I pulled up to the Arrivals curb. She craned her neck into the back seat with a smile as wide as her face would allow. "Okay, now let's get these bags into the car," my mother said, looking around frantically, as if expecting someone. "I don't suppose there's anyone here to help—" I smiled, recalling the orchestrated army that greeted me and my traveling companions visiting her airport for my baby shower. I may have had a hard time asking for help, but my mother had no problem. "Maybe I can find that nice man who helped me with the bags and put them onto this cart," she mused aloud.

By this time, I'd already pressed the button to pop the trunk and carefully exited the driver's side of my car, trying to not to wake a sleeping Evie. "Welcome to LAX!" I said, wrapping my arms around her. "We're on our own, but I think we can manage." My mother seemed flustered, briefly confused at the prospect of lifting her bags, but eventually joined me at the cart to hoist the larger roller bag and shift it to the car, heels clicking in staccato as we covered the short distance together.

"Careful, now!" she said, admonishing me about not hurting my back. Somehow, amidst all this, in a struggle of grunting and loose coordination, we managed to load the collection of matching luggage into the trunk space. My mother settled into the front, holding her purse and smallest bag in her lap. "Is she still sleeping?" She turned to look at Evie, nestled in her car seat and just starting to make the shifts that signaled the possible end of her nap.

"Not for much longer. She's been down for almost three hours, and I think the car ride bought a little more time."

"Oh? You aren't still feeding her every two hours?" I closed my eyes and took a deep breath. The question sounded earnest, but somehow it carried the same flavor that I'd been trying to escape from with Yvonne. Maybe it was the hormones, or the lack of sleep, or my raw feelings so close to the surface. When my eyes snapped open, I snapped too.

"No." I whipped my head around to face my mother. "I'm not feeding her every two hours. I feed her when she wakes up." My mother's face fell sharply. I felt instantly guilty and terrible. I caught myself and shifted to a softer tone. "She's gaining weight, and according to the doctor, it's fine. Everything is fine." I pushed down the lump in my throat. *Everything is fine*, I repeated silently to myself, as if each repetition made it more true.

"Tabby! Are you okay?" My mother had recoiled and pushed herself into the passenger side door, looking at me with an expression of surprise. "I didn't mean . . . I just . . . Well, it seems like I upset you and I certainly wasn't expecting that reaction."

I sighed heavily. "Mom, Marc's mother leaves in less than forty-eight hours. Let's just say I've taken about all the advice I can take for now. Can we talk about something else? Just for now, for this car ride?" My mother studied me for a moment, looking me over twice, as I watched her eyes travel deliberately from the top of my head down to my leisure-wear stained with milk and baby drool. I braced myself for the next comment.

"Okay," she said, finally. And only then did I set the car in drive and pull away. My mom turned her attention to

Evie in the back, who managed to still be giving us much-appreciated blissful slumber. Gradually, I could feel the energy reset between us. I imagined my mother needed time to find a topic other than thoughts and opinions about raising Evie, or children in general. It was almost as if criticism was another love language, or perhaps even its own imagined act of service, making her feel much better than it did me. At least she'd given herself the satisfaction of do-gooding. I felt at a loss, thinking about Alexis's words, that every mother had her own way of loving . . . *like a lock and key.*

That's the thing about advice; its value is mostly subjective. And at my most vulnerable, when I really wanted to be great, criticism cut deeply into my soft parts. It created wounds that festered, leaving me with large open gashes of self-doubt. "Well," my mother began again, "our neighbor started building a pool in their backyard just before I left," finally finding her words. "And you wouldn't believe how much commotion that whole thing created. The entire neighborhood has been talking about it . . ." She seemed delighted enough to speak about this third-party travesty, leaving my shortcomings somewhere back at the airport Arrivals for someone else to pick up.

IN THE EXCITEMENT OF THE TRAFFIC-INDUCED QUAGMIRE OF Los Angeles International Airport, I completely forgot to mention to my mother that on the evening of her arrival, I'd agreed, under extreme duress of course, to bring Evie to dinner at the Walker residence in Calabasas. Everything happened so quickly with her travel plans—I'd forgotten all the escape routes I'd lined up during Yvonne's stay. And so, while my mother saved me in effect by coming, she'd also created an entirely different challenge. On her first night in town, how could I possibly tell her that I'd be leaving her alone to go to my father's house and eat a meal most likely prepared by Diane?

By all appearances, my postdivorce family, blended together over time, had become a vision of relative harmony. The vast expanse of obstacles we'd overcome to even gather had started to fade into the past, obscured by more recent memories we'd created. Sometimes, I'd even manage to forget the origins of my father's relationship with Diane, how they'd come to meet and marry. Now, if someone snapped a photograph of me with the "new" Walkers, the people captured within would probably look like any other family—someone smiling, someone talking, someone staring off into space for an instant. But in the layers that don't show, there too, like an unwelcome guest, sits betrayal. And the hurt feelings that still haven't healed. And the pain that inevitably someone has swallowed.

When I'd visit Granny Tab at Crestmire, she tried in her own subtle way to create these connections for us, to keep us together as a family despite what had already torn us apart—to wipe the past away with the fresh cloth of the present. She'd ask me gently to join the family dinners, and I always politely refused. She didn't push, and if she was disappointed, she didn't show it. Each time, though, soon after she'd simply ask again, as if I'd never said no all the countless times before.

Before she passed, I started trying, we all did, even Diane, to make moments like that photograph. But after she was gone, it just felt more necessary. This was the start of healing that once seemed impossible, and a relationship with my sisters, who not so long ago would have been "Diane's kids" to me. And to be clear, that was my mother's description. Still.

After pulling into my driveway, while unloading a newly awake and very hungry Evie, pulling bags out of the car and getting settled, I procrastinated with the news that I'd need to deliver to my mother. Even Evie seemed to sense my discomfort, taking longer to take to the bottle and fussing a bit before settling into our familiar position for feedings. My mom was quietly sorting herself within the room, unpacking casual tops and folding jeans into the meager guest space that remained after I turned my second bedroom into a nursery. It was now or never. The dinner was just hours away.

"Mom," I said gingerly, hoping not to disturb Evie, still attached to her bottle. "With everything going on, I forgot that tonight I was supposed to bring the baby to my dad's house. The girls wanted to see her and . . ."

"Oh?" My mother looked up at me, suspended in mid-arrangement of leisurewear. I waited for the reference to "Diane's kids," but it never came.

"It's just that, we haven't been there yet, and with Yvonne being here and all, I thought it would be a good excuse to get a break. I didn't think to change the plans once you decided to come. I'm sorry." I could feel the pinching in my face of genuine remorse and could see in hers the building disappointment that she seemed to be trying to hide. "Do you mind? Being here by yourself, I mean? Just for tonight?" My mom shifted and sighed. Still saying nothing, she resumed folding a brightly colored cotton top, placing it gently in the open drawer in front of her.

"We? I suppose that's you and Marc?" I nodded back to her in reply. "Well, what can I say, Tabby? I'm not going to tell you that you shouldn't go to your father's house. You know that." She paused. "I hope you weren't thinking that I would go . . ."

I cut her off quickly. "Oh, no. No. No, I would never expect you to go or anything. I was just hoping that you wouldn't mind staying here for a few hours while . . ." My mom lifted herself to her feet and came over to put a hand on my shoulder, bending down to look me in my eyes in the nursing chair.

"Tabby, I came here to help. So that's what I'm going to do. Plus, it's not me that has to deal with that woman." With the emphasis on the *w* in *woman*, I knew she was referring to Diane. "Or her children," she added flatly.

I didn't bother to correct her, or even attempt to explain that Dixie and Danielle had long transitioned from being virtual strangers into something much closer to sisters. My mouth stretched into a half smile, and even that felt like a small betrayal, on both sides. Of all the disagreements that littered the jagged history of our relationship, Diane and, by extension, Danielle and Dixie, had never been one between my mother and me. On that we could always agree, or at least we used to. This wasn't the time that I wanted us to feel disconnected. For so many reasons, my mother being back and helping me with Evie made me feel like we had a second chance at closeness that I couldn't afford to waste.

"I should probably call Marc," I offered. I could feel the gentle tugging of Evie's nursing starting to ease. My mom offered to get my phone and bring it to me, allowing me to stay in position just a bit longer. She returned, dropping the phone into my freed hand, and headed back out of the room.

Marc answered with the noise of surrounding traffic in the background. "Did your mom make it in?" he asked. "I'm taking my moms to get a bite and then we're headed back to the crib." He paused for a second as if the rest of the words caught in his throat. After a beat, he continued. "You know, why don't I bring my mom with me when I come to pick you and Evie up to head to your dad's? No sense in leaving them both alone, right? My mom and your mom? Let them keep each other company." A grip of panic seized my core. There was no good excuse to tell Marc the "hell no, are you crazy?" that I wanted to. But maybe this wouldn't be such a bad thing. Maybe my mother and Marc's mother would have much more in common with each other than I did with either of them. Maybe my mother could give Yvonne the piece of her mind that I could not.

LATER THAT EVENING, HEADED UP THE 405 FREEWAY IN MARC'S shiny specimen of German engineering, I felt acutely aware of every road sound I could hear—the subtle rhythmic spin of the tires, the gentle hum of the engine, and the wind softly whistling its way through the cracked window on my side. We were driving fast, a little late. My hope was that I'd timed it right to make it to Calabasas and the Walkers' so Evie would have at least a few minutes of awake time with this somewhat neglected part of our family. The sound coming from inside the car startled me a bit and made me instinctively turn around to check the car seat. But it wasn't Evie, it was coming from Marc, who was quietly laughing to himself.

"What?" I asked, turning to him. "What's funny?"

Marc seemed surprised to find himself in present company. He turned to me briefly and smiled. Chuckling again, he adjusted his brown hands on the leather steering wheel, and one came down to pat me on my leg.

"It's just that . . . Tab, I keep forgetting that you have a whole white family. I thought about it just now, and it has me trippin' out a little bit."

"You mean Diane?" I questioned.

"I mean Diane, your sisters—"

"They're not white, Marc." I cut him off, feeling only slightly defensive. Marc turned to me with a raised eyebrow and faced the road again. More words rose in my throat, and all of a sudden, they started pouring out of me. "They're not! Sure, Diane is, but my dad's not white, and my sisters aren't." I wasn't quite sure why I felt so protective.

Marc looked at me with confusion and a touch of concern. "Tab, what's the problem? They're basically white. Your sisters look white; plus, they live in Calabasas. I mean, come on—" His hand squeezed my knee twice, which made me shift against the seat leather. "Listen, I'm not saying there's anything wrong with it. There's nothing wrong with them, just that it's not what I imagined—my family is, like, *all* Black. Family reunion and everything. So, it's just a trip for me, you know. Something to get your mind around."

I hadn't thought much about it and had never even felt comfortable enough with the situation itself to start separating the discomfort into buckets. There was always the reminder of how my first family fell apart, a forever souvenir that I didn't grow up with my father. It wasn't because he was away doing something honorable; it was because of Diane. He'd made choices about his life, and these choices were living, breathing people with names, and faces, and, sure, straighter hair, and lighter skin. If I'd had a therapist, he or she probably would have said I had some trouble along the way, trying to prove to myself that our differences had no role in my abandonment. But I hadn't even gotten to whether they were white or whiter, according to definitions outside of our family. I was still stuck on the fact that my father had chosen them over me and nobody could tell me why.

"Marc, who gets to decide—who's Black or not Black? You know as well as I do that someone can look white and be as Black as you or me. I don't think of my sisters as white, but maybe that's something to ask them—how they're seen by the world, how they're treated."

"Yeah, I guess," Marc said casually.

"I'm not going to even pretend that I'm comfortable there." I let my hand drop on top of his. "But the reasons why are so much bigger than race. So, I'm sorry . . . I hadn't thought about how you might feel." Pausing to consider it, Marc's perspective was unexpected. At the dinner table, within a family, a lot of what society seems to care so much about makes for the least concern. "I always thought that me and Danielle look alike, though," I added. "And that Dixie looks like my . . . our grandmother."

Marc smiled. "It's cool, Tab. Not even that deep. I'm used to your sisters running around, but that's at your crib. It's just now that Evie's here, we're all connected in this way, in a way I hadn't really thought about before. Like, *family*."

I felt a wave of confusion. "Wait, you mean for you this is culture shock?" I asked, needing him to clarify. It never occurred to me that Marc's life in Florida could be so different from his life I'd witnessed in LA.

"Naw, Tab, not culture shock. I was just trippin' out on

the fact that basically now, I've got a mixed-race family. And what does that even mean? Maybe nothing." He offered the last words with a shrug of his shoulders.

I hadn't considered it. "Maybe one day, it'll mean a lot less than it does now," I said to him with a smile. I hoped those words could be true, not just about race or cultures, but about everything and especially the tensions at the fragile seams of our family dynamic. "So, I guess we know who's *not* bringing the potato salad to the Brown family reunion." Marc and I shared a quick laugh. "And I'm glad you'll be there with me tonight."

"Oh, it's gonna be weird, Tabby. I mean, it is weird, and uncomfortable. But, as my mom would say, 'Family is always worth it.'" I tried to hide the surprise on my face at Marc's words. I couldn't even imagine what she'd be saying that about.

"Really? When would she say that?" I tried my best to sound completely neutral.

"All the time, growing up, even now. There's nothing she wouldn't do for any of us."

Stop judging? I wondered silently. "There's not a day I don't learn something new about your mom, Marc," I finally said aloud.

"Yes, she's really a fascinating woman." Marc turned to look at me briefly. "Just . . . like you." My mouth dropped open. And for all the reasons, I was speechless. All I could do was blink. And shift nervously again against the leather seats. The familiar blanket of guilt began its descent to rest its weight upon my shoulders—guilt for leaving my mother with Yvonne, guilt for wanting to escape Yvonne in the first place, and guilt for thinking that I might never become the version of me that Marc held in his mind, nor would I want to. Marc's free hand squeezed my knee again. I forced a smile to my face.

"I think that next one's our exit," I said quickly, pointing ahead at the rapidly approaching sign. The voice of our navigation app echoed my direction. In short order, we made it to the community gates and pulled up to the house in the cul-de-sac.

"Damn, Tab, you didn't tell me your dad was rockin' like this. This is a baller ass crib." My discomfort at arriving at my father's house had yet to fade, even as it had become more familiar with the increased frequency of my visits. But Marc's words gave me a moment to take it in anew. It was a dream home by any measure, spacious, Spanish style, on a street dotted with Teslas and electric versions of fancier car models. A verdant yard of freshly mowed grass and lush landscaping accentuated the entrance, framing heavy wooden double doors.

It was Dixie who pulled the door open this visit, almost simultaneous with my finger hitting the bell. Knowing Dixie, she'd been waiting in the foyer, timing our arrival. I couldn't imagine her being more enthusiastic about being an aunt, or about spending any amount of time with a sleeping baby. Barely allowing us an opportunity to enter, Dixie leaned into her hugs of both Marc and me, and then eyed the carrier. She turned to me with her irresistibly perfect doe-eyed performance. "Can I take her into the kitchen?" she pleaded. "I promise, I'll be very careful."

Marc turned to look at me with the look that said *your call*. I nodded. Dixie gingerly took the carrier handle from Marc in a transfer of the most delicate cargo. And with that, she almost tiptoed like a slow-motion ballerina away from the two of us, who were still standing at the door. "Are you coming?" She turned back to us to whisper as if we should have known to feel more welcome.

Marc looked at me. "When in Rome," he said, with a shrug of his shoulders. And started in the direction of the kitchen behind Dixie. He stopped briefly and turned around to me as I had begun to move forward. "And we are definitely, definitely in Rome."

Marc had met the Walkers, my dad, and Diane during the first days home from the hospital after Evie's birth. It all happened so fast, in the blur of hormones and sleep deprivation, it was unclear what had been said to whom. Thankfully, Marc had gotten the chance to meet my sisters before that, on the many nights they'd been spending at my house at the request of their mother.

Marc might have felt like he didn't know what he was walking into because of a cultural difference, but I didn't know what we'd be walking into because of a shift that started not too long after Granny Tab's passing. It was a shift that had Diane fading into the background more and more each time I saw her; an increase in my father's unexplained distance; and vacant looks and sporadic calls from my little sisters. The result was weekends spent at my house where they'd never normally leave a life ensconced in the confines of Calabasas. Sure, we told ourselves that we were bonding, spending sister time. But we didn't talk about what was going on at home, or why Diane's eyes looked like she'd gotten less sleep than I had with a newborn. But that was just it with the Walkers. We didn't talk about anything we needed to.

We caught up with Dixie in the kitchen as she so gingerly placed Evie's carrier on the floor, just next to their very expansive kitchen island and out of the way of foot traffic. The island was so expansive, if it were a table, it could seat at least twelve people comfortably, perhaps more. Danielle was milling about, grazing on grapes that she'd been plucking out of a bowl, pretending not to be paying attention to our arrival.

"Is that our baby!" Diane cooed, rushing over from the stove. Immediately, I felt sick to my stomach, and then bad about it. Diane was so genuinely excited, like Dixie. "And hello, you two! Welcome, Marc! Glad to have you over!" She rushed over to us and then paused to receive the tepid hug that I was able to offer. Marc greeted her much more warmly. Clearly, he hadn't picked sides.

"Hi, Danielle!" I called out. I caught her brief grunt of a reply. Her lean frame continued to skulk about in the shadows of the kitchen, grazing and making inconspicuous observations. Even for a teenager, she'd become much more withdrawn in recent months. But she never offered me much of an opening to ask her about it. "Where's Dad?" I asked in general. Usually he'd be right in the center of things, and often not far behind Dixie to greet me at the door.

"He's in his office . . . where he basically stays all of the time." Danielle spoke up in her deep deadpan.

"Not *all* of the time, Danielle," Dixie chirped in sharp defense.

"Okay, *most* of the time," Danielle snorted back at her.

Diane turned beet red, but didn't interject. It was also unusual for her to stay quiet.

"I'll just go say hi!" I said cheerfully, trying to break up the tension. I wasn't sure what was going on between all of them, but it concerned me.

"Tabby," Diane said, seeming to regain herself, "if you want, we'll watch Evie while you step in to see Paul." Turning to Marc, she offered him something to drink and a plush comfortable seat in the adjacent living room area, right in front of the television.

By then, Danielle had managed to maneuver herself behind her mother, peeping over her shoulder at Evie, but not reaching for her. Her face had a look of bemusement, which was a drastic improvement from the sad emo vibe.

Marc accepted the drink offer and was pulled by Dixie deeper into the kitchen while she pointed out the glassware and drink options. *Let me know if you want alcohol*, Diane mouthed to him over Dixie's turned head.

Satisfied with the settling of things, I set off in search of my father, and some answers.

"Hey there, Two!" My dad looked up from behind his ornate wooden desk, surrounded by a host of gold-topped awards and trophies displayed on the file cabinet behind him. He too looked tired, like Diane, but less so. The usual good-natured lilt in voice was dimmed, but present. He wore a USC sweatshirt, his glasses, and the neatly cropped salt-and-pepper curls of his regular haircut. He seemed no worse for the strange nature of things at the Walker residence. "Where's the baby?" he asked, standing up to walk around and hug me.

"She's in the kitchen. Dixie's on duty."

"Of course she is! I tell you, I've never seen someone more excited about being an aunt. I caught her watching YouTube videos the other day—learning how to fold a blanket into an infant swaddle." He chuckled.

"Yes, she's been asking to come over ... *a lot more*," I said, trying to create an opening for my father to tell me at least something of what had been going on.

"About that, yes, I really appreciate it—all the times before

Evie. The girls, they—" My father was interrupted by the unmistakable, insistent wail of Evie's cry. I had to breathe deeply not to instinctively run back to the kitchen. The sound was impossible to ignore.

Less than a minute later, Dixie appeared at the doorway, distressed. "I don't know what happened, Two, she was fine and then all of a sudden she started crying!" Before she finished, I had already closed the distance between us and was moving quickly toward the noise.

"I'm sure it's okay, Dix," I said, holding my hand at her back as we proceeded together. When we reached the kitchen, Diane was holding Evie, attempting to soothe her, with no success. She walked over to me, rocking her, cooing, shushing, but Evie was inconsolable. "Mommy's here," I sang to Evie, in my arms. She fixated on my face, and soon the wailing silenced. "She might be hungry," I announced, feeling the throbbing in my chest. It never failed to amaze me how connected we were.

"Can I hold her now?" Dixie asked. "I know how to feed her," she said proudly.

"I bet you do." I beamed at her.

It was a relief to have my dad join for dinner. Evie slept soundly after the latest cycle of feeding, burping, and changing. I'd become used to wearing at least some of her emissions as part of my clothing, and it never mattered the size or placement of any burping cloth. Tonight, baby goo was a stripe down my back, mostly dry by the time we got to the dessert that Diane had prepared.

The table dynamic was staggered conversation. Half was me answering the questions Dixie peppered me with about KVTV and motherhood. She was particularly interested in the mechanics of a proper diaper change.

"Um, can I be excused?" Danielle spoke up into our chatter, having already pushed her chair back. If I hadn't seen her act differently before, I'd have thought she was just bored. But instead, I could tell there was something more.

"You're not even going to eat your ice cream?" Diane protested.

Danielle shook her head *no*. I decided to save her—we needed things to wrap up early, anyway. I had no idea what showdown might have been happening at my own house between the two grandmothers.

"Actually, Marc and I need to get going too," I added. "Both of our mothers are in town, and—"

"Oh, you could have brought them!" Diane said. *What?* We all must have turned to look at her. She turned beet red again and returned her focus to her ice cream.

"Can I come?" Dixie chimed in. I had no good way of saying no. Trapped.

"Not this time, Dix. Tabby has a full house. Don't you?" It was my dad who came in with the save, already consoling a deflated Dixie with a tender rub on her shoulder.

Seeing Dixie's big eyes so downcast, her little shoulders slumped, it was heartbreaking not to be able to take her with me. Danielle too. I had no idea what was going on there, but it seemed like they needed an escape. Only I was already stretched too thin. I had no room in my home, physically or emotionally.

THE RIDE FROM CALABASAS LULLED EVIE TO SLEEP AND LEFT ME feeling spent. It wasn't so much the hour of the evening, but more what I saw at the Walkers'. And more specifically what was apparent in my dad's behavior and Diane's silences; in Dixie's eyes, and maybe Danielle's too if she'd ever managed to look up with her sullen demeanor. It was in all the conversations that we didn't have and the questions I didn't get a chance to ask.

We entered my house to find the two grandmothers still up and talking casually at the dinner table off the kitchen— the prim and proper, tightly coiffed Yvonne Brown sat nursing a mug, and the comparatively much more glamorous Jeanie Walker Williams toyed with the stem of an emptied wineglass. They'd clearly gotten familiar with each other, and it took some time for them to notice us. I waved my hand and signaled quiet as I broke off from Marc to head into the bedroom. I could hear his muffled greetings as I settled Evie on her back and positioned the monitor. For some reason I wanted to linger there, to stay a little longer in the one place that always seemed to make sense. When it was just me and her, and everyplace else ceased to exist for just a bit.

The glow of the night-light illuminated my path back to the hallway, and the voices were my beacon to the kitchen. Marc leaned against the countertop casually, reminding me that my mother wasn't a stranger to him. I admired the relaxed and natural ease with which he spoke to both women, because both of them made me feel on edge. It was a wide departure from the Marc I'd first seen at dinner with his parents, the little-boy version of the grown man who should have let me know what to expect from Yvonne.

"Everything all good with Evie?" Marc turned his attention to me as soon as I crossed into his line of sight. I nodded and gave him a smile.

"Well, I know it's about my bedtime," Yvonne said, with a

yawn following. "You gonna take me home, son?" She looked expectantly at Marc.

After a slight pause that seemed like a hesitation, he perked up, straightening himself from his slouched back leaning on the counter. "Of course, let's get you ready to go. Maybe we'll get back over before your flight tomorrow." He gave her a wide smile.

Yvonne turned her attention to my mother. "Well, I have to say, Jeanie, I'm glad you're here. And maybe you can get Tabby to stay at home a little more with the baby. I swear, my mother would never have let me out of the house with a newborn." Never so much as turning to look at me, she said it as if I weren't standing right there in the room. I felt the blood rising in my face and my eyes narrowing. I took a deep breath, unsure what I was going to say or what the fallout would be.

"Oh, now, Yvonne, what our mothers would have done is long gone. Those are old wives' tales." My mother waived her hand over the table with a flash of her glossy manicure. "This generation has all kinds of other options. And *my* Tabby is an *excellent* mother. Just excellent." My mouth dropped open as I sucked any of the words I had back in, in a breath of pure surprise. It was the most gentle version of a "read" I'd ever heard. Who knew that Jeanie Walker had it in her?

My mother stood up, taking her wineglass in one hand and Yvonne's mug in the other. "Come, I'll take these to the sink so you can get your bag. I know you have a full day tomorrow getting ready to head back home. We'll certainly have to see each other again before too much time passes, right?" My mother gave her smile, the one I knew, the fake one. The one that held back everything she wasn't saying.

"Where's your bag, Ma? On the sofa?" Marc sprang into action, heading toward the living room, as the group of us slowly moved behind him, my mother ushering a now standing Yvonne with a hand on her shoulder.

With awkward goodbyes, thank-yous, promises to see each other again soon, and just after Yvonne's last look in at a sleeping Evie, the door finally closed behind Marc and his mother. With a loud and heavy sigh, I leaned my whole body against it and closed my eyes.

"You are, you know." My mother's voice broke into the silence. My eyes slowly slid open as I turned to look at her, standing in the middle of my living room, between the light and the dark, the glow from the kitchen giving her a slightly ethereal appearance.

"I'm what?" I turned to my mother, my eyes starting to brim, blurring my view just slightly. My mother closed the distance between us, reaching her hands toward my face. The warmth of her soft palms made contact just beneath my jawline, holding my gaze.

"You *are* a good mother, Tabby." I swiped at the tear that streaked down my face, first just one, and then the others that followed. For once it wasn't that I didn't want to cry; I only wanted to hold on to the moment. To keep it so pure that it could last just a little bit longer, not be interrupted by the instinct of comfort or overwhelmed by the weight of doubt I'd been carrying. I wanted her words and the fullness of possibility that they might be true. Even just for a second.

The only response I could muster was to shake my head. The spirit of Yvonne hadn't yet left the room, and all the judgment I'd encountered from everywhere else, from the very first moment of my pregnancy. It was the most important question I asked myself: *Am I a good mother?* The answer could deflate me instantly, reduce me to tears, or rebuild me from ashes and disappointment. Would this forever be my one defining accomplishment?

"Mom, is this it?" I asked. "Does everyone get an opinion on my parenting from now on? Is *this* what it's like? If so, it's too much. I don't think I can handle it." My mom brought her arms around me, pulling me close, nearly cradling me into her own shoulder. We stood there for so long.

"Oh, Tabby Cat," is all she said, stroking my hair.

Sometime later, we'd finally found our way to my sofa. In the quiet of the living room, my mom sat next to me, her hand on my leg, then my shoulder, then my hair, seemingly dissatisfied with her ability to be as soothing as the occasion required.

"You know, being a mother, being a wife . . ." She spoke slowly, breaking into the silence. "That wasn't always all I'd wanted to be. I guess there was a time I'd started with other dreams for myself too."

"Other dreams like what?"

My mother shifted and brought herself around to face me more directly. "Oh, the dreams that come from questions I used to ask myself. When I was younger. When I was in college and wondered who I wanted to be . . . and believed for just one moment that I had a choice." With a slight smile, I could see her eyes gloss into a remembered time. "I had a dream of working in advertising. I was going to be fancy, fabulous, clever, successful . . . an independent woman calling my own shots. I even managed to get hired. But early on I had to choose . . . I had to choose that job or your father. That was my choice." She patted my hand again, with the same soft palm that had held my face just earlier. "Paul Walker . . ." she said on the breath of a deep exhale. "I don't regret any- thing, Tabby. This was what life was supposed to look like, at least for me. But you, I see you and all that you're able to do, everything that's in front of you. You can be anything. You can choose *anything*, Tabby. But don't ever doubt that you're a good mother. Don't *ever* let anyone make you doubt that."

I brought my arms around her and whispered my thanks. After, I became curious. "You never told me that you wanted a career in advertising," I said. It was like meeting another person, or another side of the same person that changed how you saw them. "I just never knew that. I—"

"You thought all I wanted to do was be someone's wife?" my mother said, cutting me off. "Well, maybe that's fair. Be- cause once I chose that life with Paul, I leaned into it and I never looked back. I never even tried to remember or imag- ine who I might have been. Because that person would never be. So I became Jeanie Walker . . . the best Jeanie Walker I could be. Paul's wife, Tabby's mom. And that was enough . . . until it wasn't.

"But you, Tabby, *enough* isn't driving you . . . something else is. And whatever it is, keep that thing. Because it's my greatest joy to watch." She beamed at me, stopping for a sec- ond to study my face, and then continued. "That woman I left behind, it's like you picked her up and took those dreams further than I ever imagined I could go." She shifted on the sofa next to me, uncomfortable in all that she'd just revealed. As she turned back up to face me, she took a deep breath and added, "I'm proud of you."

"You are?" Without my realizing it, the words had come out of my mouth. Watching the look on her face as it fell made me feel like I'd said the wrong thing. She looked hurt, crest-fallen, confused. And it wasn't that I'd never heard her say she was proud of me before. There'd been the graduations, the promotions, the celebrations—even my speech at Granny Tab's funeral. But now, we were talking about the failures, the missteps, the bad and questionable decisions that meant I'd had to fight through a wilderness of my own creation. This conversation was about my scars. This pride was about my ugliness.

"Tabby," my mother said softly as she took my hand, the concern pooled in her eyes, "of course I'm proud of you. I haven't always understood or agreed with every decision you've made, but I have been able to watch you see it through with more courage and strength than I could have."

Before that night, I had no idea how much I needed the care and protection of my own mother. But there's a perfect time for the right words. Finally, it felt like we were coming back into orbit.

15

"LEX, DO YOU EVER FEEL LIKE WE DON'T SAY THE THINGS TO each other that we really need to say?"

Alexis's puzzled expression stared back at me through my phone screen. We'd agreed to a video chat to continue planning for Laila's so-called "business shower." The question had been on my mind since the conversation with my mother, who still couldn't believe that I didn't know she was proud of me. It wasn't that she'd never said it before, just that the nature of the circumstances were usually different. There were always critical words for what wasn't done right, corrections offered, but not grace. I started to wonder if I'd learned to model her example.

"Girl, *what* are you talking about?" Alexis said, face crinkled. "What is there that we *don't* say to each other?" I set the phone down on the counter in my kitchen as I reached up to grab a mug from the cabinet and then turned toward the stove to heat the kettle. I had to make a mental note to catch it before the loud whistle of boiling so as not to disturb the sleeping newborn or my napping mother. With my hands free again, I picked up the phone to see that Alexis had now put the phone down on her end, giving me a view looking up at her as she applied mascara.

"Lex, I was just thinking that with all this planning and this big event, is it really necessary? What if we're missing the point? I mean, maybe Laila was just telling us that she doesn't feel seen, you know? What if it's as simple as that?"

"Tab," Alexis said, picking up the phone again to face me with newly defined eyelashes, "I don't know what you've been doing over there during your maternity leave, but clearly you've been doing too much thinking when you should be sleeping. What we're doing is simple. What better way to say 'I see you' than to do something helpful? Being a friend doesn't mean solving all your friend's problems."

"But is it really helpful to have a bunch of people Laila barely speaks to stand around in my backyard and hand over gift cards for office supplies?"

"I think it's just the gesture, Tab. There's nothing wrong with gestures. Some things are just about making another person feel better, even for a moment. And if that's not an 'I see you,' I don't know what is."

"Don't you think you're being a little tough on her, Lex? I mean, there's no room for any slack with you."

Alexis gave a sigh and rolled her eyes with a brief shake of her head. "I don't think I'm being tough on her; but, if I'm honest, I think she's being kind of selfish. And nobody else gets to be that selfish, Tab. I don't get to be that selfish. You don't. So why does she? I love Laila, truly, but it's not my job to be her mother."

I paused for a second to process what Alexis said. Sometimes her view of what was selfish could be pretty broad. "All

I'm saying is, are we doing what she really needs us to do, or are we just doing something to make ourselves feel better?"

"What's the difference?" Alexis replied quickly. "We're doing something. You're at home with a newborn. I'm a working mom with three children."

"Three?"

"Girl, Rob counts. Look, we all have a lot going on, and sometimes the gesture should just be enough. Stop doing everyone else's worrying. Don't you already have enough on your hands?" Alexis had a point.

"I'm already worn out, honestly. I'm team no sleep, practically a zombie."

"Then just do the best you can." The background of Alexis's phone spun as she swung her purse onto her shoulder. "It's already above and beyond," she said, flipping her hair with her free hand. "Really."

As almost inadvertent punctuation, I let out a yawn I couldn't manage to stifle. With my mom visiting, having the extra help was a lifeline, but not enough to make up for the sleep I wasn't getting. And I didn't have the energy to defend Laila to Alexis, nor was I sure why I felt like I needed to. Maybe because there comes a time for all of us to be a bad friend. And the demands and isolation of new parenthood had me feeling like I was being terrible at it. The most I could do was try to support where I could.

AT LEAST ONCE A DAY, HAVING MY MOTHER IN TOWN FELT LIKE finding an extra twenty-dollar bill on laundry day. In the heart of my maternity leave, when most new mothers were quarantined in the cave of their home, I managed to escape for the meeting with Lisa that we'd agreed to the week prior. We could have made our meeting a call, or she could have stopped by, but I needed to get out and find some semblance of the woman I used to be.

Giving birth had made me feel like a champion, but the demands of motherhood that followed were proving harder than anything I'd ever imagined. And I wasn't even remotely prepared for the guilt. Guilt trailed me everywhere. Even in my driveway, as I reached for the handle of my car door, waving to my mother, the little voice inside whispered, *Who are you to leave your baby?* But I knew I had to. Our future depended upon it.

I met Lisa at a quaint coffee shop on Larchmont, near her house and decidedly close to the station. The route there was a reminder that my maternity leave would be ending soon and I needed a plan. I'd put so much effort into my career and never expected that a short time away would threaten my future or jeopardize the trajectory that I'd worked so hard for. But I had taken risks that come with consequences.

As I entered, I found Lisa sitting at a table reading a paper. Unable to take the time to create a public-facing appearance, I was in my version of disguise. My hair lay flat against my head in twists under a baseball cap. Wearing flats and baggy clothes, walking with my head down through the milling crowd of midday café patrons, I was unrecognizable. As I approached the table, Lisa's startled expression seemed to tell me my disguise worked a little too well. It took a long second before the flash of recognition and then affection crossed her face. Suddenly, she was all smiles, standing up to pull me in for a warm hug.

"Tabby!" Lisa sounded as if we hadn't seen each other

for months, not just the week that had passed since our last meeting. "Girl, you look like you're going through it! Barely sleeping, the baby's crying; you're crying, diaper changes in the middle of the night, all that, right?"

I nodded. "I barely made it out of the house. If it wasn't for my mother, I don't know what I'd do."

"Well, I can tell you this, I think your top is on inside out." Lisa tugged gently at the tag, which I instantly realized was on the outside of my shirt. I felt my face flush as I looked down to examine my sleeves. Sure enough, the stitching of the seams mocked me. Lisa couldn't hold the laugh in as she wrapped her arm around my shoulder. "Don't worry, I know exactly what that means, I've been there. I'm impressed there's no visible baby poop or spit-up stains."

"Look closer," I said, shaking my head. "I'm basically a walking burping cloth." Lisa laughed louder and ushered us to a chair.

"Burping cloth, baby gas station, favorite cushion, and pacifier. We're all things, aren't we?" Lisa gave me her megawatt smile and reached down for her coffee cup with the signature straw poking out of the top. With her French-manicured hand she pulled the drink to her lips and took a sip. "I ordered you a green tea when I got here. Still green tea, right?" I smiled.

"Thank you," I said. "At this point, I'm dying for a coffee, but I'm going to wait until Evie gets a little older or I stop breastfeeding, or at least, trying to. Every day I think—okay, this is going to be my last week."

"I understand that too. I had so many problems getting my son to latch. It felt like constant failure. I had to just give myself some grace. I'm not ashamed to say he was a formula-fed baby. But there's been plenty of opportunity for other sacrifices." Lisa's words trailed off as she turned away from me briefly and took a deep sigh. I reached my hand across the table to her, raggedy nails and all.

"Lisa, are you still one hundred percent sure you're leaving?"

Lisa straightened her posture quickly. "Oh yeah, Tabby, that's a done deal. Listen, about that. I've been meeting with Chris and Doug. They want to name my replacement as soon as possible. They've scheduled all of these prospects from all over the country, *and locally*, but I've been saying they need to just promote someone that the KVTV viewers already know, *specifically*, who has a perspective, and real roots in this city." Scott Stone's golden-boy image flashed briefly in my mind, triggering a pang deep in my core.

"But they don't want it to be me," I said, almost to myself.

"Oh, no, it's not just that, Tabby. I think they're trying to hold the market position and stay number one. And it's been a battle between convention—let's just do what we've always done—and doing something that seems so obvious to me as the right thing to do, but is new. It's all about—"

"All about ratings."

"Yes, ratings." Just as Lisa spoke, a casually dressed barista slid between us and dropped a mug in front of me, followed by the thud of a teapot in the middle of the table.

"It just needs about another minute and then should be all set to pour," he said.

Lisa and I both said our thanks and fell into a brief silence. I wasn't in any hurry to speak again. *Ratings* had been the word used to hold me back, to justify the unjust and unfair, to excuse viewer comments about my hair, and to discourage me from believing that I'd ever be given a fair shot at KVTV. If I came back from my maternity leave and lost my job six months later, it would be blamed on ratings, no matter what the real reason was. It was the excuse that always kept the light on.

"I got us the meeting." Lisa said finally, as if she'd unveiled a surprise from behind her back. "Tabby, don't get me wrong. I know it's a long shot. And I know it's your maternity leave. But you have to . . . You'd have to come back to work." Lisa ran her fingers through her blond highlights, glossy enough they seemed to sparkle even in the darkened corner of the café where we huddled. "But just for a meeting," she added quickly. "If you could just come in for the meeting, I really believe we can get you the test. If you're there, if you show how badly you want it, I just know they can't say no to your face. With you sitting right in the room? No way."

I sat for a second contemplating my tea and then suddenly remembered to pour it. The lightly tinted liquid fell in a steaming stream into a pool at the bottom of the mug in front of me. Cup filled, I pulled it to my lips and took a deep inhale. There was only one word my mouth wanted to speak. In the midst of all the thoughts and ideas, the swirl of feelings, and the pang in my gut of anxiety, all I had was a single question that blocked the path of every other thought from moving forward.

"Lisa . . . why?" I said it simply. With full innocence and curiosity. Unguarded, with no assumptions about the answer. But I needed to know, because if I didn't, I couldn't afford to get my hopes up or to trust something that had let me down so many times before.

"Why? Why what?" Lisa asked, her face a display of pure confusion.

I shook my head gently. "Why me? Why do all of this for

me? I guess I just don't understand." Almost immediately the guilt came again, flooding me. She'd think I didn't trust her. And that wasn't it. That wasn't it at all. But I didn't have any more words for the moment. And as much as I wanted to drown out the awkwardness, I could not. I had to sit in the stillness of it, in my raw honesty, and wait.

In response, Lisa's mouth dropped open as if she were going to speak, but she did not. She took a breath in, but again, said nothing. Finally, I saw her chest rise, and I knew that she'd reached deep enough to find her own truth. And still, the seconds that passed felt like tiny forevers.

"Tabby . . . I . . . it's just that leaving this behind, all this, everything I worked for, everything I sacrificed . . . I keep asking myself what's left. And every time I ask myself what would make it all right, or even just a little bit better—it's that I need to know this business isn't empty. That there's some meaning to what we've been doing—what I've been doing this whole time. Part of that, a real part of it, is just that I need to see *you* win. I need that. Because then I can feel all right about it. That it's not just all evaporating. That . . ." Lisa straightened herself again and brought her hand up to her mouth and held it there for a minute. After a beat, she brought her coffee to her lips to take a sip out of the straw.

"My natural hair color is brown," she said slowly, looking me squarely in my eyes. "Dark brown. Mousy, even. I've been coloring it so long, I almost forgot the original shade." She placed the coffee cup back on the table and examined her hands, as if she'd never seen them before. She closed her eyes briefly and then continued, fingering a loose bit of her golden hair near her earlobe. "Even when the roots started to grow in gray, it just became another thing to hide. And it's curly, you know? When I was a kid, I called it frizzy and tried every way to make it sleek.

"And my teeth." Lisa waved a fan of her fingers in front of her lips. "All the work to cover almost everything I was ever insecure about to become *this* . . . this ideal of something. On television. And it worked. It worked and I've been very successful at being this. But what part of that is me?" Lisa paused and looked at me as if I had the answer. I gave her a smile of recognition, but stayed silent. Eventually, she continued. "Tabby, I need to know that some part of it was still me. Was done by me. And that's why. Because if I can see you win, doing it the way you have been—then I'll know that somewhere, some part of me hasn't been an illusion. Because when I leave, when I'm no longer Lisa Sinclair at KVTV, that's going to be all I have."

I leaned back in my seat, taking in her words. The din of the coffee shop around us faded out of focus. I hadn't expected the answer Lisa gave. I thought she might have felt guilty about Chris's reaction to our natural hair interview. But somehow, knowing that her why had more to do with her than it did with me made me trust it more. It unlocked a piece of belief I'd been holding back since the first day we'd collided in the ladies' room—what felt like a lifetime ago. And now that we'd become friends, to know that the impossible standards for me had cost her too, it felt like we'd finally started speaking the same language.

"Wow, so you're really leaving." I said it low and quiet, not to her as much as it was my final acknowledgment. It was true.

She looked surprised. And then the cloud of resignation washed over her. "I'm sure," she said slowly. Her head bobbed slowly in affirmation of her words, seeming to build confidence in her body. "I'm sure I have to, Tabby. My husband and I had a deal, and it's my turn. If I don't live up to my end, then we're not a team."

"A team," I repeated. Maybe I expected Lisa to speak about love. And maybe this was her way of doing it. Perhaps this was a different kind of love, of partnership. One that lasted—the kind I hadn't seen yet. The kind of partnership that I could best remember as Granny Tab and Ms. Gretchen at Crestmire, the times that my grandmother's swollen legs weighed her down into a slower pace that Ms. Gretchen matched without complaint.

I made it a point to meet Lisa's eyes. "Thank you." I offered the words sincerely. I wasn't sure of her plan, but I knew I was going to go along with it. If she was willing to try, so was I. We were a team.

16

TWO DAYS LATER, TRUE TO HER WORD, LISA ARRANGED A MEET-
ing at the station with Chris Perkins, and more important,
Doug Reynolds, KVTV's general manager. Chris might have
acted like he was the center of gravity in the newsroom, but
Doug was the sun, and all things rotated around him. If he
was in the room, Chris was as good as invisible. For me, that
was a good thing. Chris was the news director who told me to
use my voice, then backed down later when I needed an advocate. He was the voice of the viewer when there was criticism
about my hair and left it to me to figure out how to reconcile
ratings against my rights.

After my last broadcast, right before my maternity leave,
Chris and I were far from being on good terms. Lisa and I
had openly defied him, which I was sure was more than just
a knock to his ego. I could only imagine whose idea it was to
hire another anchor while I was away. Who'd orchestrate my
return from leave to find my position had been all but filled
by someone who was supposed to be a temporary stand-in.
Truly, with Chris at the helm at KVTV, if I didn't find a way

around him, I was going to have to find somewhere else to build the rest of my career.

Sleep deprived, and still considering a full shower a luxury, I prepared for battle—the new mother version of it. I'd pumped, pulled my hair into a reasonable puff, and slapped a decent polish job on my filed-down nails. As a finishing touch, I managed a little war paint—a reasonable application of makeup in most of the right places to look like a recognizable version of myself

"I'll be back in a couple of hours, I think. Milk is in the fridge," I whispered to my mother, my head popped in the den's doorway. She had the television on a low murmur with the voices just audible. I remember her saying once she thought the sound soothed the baby. To me it seemed like it lulled both of them to sleep.

"Good luck," my mother whispered back. I waited for the follow-up to come, an *Are you going to wear your hair like that?* Or some other echoing of the doubts that had taken residence in my own mind. The always-on internal assessment of the risks of nonconformity. I'd stood in the mirror and thought as much, wondering whether I was disadvantaging myself. I considered the idea of wearing a wig, or if I had enough time for a blow dry and flat iron. I wondered if this meeting needed me to be somebody else, to pretend once again, to wear the mask. But once motherhood makes two of you, the eyes that you know are watching every move you make are so much more important than the pair staring back at you in the mirror. The message I would convey to Evie was much more meaningful than me being judged.

It wasn't a risk I could afford to take. I couldn't go backward.

I blew my kiss to Evie. "Always be yourself, Sweetpea, even when it's not convenient," I whispered on my way out. And then I knew for sure. Any yes that I got today, any test broadcast that I'd have, it would have to be as the me I wanted my daughter to be proud of.

My mother's presence for once gave me a guiltless departure. And I had Yvonne Brown to thank for my level of appreciation. For all the complexities of our relationship, my mom and I needed this time together more than either of us knew. Her help was a quiet confidence. An embodied assurance that everything I was afraid of, everything I thought I'd screw up or couldn't be trusted with, was going to be all right.

Driving into the lot of KVTV for the first time since I left Chris Perkins's office after my and Lisa's rogue broadcast, the knot of anxiety in my core delivered a shot of adrenaline through my sleep-deprived body. I took a deep breath, drawing my shoulders back and straightening my frame. I would walk in with my head held high. I couldn't control the outcome, but I could control how I showed up. For once, I was asserting my value and insisting on my authenticity. And it was as frightening as anything I'd ever known.

Barely two months into my maternity leave, I had no business back at the office, unless I'd planned to bring Evie for a quick friendly visit with colleagues, or to meet someone for lunch. Instead, I hoped to avoid my coworkers and accomplish the near impossible feat of walking through the halls invisibly, unseen and unquestioned.

Lisa and I, in our pregame, decided to meet in her office for a few minutes before we were scheduled to see Doug and Chris. True to form, she had a tea sitting on her desk in a steaming cup waiting for me. As I entered, she looked up only briefly from her computer, nails still typing staccato clacks on the keys.

"Hey," she said quietly over the noise of the keyboard. I smiled my greeting. She reached up with one hand to gesture toward the door, which I understood meant that our conversation would require privacy. I braced myself for the news she had to deliver. Closing the door behind me, I entered to take the open seat facing her desk.

A few quiet seconds had already passed before I realized that I was holding my breath. Lisa turned away from the computer, seemed to change her mind, stood up, and then made her way over, arms extended for what turned out to be an awkward and slightly off-balance hug between us. Lisa settled into the visitor chair next to me and sighed loudly.

"Tabby, I have to tell you, I'm not sure how this is going to go. You know they've been moving folks around to cover for you at the anchor desk on weekends. They brought in a temp, and they also hired a new senior reporter. I'm sure Chris is watching the ratings every broadcast and has already discussed his staffing vision with Doug. But this all looks suspicious. You'll have a job when you come back from maternity leave, but I wouldn't trust it, I just wouldn't."

I'd never heard Lisa speak that way before. Two months away from a place was enough for changes to happen, for shifts that come with jockeying and ambition. My absence made the situation ripe for people I'd never suspect to do something of the "hey, it's not personal" nature. I shifted the soles of my sensible flats along the tiny, tufted lumps of the carpet.

"So what are we going to do today? Fight back?" I asked earnestly. I was uncomfortable and felt it in many ways. Sometimes, it was aching in my hips shifting back after childbirth, or sore breasts and nipples from what seemed like unrelenting pumping. My feet that were still wider than I'd ever imagined and needed to be squeezed into my slippers. And all this was aside from the constrictive tug of clothes that used to fit me loosely. I longed for my at-home uniform of elastic-waist pants and pullover tops.

Here I was, in Lisa's office, still needing to heal, but present and ready to lay claim to my future—everything that my past self had struggled to gain. The courage that I remember feeling in my pregnancy felt like a memory of flooded hormones and misplaced optimism.

Lisa leaned toward me, her hands folded between her knees. As her eyes met mine, she spoke earnestly and firmly. "Tabby, what we're going to do today is fight forward."

LISA AND I WALKED DOWN THE HALLWAY WITH THE PACING and energy of our very own theme music. A few familiar and friendly faces noticed me and waved their greetings with slightly confused expressions. I gave quick, awkward acknowledgments and ducking glances as I continued with speed toward the elevators. Doug's office was on a different floor—a higher one with all the other execs. The ding of the elevator door brought another wave of flutters to my belly. But Lisa moved us forward deliberately, leaving no room for hesitation. Another ding and a few steps more delivered us to the waiting area for the executive suite. Doug's assistant gave a nod of acknowledgment to Lisa and me, signaling "one minute" while on the phone.

"Okay, you ready?" Lisa spoke the words on a quiet exhale, seeming for that one moment, in spite of all her confidence, to be as nervous as I was. Still, I nodded.

We barely had time to sit down before a door opened in the frosted glass wall, revealing a tall and jovial Doug Reynolds, his booming voice directed toward someone inside his office. And then suddenly his attention was upon us. "I didn't keep you waiting, did I? Sorry, we were running a few minutes late," he offered in the same loud and deep tone, cascading authority yet giving off a friendly air. He pushed the door open more widely and ushered me, followed by Lisa, inside. Seated at the round table—a spacious distance from his desk—was Chris Perkins, looking as pallid as ever. I wondered if, even living in Southern California, he ever actually made it into the sun. He was wearing his glasses, and I could see dark circles under his eyes, making him look somehow less healthy than he did just a couple of months prior.

"Thanks for joining us, Tabby." Chris stood up with his hand extended to me. I took it.

"Good to see you, Chris . . . and you too, Doug," I offered. I was grateful that none of my interactions with Doug Reynolds had been substantial enough to match the complexity of my relationship with Chris. But if I was going to have a shot at the weekday anchor desk, *this* was the table where I needed to be sitting. Not across from Chris several floors below. He couldn't make this kind of decision. But he could certainly do his part to keep me from attaining it.

"Well," Doug said, settling into his seat. "Let's get right to it. I'm aware that this is your maternity leave, so I want to respect your time. And I thank you for coming in person to meet with us. I've had three newborns, so I know how challenging this period can be." Instinctively, I turned briefly to Lisa, who was also looking at me, exchanging paragraphs of silent commentary in a glance.

I forced a smile at Doug and cleared my throat. Running my hands over the smooth polished mahogany wood of the table, I brought them to rest in front of me, anchoring myself. "Thank you, Doug, Chris, for taking the time to meet with me, and for giving me the opportunity—"

Before I could finish my awkward introduction, Doug cut me off, reclaiming control of the conversation. "Opportunity, yes, that's what we're here to discuss. The anchor position. Of course, we hate to lose such an incredible and *seasoned* talent as Lisa Sinclair, who has been so popular with viewers here in the Southland. She's leaving very big shoes to fill. We do have a number of candidates with significant experience and success in this and other markets, but Lisa has been a relentless advocate for us to consider someone homegrown . . . with history at KVTV."

"Tabby has been absolutely fearless when it comes to sharing her views, her journey, and her perspective," Lisa interjected. "I can only imagine how far that can go with a true platform and positioning on the station."

"But as I'm sure you understand, we would like to see someone with more experience in the position," Chris said. Both Lisa and I whipped our heads to look at him. I was almost surprised he didn't burst into flames that instant.

"What Chris is saying is true," Doug said with the same practiced friendly tone. "We would like to have someone with more experience. You were just promoted to weekend anchor, and there's still room for you to grow in that position."

My spirits fell. I recalled seeing Scott Stone sitting in the midday anchor seat. Same experience, less even, but just by going to a competing station in the very same market, he was promoted in the same amount of time that, according to Chris and Doug, I was still proving myself at KVTV. Scott didn't succeed at KVTV, he failed. He didn't have ratings behind him. Instead, he had the expectation of success that traveled with him, just because. And for me, for me there was always more to prove; there was always more evidence needed, and one more thing to demonstrate.

"And that's why we decided to give you the test slot," Doug said, breaking into my thoughts. I sat in stunned silence wondering if I'd heard what I heard. *Had I heard that?* I scanned each of the faces looking at me expectantly.

"Thank you?" I said. I looked at Lisa, who was beaming more brightly than I'd ever seen joy represented on a face. Doug looked like he expected to be congratulated, and Chris looked flush and uncomfortable. And in the middle of it all was me, the same me who had decided not to change my hair, the same me whose body had been changed by pregnancy in ways that weren't just "cute," and the same me who maybe was punching above her weight, but at least was going to take the shot.

"We're not number one for no reason," Chris said, looking to Doug for his nod of approval. "There are no promises here, of course. But Lisa made a good point that our audience might want to see more of someone they're already familiar with. And . . . you've already shared so much with all of us." Chris pushed his glasses up on his nose. "*Much more* than we expected," he said.

"Much more!" Doug echoed with a bellow. "So it makes sense to give you the test slot, see what the ratings have to say. Then we'll make our decision." Doug patted Chris on the back with a heavy hand. "Number one in the Southland, that's right. Gotta keep it up!"

Our meeting ended, and Lisa and I could barely make it to the elevator before our excitement spilled over. Thankfully the doors opened, revealing an empty cabin.

"Lisa! I can't believe it!" I whispered as soon as the doors closed in front of us. I wanted to grab her hands and jump up and down with excitement, like Alexis and I used to do as girls.

"Actually, me either," Lisa said, looking somewhat bewildered. "They said they were going to give you the test slot! Wow . . ." She turned to me with a brilliant smile illuminating her whole face, lightly shaking her head side to side. "You deserve it, Tabby." She put her hand on my shoulder.

"Thank you, Lisa." I said it as the doors opened. I meant it so deeply that the weight of the words froze me in place. Lisa had to nudge me forward to exit.

She hugged me tight and close. "Tabby," she said as she finally pulled back. "This is just the beginning for you." And in my mind, the bittersweet end of her sentiment continued. It was the beginning for me, but her finale.

And just like that, I had a date with my dreams set for two weeks from now. Somehow, I knew to hold on to that fleeting moment of victory. I felt that I needed to cradle it close to my chest. Not just because it was the biggest thing I'd had truly to myself since Evie had arrived, but because somehow I knew that wouldn't be the last challenge. Because nothing ever came easy, and this was far from my final stand.

17

MAYBE THERE IS SOMETHING TELLING ABOUT THE FIRST CALL you make to share good news. Maybe that decision tells you something about your relationships. Or maybe it's as random as the winds of change and circumstance. My news about being given the opportunity to do a test broadcast for the evening anchor position was still an incomplete triumph. There weren't many people in my life who could understand the nuances of the development. In truth, it wasn't that there weren't *many*—there was only one.

I needed to talk to the same person who'd stayed up with me until four a.m. with chocolate sandwich cookies and cola only to switch over to cold pizza and coffee, cramming to beat the sunrise. There was only one person who was more convinced than I was that I could get a starting reporter position in a major market and made sure that I wasn't alone in preparing for it. There was one person to call who would take this news as a win for "us." Because she'd know how rare the view was on this side of the professional hill we'd both climbed.

"Call Laila," I instructed through my car's speaker system. My car ride home was my last moment of belonging to only me. And Laila was the person I wanted most of all to share my news with.

"Hey, girl, whassup?" Laila sounded mildly distracted. I realized then that I couldn't remember the last time that just the two of us had even had the chance to talk since I'd entered the world of mothering a person. And she'd been deep in the world of birthing a company.

"Lah, I . . . They're going to give me the test for anchor." I tripped over the words excitedly, and even as I was speaking them, I could hardly believe they were the truth.

"Tab, anchor like anchor, anchor? Like primetime show-time?" I could hear the excitement in Laila's tone escalate. By the time she'd gotten to the actual question, her voice was as high-pitched as a small girl. "I'm so excited for you!" Her words amplified the warm feeling of accomplishment so much that I almost didn't notice the pause and lull that followed them. Finally, she spoke again, this time in a much more sober tone. "I mean . . . this is what you want, right?" And suddenly I was confused.

"Girl, what do you mean? Of course this is what I want. This would be everything, I mean if I got it, can you imag-ine? And can you just see the look on Chris Perkins's face with me really, really having a seat at the table?" At some point, it started to feel and sound like I was past the point of just answering the question. And just briefly, in a quick flash, it wasn't clear, even to me, whether it was Laila I was trying to convince, or myself.

"I was just asking," Laila replied, her tone much more cautious than before, "because in our industry, especially the way that it's going now, I think we have to wonder some-times, what's it all for? But maybe that's just me projecting."

I asked her what she meant.

"Tab, you're so talented, and this industry . . . it's so thankless. I just remember how easy it was to one day be afraid of getting fired and then the next day gunning for what seemed like the next big step forward. It was that wheel of fear and then fighting, then fear and . . . well, then I got laid off. In the end, no matter what I did, how hard I worked, I was still confronted with everything I was afraid of."

"But you made it happen, out of all of that." I realized how heavy the *that* had been, just a couple of years prior for Laila. She'd come so far past it. "I know exactly what you mean, that endless cycle, the back-and-forth of it all. I literally just had a baby and I'm back at the office. I'm fearful and fighting at the same time. Because I've been afraid that if I don't move up, I'm going to get moved out of the way."

"Right, because you're an inconvenient person." Laila sounded so defiant, so strong. I tried to borrow her confidence.

"Yep, with inconvenient hair and an inconvenient attitude." We both laughed.

"Rude gal!" Laila teased, bringing back memories of our days in school, listening to music and feeling rebellious, promising each other we'd take over the world together. She'd be the editor in chief and I'd be primetime at the anchor desk. And somehow, we'd made it there—some version of it. But dreams do shift on you.

"Do you ever think about it, Tab, getting paid for your perspective—really paid to do it? That's what I'm about now. I see the potential of it, how far it can go. And now, there's nobody to tell me no. All I have to do is find enough people who are willing to pay me. But at least it's a measure of something real, not just *ratings*. Girl, I see that for you too."

I gripped the steering wheel tighter, halfway home and remembering my rush as the throbbing started in my chest. It was the call of motherhood and a reminder of the responsibilities that accompanied it. The freedom that Laila described had been paid for by risk that I could no longer afford. The pang in my chest balanced the one in my gut that knew she was right. "Girl, I'm stuck in the hamster wheel. This is my life for now. I don't even get to take my full maternity leave. Nobody tells you that leaking through your shirt in your car leaving the office is one of the squares in 'Having It All' bingo."

"Or that another one is struggling to prove yourself to investors in an industry you've worked in for a decade." Laila laughed. "Nothing is ever what people tell you it's going to be. Nobody talks about the hardest parts."

"Bingo!" I shouted. "Congratulations!" I began, thinking of the game shows I used to watch with Granny Tab.

"Tell her what she's won, Sam!" Laila continued our riff, sounding like a perfect imitation of a game show host. "That's right, Tabby Walker, after all of your hard work and accomplishments, you've won the grand prize—even more work!" Laila continued in her even more perfectly honed announcer voice. "You'll get to work harder than your counterparts for less pay and higher expectations! And that's not all! You'll also get to come home to full responsibilities for your family!" Laila laughed so deeply it was immediately contagious.

"Exactly!" I said, enjoying our moment. It was great to have the Laila I knew back. And to be on the same page doing what we'd learned to do so well. In the hardest times, we always managed to turn our pain to laughter. Laughter was the sugar for our lemonade.

When I reached home, I heard the unmistakable rhythmic wailing of Evie crying before I even opened the door. I walked in to find my mother trying to console her with pacing strides and bouncing arms. I knew that babies cried, but I wondered in that moment if in her big eyes she was somehow able to see all that awaited her later in life. I wanted to cry too, from both joy and exhaustion. The tears welled, but I wiped them away as I walked into my house, remembering that I was happy.

"THAT'S WHAT YOU WANTED, RIGHT?" MY MOTHER PERCHED on the seat at the island in my kitchen, fingertips curled around the stem of the wineglass I'd delivered to her moments earlier. Resting my elbows on the smooth, cold surface of the countertop nearest my stove, I fidgeted with my ceramic mug handle, quite literally waiting for water to boil.

"It's everything I've been working for," I told her confidently. While true, it didn't mean I had no second thoughts; I just hoped she didn't pick up on them in my voice. Like so many steps forward, this latest didn't feel like I'd imagined it would. "The truth is . . . Chris was right. It's really soon for me to level up, especially as an anchor, but it also seems like it's the only option I have to keep my momentum at KVTV."

"I thought your job was protected with maternity leave?" My mother's face scrunched with confusion. I sighed.

"It's supposed to be, but just like so many parents who can't afford to take time off financially, I can't afford to have viewers getting used to seeing someone else in my place. It's always about ratings. Always, always, about 'ratings.'" I showed my mother an air quote and walked over to check the baby monitor. *Still sleeping.* Even while Evie slept, the demands of parenting did not. Not in the middle of conversation, not when I crossed the threshold of the office, not even when I faced the television cameras once again, as they broadcast some version of me into millions of homes in the Southland.

The whistle of the kettle started and I rushed to pull it off of the burner in well-rehearsed choreography, flowing into my evening tea ritual of just a tiny little something for myself, especially on the rare evenings that Marc didn't join for bedtime. While my mother was visiting, he made his way over nearly every day, but didn't stay the night, both because of the amorphous state of our relationship and the awkwardness of modesty. With my mother's presence, even with a mortgage and two decades of living apart from her, that twinge of shame came into my belly about having a boy in my room.

My mother sighed softly, her shoulders slouching as she lifted the wineglass to her lips. Tea in hand, I walked over to take an open seat beside her. It was a moment that looked like so many after my father's departure—both of us, in the kitchen. My mother was eased by wine then, and the child version of me often observed her with worry. This time, it was her observing me. This time, it was me overwhelmed by motherhood and everything else meant to ensure a life of stability and comfort. And all the while, grasping to hold on to some semblance of my own identity, trying not to give up the same things she did.

Up until a short time ago, measured now in the development of a tiny human, I was a woman defined by my own accomplishments. I woke and slept according to how well I performed in the workplace and no other measure. As long as that was going according to plan, I believed so deeply that everything else would work out.

With a healthy career, I was free; I was safe; I was valuable in ways that allowed me to be more than an object. It was a value that could be measured by salary, promotions, and of course at KVTV, ratings. But now I could fail in a new way—the worst way. I could fail *someone*, and it would matter—more than just feeling bad about it. It was a whole life that I was responsible for—the life of someone who needed me.

In the silence that settled between us, sitting in the kitchen that connected past and present, I felt moved by the growing realization that the parent in front of me was a human apart from the name "Mom." That there was a Jeanie, and that there'd always been a Jeanie, and that she'd at times failed miserably even while doing the best she could. That knowing stirred inside me. The knowing that I could fail too. I could fail Evie. And I wondered if my mother felt like she failed me. That maybe in the second that our eyes met, in the lifetime of words that crossed between us, I could hear in the air the constant apology that is every breath of motherhood.

Leaving my mug on the top of the island, I gave in to the awkward compulsion that moved me toward her, almost like a gravitational pull I couldn't resist. I stood up and walked the few steps over to her where she was seated, still slouched. I found my arms opening to her, wrapping around her and pulling us close together. "I'm glad you're here," I pushed out in muffled words into her shoulder. "Thank you for coming." Her arms came up to embrace me, and we stayed like that for a long while.

18

WITH TWO DAYS LEFT IN MY MOTHER'S VISIT AND A WEEK AND a half until my "back to work" opportunity, it should have been smooth sailing, as far as new motherhood could go. But instead, I unexpectedly found myself driving a little too fast northbound on the 405, heading to Calabasas to retrieve my sisters following a concerning text message from Dixie.

> Can u come get us? They r fighting again n now Dad is leaving.

My heart dropped to my stomach at the sight of the message, all my worries confirmed. The memory of nine-year-old me on the day my father left made me want to protect Dixie with all of my being. Danielle too, if she'd let me. Since Granny Tab's funeral, I'd watched the strain build between my father and Diane, reflected in its effect on the people in the new Walker household. I could see it in the darkening circles and slowly billowing skin underneath Diane's eyes, how she'd withdraw from conversation to busy herself with something trivial at dinner. The timidity and almost embarrassment she showed when asking me if I could again host the girls at my home for the weekend. And Dixie and Danielle, the words they didn't speak when it seemed like so many times they wanted to say more, all filled my mind along the drive to their home.

I was sure that I would make it in time to confront my father; to make him see that he couldn't just break apart another family. I wondered how much of me behind the wheel, racing against time, was the nine-year-old me trying to outrun the past. The exits rushed by in a blur of green and white until I reached the one that I'd begun to instinctually recognize.

I wasn't sure what I expected to see when I reached the door of the Walker house. It very well could have been a moving truck with brown boxes trailing off the landing like a caravan, or an open trunk of an SUV with lamps, papers, and odds and ends strewn about, loaded in armfuls by my father in a rush to depart. To me, all of that was what leaving looked like. So it was a complete surprise to pull up to a nonevent, and a home that looked as undisturbed and peaceful as on any other ordinary day in the Southern California sunshine.

Dixie must have been waiting for me or monitoring the cameras, because she cracked the door open even as I was exiting my car and stood patiently waiting for me to approach, peeking neatly through the opening. I moved hurriedly toward her with the ready embrace that I would have wished for at her age. From far away, she still looked so small, even though she'd started to grow in height like Danielle and would be taller than me before I knew it.

"Hey, Dix, what's going on?" Moving so fast, I was breathless. My words came out in a rapid stumble between us. I hugged her narrow body toward me, and felt gangly limbs cross my back. Slowly, eventually, Dixie stepped back-ward from me.

"I'm glad you came, Two." Dixie pushed a shiny strand of brown hair behind her slightly sunburned ear. I surveyed the foyer behind her as we moved farther inside, listening for the sounds of conflict and disarray.

"Of course I came, Dix." I bent down to meet her eyes more directly. "Is everything okay? Dad already left?"

Dixie looked at me with confusion, her face in a small, crumpled expression. "No, he's still in his office. He's not leaving until later." Immediately, I was the one confused.

"Later? You said that he and Diane had a fight and he was leaving. He's not leaving?"

"No, he is leaving, but his flight is later. So I guess he's just getting ready to go."

"But I don't understand, Dix, you said you needed me to come and get you and Danielle. Dad was leaving and . . . I thought . . ." As I struggled to find the right words, Dixie continued.

"We wanted to come . . . I mean, it's been happening a lot and our mom gets sad. We just wanted to stay with you this time while Dad was on his trip." As the realization hit that I'd walked into a situation I didn't understand, I managed to stop myself from saying more. At least until I could assess for myself.

"Ok—grab your things. I left Evie at home with my mother. Get Danielle. I'm going to go speak with Dad for a second, okay?" Dixie nodded at me and headed off, shouting her sister's name into the back of the house. I made my way toward the closed mahogany doors of the study.

"Yes?" my dad called back to my knock on the door. I

pushed the heavy door open and peeked my head around its edge. My dad was standing behind his desk, sorting through papers, with a small computer bag open in front of him. He looked up to see me with a bit of surprise. "Hey, Tab! I didn't know you were stopping by. Where's the baby?" His voice sounded nothing like that day so many years ago in the kitchen. This wasn't a man leaving his entire family for good. This was a man going on a business trip. But somehow, either Dixie or I had misread the situation. And the only way to find out was to ask. I made my way deeper into the office, heading in the direction of the weathered leather sofa against the wall.

"She's . . . at home . . . with my mom."

"Ah, so Jeanie is still in town? That's great. Getting some bonding time in." He sounded good-natured and pleasant. I was even more perplexed. Why had Dixie asked me to come?

"I guess so, yeah," I said, as slowly as I could, drawing out the words to find the courage for more. "Dad, can I ask you a question?"

"Of course, sure." He looked up at me over his glasses, and his eyes met mine directly. His hands paused in midair, still holding the papers. I could see him contemplating. And between us, there was still a lifetime of unspoken words.

"It's about you and Diane."

"Oh." He seemed to freeze for a moment, and then took in a deep breath. So deep I could actually see the outline of his chest expanding under his shirt. And then his shoulders seemed to lose inches of height and sank downward. "Mind if I join you?" he asked. He had already started toward the sofa, so I simply nodded and took my own deep breath. There was something I needed to know.

"Dixie asked me to come. She said you were leaving, and I thought it meant that you were *leaving* leaving . . ."

"Like, leaving for good?" My dad's voice sounded like I'd just said the most unthinkable thing. But it wasn't unthinkable. It had already happened. And if it had already happened, it could happen again. And after a momentary recoiling of his entire frame, he leaned toward me and touched my hand. "Why would you think that?"

Why would I think that? my thoughts echoed. There was so much I could say, but I managed to stay in the present. "Because I know lately things haven't been going well between you and Diane, and I guess . . ."

He settled backward into the couch as if yanked by an unexpected pull of gravity. "Ahh . . . and you think I'm a runner. You think I'm going to run away. Right?"

I had no idea what to say next. Because he was right. But I also knew that he thought I was wrong. So I only nodded, trying to hold on to the slippery courage that had brought me in the room in the first place.

"Well, just leave, kinda like you left . . ."

"Because you think that's just what I do, Tab? Really? Is that what you think?" His tone sounded so sincere, his expression crinkled with confusion.

"Why wouldn't I?"

He looked wounded. "Can I tell you a story?" he said softly. I nodded and he continued. "I know we haven't talked much about the time since your mother and I split." My dad adjusted and removed his glasses, seeming to blink me and perhaps his next words into focus. "Around that time, Granny Tab said to me once, 'How can you ever know what anything is if you keep doing everything the same way?' It took me years to understand what she meant. It's so easy to think that just because you seem to be moving forward that you have things figured out." He squeezed the bridge of his nose. I couldn't tell if it was still squinting or if he was holding back the emotion of tears. It felt like the latter. But the tears didn't come.

"That's what I thought, until recently," he continued. "And sure, Diane and I are having some problems. Hell, *I'm* having some problems. I lost my mother. But I'm not leaving."

Not leaving? I was baffled. He sounded so definitive, so clear. Nothing like what I expected based on everything I'd been seeing and hearing. The clouded lens of the past made it impossible to interpret the present, sitting there on the creaky and worn brown leather sofa in a house situated right in the center of my father's new life.

"You left us." It was all I could manage and so difficult to say, I whispered it. I wasn't even sure if I'd meant to say it out loud. It wasn't a door meant to be opened. "You left us, and now things look the same." My father's face looked as if my words had physical form and they had just settled onto him like a weight.

"Tabby, that was years ago." He reached for my hand to hold it. His skin was only slightly lighter than mine. Sprinkled on it, I could see the hairs that time had turned gray in the years that I'd missed with him. The salt-and-pepper curls of his hair had receded past his temples, changing the shape of his face. Without his glasses, the extra skin of his eyelids weighed them down farther than I remembered, with some white hairs sprinkled within his eyebrows and lashes. Time had had its effect and made its mark on the outside, but how could I know whether anything at all had changed within?

"Well . . . Dad, what's different?"

He said nothing, and yet his mouth opened, once, twice, and closed. He took a deep breath. I waited. And in the silence, what I heard was Granny Tab, the quietness of her voice. I recalled the times spent by the window at Crestmire, her faded blue eyes looking out at the willow tree, when she told me that my father was what she called—*the rare type*. She said that he'd never give up trying to be better, no matter what the past had looked like. And I'd wanted to believe it.

"It's . . . it's different." With a start, he pushed himself off the sofa and began to pace a small slow circle in the direction of his desk. "I'm different. Diane's different. We started counseling. And I know there are the disagreements and it feels rough." He pulled his hands to the top of his head. "But we're not giving up. I'm not giving up." He said it with balled fists, in a punch to the air beneath him.

"Maybe it's harder on everyone else around you than you realize," I said. "The girls have been asking to stay with me. I don't know how to reassure them."

"Just give it some time, Tabby. Trust me. There's a lot of catching up we all need to do." His words halted as a soft knocking sounded at the closed door. I'd lost track of how long I'd been in there. I knew that it was Dixie at the door. And the surprise wasn't that she'd shown up, but that it had taken her so long to come. The realization washed over me all at once—the curious text. She'd wanted me to speak to our father. And I'd done so for the nine-year-old me and for her and for Danielle.

Leaving that office, I realized that I was stuck in a loop of the past. And as long as I stayed there, no matter what was happening, or what kind of music played in my life, I'd keep doing the same performance. I'd make the same moves, respond the same way—dancing with ghosts. It wasn't just my father who Granny Tab was talking about with her "rare type" label. It wasn't Marc either. She was talking about me.

19

"TELL US MORE ABOUT KVTV, TWO!" DIXIE WAS THE TALKATIVE one next to me in the front seat in the car heading back to my house. As usual, a brooding Danielle sat in the back, next to the empty baby seat, looking out the window at the blurred scenery as we zipped down the 405 Freeway heading south like two Thelmas and a Louise. There are moments in life when we all need a getaway driver. We want to believe there's an escape—somewhere else we can go and be safe, no matter what happens. Granny Tab had been that for me in my childhood. And in the most unlikely series of events, I'd become that for my sisters.

I told the story again of the meeting with Chris, Doug, and Lisa, and how the test, now ten days away, would work. And I told the much more engaged Dixie about what could happen next. How things would change for me at the station and why I couldn't just keep doing what I'd been doing. Explaining workplace politics to a preteen was exactly the experience I needed to understand how juvenile the entire situation was. And my relationship with Lisa, which was like being best friends with the most popular girl in class, was going to be different. She was leaving and I'd be on my own, potentially in her position if our audience liked me enough.

"But aren't you already popular?" Dixie's innocence and sweetness radiated from her in ways that made me regret the years I'd missed out on knowing her. She rejoiced in any sliver of involvement in my life and seemed like she would pop with excitement every time the topic of her new title of "Evie's aunt" came up. It was so much more than just her big blue eyes that reminded me of my grandmother. Our grandmother. It was almost like the best parts of her, the faith in other people and the aptitude for love, were part of her own genetic inheritance. Danielle, I would continue to believe, had more of the personality of her mother. But maybe it was more than that.

"I want you two to know I spoke with Dad." I kept my focus on the road, but checked my rearview to see if anything I'd said had registered with Danielle. "And you know you're welcome to come over anytime, always. But maybe things aren't as bad as they seem at home." I paused, waiting for some acknowledgment from either of the girls. But there was only silence. I continued. "Dad and Diane are trying to work out a few things. It isn't always easy for adults to understand each other, even when they're married. But they do love you both very much, and I don't think you have to worry . . . about anything, okay?" I looked over at Dixie, who looked back at me with a quizzical expression.

Oh no, my mind warned. In the pause of conversation, it occurred to me that even as I consoled my sisters about the state of their parents' marriage, we were headed to my house, with my mother. I hadn't thought about what it would mean to bring Diane's kids into the same environment, or if it would be beyond awkward. When I mentioned it to my mother during my hasty departure, for reasons that felt quite ridiculous in the car ride back, she said very little. And as a black woman, I'd learned over time to listen to the silence as much as any verbalized response. In that quiet was the work of extreme concentration, holding one's mouth shut.

"I just don't think they love each other very much anymore." If Danielle's voice weren't so much deeper than Dixie's chipper squeaks, I wouldn't have believed she finally spoke. And then it was my turn for the silence. Silence of my own and a desperate search for what to say from the comingling truths that swirled in my mind.

"People . . . sometimes love differently at different times," I said. "Maybe, as long as they're fighting, they're still trying. And maybe sometimes that's what love looks like . . . even when that's not what it seems like." Granny Tab's reassurance of my father's ability to change sat in the center of my mind, but I didn't dare repeat it. I hadn't seen enough to believe it yet. *Leopards don't change their spots*, my mother would always say. That message felt safer. And who was I to promise a twelve-year-old and a fifteen-year-old a world that was better than anything I could prove?

"Hmph," was the muttered sound that came from the back seat. In a brief glance in the rearview, I saw that Danielle had already turned her attention back to the passing scenery.

At a certain point, before pulling up to my home, the space inside my car had fallen quiet, the only noise coming from the radio. I'd been using the time to figure out how I was going to give my mother some grace while forcing her to share space with who she most likely saw as the spitting images of my father's betrayal. Perhaps she'd busy herself with

Evie. Or maybe she'd focus herself in the kitchen and the girls would be otherwise occupied. I'd let them order food delivery with plentiful carbs and then fall asleep in front of the television in a pile of pillows and blankets on the floor.

It was almost as if she knew exactly when we'd pull up. As we entered the front door, my mother greeted us all like it was her own home, fully made up and under cool, calm control. A quick finger to her lips signaled that Evie was sleeping down the long hallway, where sound could travel. A wonderful rich and unmistakable smell wafted toward us. "Is that mac and cheese?" I whispered incredulously. My mother just smiled a knowing smile that creased her face and crinkled the skin around her eyes. A smile that showed no teeth. A smile that was silence. I could only hope that I'd inherited a fair measure of the Jeanie Walker poker face.

"Let's go into the kitchen," she said finally, as if I had forgotten the layout of my own home, or simply how to operate at all. We all obeyed—perhaps easily beckoned by the melding aromas of food. "I made a small dinner, thought you'd all be hungry after that drive." She spoke cheerily. Danielle and Dixie each looked on. She turned to face them with outstretched arms, reaching each girl with a hug. "Now, you must be Danielle." She squeezed Danielle warmly until I could see her frame relax a bit. "And you . . . must be Dixie," she added with a brief tug at the blunt end of Dixie's silky-straight strands. Dixie melted into my mother's arms like butter and cheese into noodles. The girls settled on calling her Ms. Jeanie, which seemed to suit all parties, and everybody hovered naturally around the kitchen island like usual.

"Now, let me ask you girls, do you eat milk? Cheese? Chicken?" To each food item named, both Dixie and Danielle nodded hungrily. The kitchen smelled glorious, a master mix of deep, silky, rich aromas that couldn't be refused. I felt my own head nodding too, even though she wasn't speaking to me. I was being hypnotically seduced through my sense of smell, through the mixture of warmth from the oven and the fragrance of garlic and butter, cheese, and something earthy that I couldn't place. I didn't have to wonder long. "I made a little mac and cheese, some smothered chicken with mushroom gravy and mashed potatoes . . . does that sound good?" Her punctuation was a perfect smile.

All I could do was look on in awe, as a daughter, as a woman, and as a mother, in seeing my own mother perform a kindness, a generosity of spirit so extreme that it briefly took my breath away. How had she steadied herself in spite of the years of resentment, the unhealed wounds, the justifiable bitterness, and allowable anger? I had no answers. Maybe peace was made through service, through the practice of doing for others, of caring with such intention that you're forced to forget yourself. So you don't drown in your own shit. My mother had won something, an invisible prize. She too was the rare type. For now, before Evie woke up, together two families of Walkers would eat together.

HOURS LATER, THE GIRLS AND EVIE WERE FED, AND JUST MY mother and I sat at the kitchen island together. Danielle and Dixie were happy and full in front of the television in the den, having their own disjointed sleepover—Danielle pretending like she wanted to be left alone, but not really wanting to be alone, and Dixie pretending not to be watching her closely, waiting for any opportune moment to say something about

the program they were viewing. My mother and I had created a similar routine during her visit, in the evening time
that Evie was down, sometimes sharing a dinner and conversation with Marc, but usually ending in both of us falling
asleep in front of the flickering light of the screen. It was
comforting to know that we still fit together in time, like we
used to when I was Dixie's age, before my mother and I both
began to insist on our self-preservation over our proximity.

Tonight, there at the kitchen island, we shared the space
for stolen privacy in a house full of Walker women. Sitting in
the dimmed light of the nighttime kitchen, there were still
things that needed to be said.

"Things over at my dad's weren't what I thought."
I leaned in to make sure I delivered my words quietly. "I
hope it was okay for you that I still brought the girls here. I
misunderstood . . ."

My mother stiffened her shoulders a bit, straightening
her posture to square her neatly styled shoulders. "Mind? It's
your house, Tabby. I don't get to decide your visitors."

"But I know . . . I know that . . ."

"They're just children," my mother said with a casual
shrug. "Nothing that's happened is their fault. I can't blame
them. They're nice girls." She broke off a piece of the cookie
that sat in front of her. It smelled of sweet, creamy vanilla
and the dark chocolate chunks that dripped in a few glossy
glops down the broken edges.

"But it doesn't bother you? To see them. It's not hard?"

My mother slowed her chewing and let her hand drop
down to the cold smoothness of the marble surface in front
of us. "Hard?" she said. She shook her head with a slight
chuckle, turning to face me more directly. "Tabby, divorce is

hard. Having a child, a newborn, that's hard. Losing parents, jobs, opportunities in life . . . *that's* hard. This . . . this is just uncomfortable. That's all. And uncomfortable I can manage just fine." She patted my sweatpants-clad leg that was next to her. "Just uncomfortable," she said more softly.

"Maybe I don't understand the difference?" I studied the cookie half in front of me. Rather than starting a new one of my own, I broke off another piece of hers, lifting it to my lips from among the crumbles, smelling the caramelized sugar but immediately tasting the salt.

My mother smiled at me and took a deep breath. "Tabby," she said, "uncomfortable is when you know what needs to be done. It's just not the thing you most want to do. *Uncomfortable* doesn't feel good, but at least you know what's supposed to happen. But whew, *hard?*" Her hands flew up to the sides of her head, as if to protect her temples from a flood of memories. "Hard is when you have no idea what needs to be done, or how to do it. And *no idea* how you're going to make it through."

She sighed, and then slid off of the stool to walk toward the half-empty wine bottle that sat on the counter next to the kitchen sink. She pulled it down by its neck, dragging the bottle behind her in the air as she returned to her vacant stool. "*No idea,*" she said once more, then refilled her wineglass and placed the bottle upright again on the island. It was a scene like so many in my girlhood—my mother and me, in the kitchen, her with a wineglass, me without one, dealing with the heaviest of life issues, somehow still involving my father.

But here and now, we were different. I was a woman, not a girl. And my mother—she was just different. With this version of my mother, I knew that the wine would stop flowing, that the bottom would be reached soon, of the glass and of the mood. And then, she'd bounce back. Before, when my father left, there'd been no bounce. There'd only been a sinking, further and deeper, to a place where neither of us recognized ourselves. This was what better could look like. The way she'd treated my sisters was a feat of strength that I could only struggle to comprehend. As I unpacked the layers of grace and compassion my mother showed in that evening, my eyes began to fill with water. She'd made dinner, she talked, she comforted. It was more than strength.

"Marc decided not to come this evening?" My mother's voice broke into my thoughts. I looked up at her, head tilted reflexively. "It seems like he's been here every day in my visit." She was right, other than this evening, Marc had more or less kept to our usual routine. This evening, he'd messaged to say that he had a late meeting, so he'd see us the next day.

"He had a late meeting . . . and . . . and I have a full house so he said he'd just see us tomorrow," I said. My mother shifted to look at me directly.

"How are things going with you two? I know it was rough with Yvonne in town. Do you have any more thoughts about how you feel about him?"

"I feel fine about him." Knowing I'd answered too quickly, I gave my mom a slight smile and side eye. She knew what I meant. I could tell by the way her own mouth pinched to-gether in a tight line. She wanted more information. "I mean, I still don't feel compelled to be in a relationship with him, but then again, I also know what that means if I'm not. It means that one day . . ."

"One day, there will be another woman," my mother said,

completing my thought. "Maybe other children, other prior-ities. One day, you might be the one visiting. You realize?" The words were difficult to hear, but weren't so different from what I'd already thought. The idea that things would only be-come more complex over time haunted me. It wouldn't just be about the logistics of a schedule. It would be about who would be around my daughter and what they would be doing without me present.

Motherhood had birthed in me the strongest desire to protect, more than I'd ever imagined. And it had also birthed in me another feeling, which ignited every time I looked into the beautiful sparkling eyes of my child. It was a burning question that I carried with me into every decision: When she looks at me, watching, learning, what will she see? Who will she see her mother be, and become? And what am I teaching her? Because my lessons will be the important ones. The examples I set against a world—once she leaves my arms, my doors, and my purview—that will constantly be trying to teach her she is not enough. And those will be the lies I will have to inoculate her against. It will start with me, like the immunity that passes between mother and child in the womb. My vaccinations become hers, my antibodies, my body's learned defenses—the same as I learned to guard my spirit, my desires, and my wholeness. In doing so, I will protect hers.

"I realize, but maybe figuring all that out now might be better than . . ." The rest of the words caught without exit-ing. We both knew what was on the other end of it. It was the memory of years of moments like this, in the kitchen we used to share—a testament to the devastation of a broken family. So far, it was impossible to tell the broken bonds apart

from the broken people. It was a path I didn't want to repli-
cate by my own choices.

"Better than divorce?" My mother lifted her wineglass
to her lips and took another sip before putting it back down
again. The delicate stem perched perfectly between her elegant, manicured fingertips. Before I could answer, she continued. "Yes, divorce is hard." Then, she turned to me, leaving
the glass behind and looking at me so directly that it made my
breath stop for a moment. "Tabby, it's time for me to go back
home. You . . ." In the pause, she reached her hand over to
mine, lowering it gently, the brown of her skin matching my
own. It felt like the soothing of Granny Tab. "You are going
to be okay. You and Marc need your time together as a family,
and then you can make your decisions."

For a moment, I struggled with a response. But what was
there to say? So, in the kitchen, in the dark, we just sat there
sharing space, wishing that the hard things were just uncomfortable after all.

20

THE NEXT DAY, I TOOK DIXIE AND DANIELLE HOME. THE DAY
after that, Evie and I said goodbye to my mother at the airport. And finally, on that same evening she left, Marc and I
spent time together as alone as new motherhood could allow,
on the sofa of my living room. We were just days away from
Laila's business shower and a week from the scheduled date
of my on-air test for Lisa's anchor position.

In the minutes before he was set to arrive, delayed panic
set in. I worried about small things, like should I try to cook
something, or should we order, and larger ones, like would
he want sex and how could I tell him that I still didn't feel
ready and maybe needed more space for different reasons.

Much of the time lately, my life no longer felt like my own,
but all of the time my body felt like it was someone else's.
Not only was it still unrecognizable to me, but it felt like the
purposes I'd always used it for had been long abandoned. My
breasts were attuned to an infant, nipples large, throbbing, and
raw. The sole kindness of breastfeeding for me was simply that
I'd been one of the moms who'd been able to do it at all. None of
my regular clothes fit, especially not jeans, or any items I'd pick

for a date night or an evening out with friends. My midsection was more pear-shaped than I'd ever known it to be, with a bulge in the front that still looked like early pregnancy.

And still, even after a near lifetime of scrutiny, I didn't always feel insecure about my appearance. Especially not when I was with Evie. Her smallness, her large brown eyes, her soft scent of milk mixed with the gentle rose and iris of powder and baby shampoo, and my fascination with her coos and gurgles gave me the sense of belonging that made me feel exactly right. There was nothing else like that, and it made everything else worthwhile.

Soon, I would hear his key in the door, notice of his arrival. He didn't live or work far, and would come to steal as much time as he could as often as possible. In my mind, he was simply spending time with Evie, but in my heart, I worried that he also wanted more from me. Perhaps, more than I could give, now or ever. He wanted a picture-perfect family. I wanted something that could sustain, endure, and be solid against the crashing tides of life.

My love for him came in waves as well. When I'd catch a glimpse of him holding our daughter, seeing him in her face and hers in his, I'd feel so overcome with raw affection that at times it made me want to weep. And other times, I'd look at him and see a stranger, someone who I could not say I knew. But he was here. And he was consistent, and he showed love.

When I heard the unlocking of my front door, I straightened myself and walked over to greet him as he walked in. Marc spoke to me in our rehearsed whisper. "How's my girl?" For a moment, I didn't know if he meant Evie or me, and the minor panic of that gave me a jolt in the center of my body.

"She's fine. Sleeping. In the bedroom this time." I motioned in the direction of the hallway and headed to take a seat in the living room. In the times that Evie was sleeping when he arrived, Marc would take his shoes off at the door and tiptoe clumsily down the hall to look in at her. Sometimes, I'd catch him watching her almost suspended as she slept, like people in museums finding deliverance in the presence of masterworks. I could understand. Looking at her, it was so hard to believe that my body could create something so beautiful, so perfect, in spite of everything I ever did wrong in life. Like a blank slate for all of my mistakes. Evie was a new beginning.

"Be right back." Marc flipped his shoes off, bending down to arrange them one next to the other beside the doorframe. He walked over to where I was seated, and rested his hand gently on my shoulder. After a hesitation, he bent down and placed an only slightly awkward kiss on my cheek. I moved my hand to glide over his and then watched him walk away, dancing around the creaks in the floorboards.

Hours later, in our usual places on the living-room sofa, Marc and I were alone-ish, again. "So, we survived the grandmothers, the sisters. And now who else is coming? You have some long-lost aunt somewhere? Mary Poppin?"

"Marc, you mean Mary Poppins?"

"Nah, I mean Mary Pop-In," he said with a laugh. Seems like there's always someone here. And we still need some alone time." With lowered eyelids showing his long, dark lashes, he scooted closer to me, one arm stretched across the back of the sofa. I put my hand up between us, resting my palm firmly in the center of his chest.

"Not yet, Marc."

"Oh, word? So how long are we supposed to . . ."

"There's no time frame," I said quickly.

"Well, of course." He sighed and leaned back, stretching his other arm across the sofa back, looking like a seated crucifix. After a pause of silence, his energy seemed to shift. "You have what, about a month left in your maternity leave?"

"Not even that long, and you know I have to go for the anchor test broadcast in a week." I brought my hand up to the tendrils of my still passable twist-out and allowed my fingers to play in the curls.

"Yeah, I still think that's ridiculous." Marc shook his head slowly. "You shouldn't have to prove anything to them." I felt the pang again. And for some reason, I felt angry, but without clear reason.

"The timing sucks," I said with a sigh, trying to calm the bubbling angst. "But Lisa's leaving, and so what else can I do? I need a job to go back to. Since they hired that other weekend anchor, I know how things go. If I don't come back on more solid footing, it'd just be a matter of time. Probably another Scott Stone situation."

"You know he's a midday anchor now on KT—"

I cut Marc off quickly. "Yeah, I know." I did know. Chris Perkins was right when he told me a long time ago that Scott Stone would fail upward easily. And for me, I would fight my way forward, as I had my entire career.

"Well, I don't know why you feel stressed. You know I got you, right? I mean, if you wanted to dial back, take some more time, why not? I'd support you in that, one hundred percent." There it was that pang again—a flash of heat. And I knew so clearly that Marc thought he was being supportive. But all I felt was a rush of anger that I swallowed down with an obvious effort.

"Are *you* going to dial back?" I asked quickly. Too quickly. But the words had started to flow and I couldn't hold them back. "Marc, you didn't even take your full paternity leave. Why *would I* want to dial back?"

"I'm just saying, you have Evie, you might want to make some adjustments. Maybe some things are more important than your career now."

"See, Marc, this is what I mean. Why would you think that? Are there some things that are more important than your career?"

"Well yes, of course but . . ."

"But what?"

"Why is this test and all the stuff at the station so import-ant to you?" And then, once again, I felt like I was sitting next to a stranger. Someone who looked familiar but didn't know me at all.

"Marc, this is everything I've spent my life working for. It's who I've wanted to be in the world. It's been my dream since I was a little girl. And why would you even ask that question? Why is your job so important to you?"

"I don't know . . . income I guess?" Marc said unpreten-tiously. "I work for money. Is that so bad? It's what allows me to support my family, you, myself. And it's not like I have any other option. There's not someone offering me anything close to what I offered you. I thought you'd feel more com-fortable, secure." Mark punctuated his words with a huff. "I'll tell you this, if I had someone who was willing to bankroll me to chill and be a dad, I'd take it, easy." He reached over and took my hand with a big smile on his face. "I'm sayin', you tryin' to put me on payroll? I'm happy to sit back and be a supportive partner." He pulled his arm back and laced both hands behind his head as he stretched out, seemingly trying on the idea.

"Marc, you'd last about five minutes." I tried and failed to imagine him taking on just half of the roles I'd assumed during my maternity leave. He'd lose his mind. I was sure of it.

"You think so? Try me," he said with a chuckle.

"You wouldn't last a day," I said, poking him in his arm. Still, I wanted him to understand my real concern. "Marc, I worked hard to follow my dreams. I made so many sacrifices. And I need to do both. I need to be a mother, and I need to be Tabitha Walker. I need to be myself, and I just don't think that I should have to choose one or the other. I want do to it all."

"You know what they say, *you can't have it all*, Tabitha Walker."

"Well, Marc, if I can't have it all, I guess I'll just have to settle for most of it."

Marc laughed, and so did I.

"Okay, Tab. Get yours, all you can. I'm wit' it." I swatted at him with my hand. In one conversation, we were two people grappling with years of baggage, wading our way through the heavy and murky waters of societal convention. "Well, maybe with some of your maternity leave that's left, we can take Evie to Florida to see my pops. He's the only one who hasn't gotten to meet her yet. And sometimes I worry that he's fading so fast, she won't know him."

"After the test broadcast, we can go. We'll plan it." I touched his leg, feeling the flood again, this time of affection for him. The possibility was there that my connection to him and the understanding between us could grow. I felt like I owed it to him and to Evie to try. And I did try—for three days. And then, it all started to fall apart.

21

"GIRL! WE HAVE SO MUCH TO DO!" ALEXIS SCREECHED HER WAY into my house so loudly that I thought Evie was going to burst into tears. Her characteristic jingle and clack of heels was comforting and brought with it the excitement of our project. It was finally the day of Laila's business shower. Even though Alexis was right that there was much to do, I was so happy that we'd decided to host it in the backyard of my house. I couldn't imagine having to plan an event and then also shuttle a newborn to some other destination.

Alexis and I agreed that we'd do decorations ourselves and pay for catering. I also asked Andouele to come to support me on the day, both with watching Evie and in part to keep me sane as I tried to navigate the multitasking experience of being more than only a feeding and soothing station.

"Tab, you would not believe how much the balloons cost! And how hard it was to find the colors of her logo! Whatever happened to just basic red, yellow, and blue? She had to get all fancy with it." Alexis performed an animated exasperation. "I spent hours in the party store, trying to get all these decorations! I had to say to myself, Alexis Carter, you need to chill!"

"Lex, how much did you spend?" I looked up to survey the damage, reflected in a wide assortment of bags and other items she walked in with.

"More than I needed to," she said, pulling down on a thick cording of ribbon that hung from the ceiling. The balloons she purchased had floated upward to create a spreading oasis of turquoise, lavender, and lime above us. "It's all coming out of the same place, and I'm still trying to write this girl a check at the end of all this. I can't afford to spend the whole budget on plastic cups and utensils! I mean, you would not believe . . ."

"I get it, girl. I get it," I said absentmindedly. While we talked, I finished my last steps of tidying the kitchen.

"Well, Rob is going to bring the boys over later, and they'll have the rest of the stuff, but I'm going to head to the back and start with these expensive-ass balloons!"

"Make sure you secure them tight!" I called after her. From what I could see, she had enough balloons billowing after her to lift a small child.

Lexi and I decided to spend half the budget on the party and then give the rest to Laila in the form of an "investment" in her new community news platform. After many conversations and glasses of wine for Lexi, we finally reached an agreement to rent chairs and tables and pay for a caterer, but otherwise try to keep costs down—make things nice, but not too nice.

Our goal, after all, was to empower Laila as an entrepreneur. Still, Alexis Templeton Carter could not resist the urge to throw an over-the-top party. It was like the ultimate challenge for her. I thought back to her champagne-and-cream-themed birthday party at Fig and Olive that was more elaborate than a juiced-up scene for a reality television show—complete with the obligatory surprise gift of the Mercedes she'd been wanting. And then, there was the "re-wedding" to Rob that Evie accidentally upstaged with her early arrival. If party-throwing had an advanced degree, this project for Laila would be Alexis's thesis. We were both so proud of her and happy to have a chance to show it.

"Where are we setting up the food? In the kitchen or outside on the long table?" Alexis's voice broke into my thoughts. The caterer was set to arrive in thirty minutes, and I'd happily allow them to take over my kitchen and turn my attention elsewhere. For a moment, our event preparation started to feel like everything was under control. I'd prepared extra bottles for the day so that Andouele could easily take over for feedings and I could focus on guests. It was also one of my first times entertaining and I wanted to enjoy it.

"Let's set up the table and wait for the caterer. Don't you think we've pretty much prepared?" Lexi stopped her frenetic pacing in a flurry of clicks and jingles and stood still, released a large sigh, and brought her arm to her forehead.

"Really? You think so?"

"Lex, you've arranged the tables and chairs three times. You spent a month's preschool costs on balloons and decorations. Maybe we're in good shape?" I watched her shoulders relax.

"I just really want this to go well for Laila. I *still* think she's selfish as hell, but I know how it is to get a business going. How it can feel impossible. When she said that she didn't feel like we were supporting her, ugh, that just broke my heart!" Alexis cringed, crossing her arms in front of her in a dramatic self-embrace. "I remember what that felt like for me. It doesn't mean I agree with all of her decisions, though, because—"

"Why don't you pour yourself a glass of wine," I offered solely to cut her off.

"Maybe I will . . ." Alexis slowly headed in my direction from the living room to the kitchen. "Oh!" She stopped abruptly. "We need a playlist!" And with that, she spun around, heading in the opposite direction. She returned minutes later face deeply absorbed in her phone, scrolling and pacing. Each time she passed by me, I could hear her muttering to herself about "Afrobeats . . . oh, Kendrick, definitely . . . Mary? . . . Riri? . . . Alicia? . . . Jill? . . . Ohh! I need Solange . . . and Syd . . . oh, yeah, for sure that one from Ari Lennox . . ." And then I heard, "Oh, yes! And of *course* we *gotta* have some Beyoncé—" *Of course*, I thought to myself with a smile. Leaving the playlist-making to Alexis, I found an open bottle of white wine in the fridge that my mother had left behind and reached for a glass to pour for Lexi anyway—at some point she was going to realize she needed it.

A couple of hours later, my house was buzzing with the final preparations for Laila's business shower. Balloons formed a well-secured and graceful arch in the backyard, tastefully reflecting the arrangement of the lime, lilac, and ocean blue of her company logo. The catering team in the kitchen was hive of activity, and I felt doubly proud to support another young black woman's business. They'd prepared a tasteful mix of richly spiced jerk chicken skewers, an assortment of salads, sautéed vegetables, crudités, and homemade rolls that smelled like someone's grandmother's recipe. Rob was contributing the champagne, which we decided to feature as a mimosa bar, complete with orange juice, bright yellow passion fruit purée, and fresh red strawberry juice that was being churned out in a consistent stream by the whoosh of the juicer.

Andouele arrived, and that was the first moment that I felt myself relax a bit. Only then did I start to feel like maybe I could balance this life and these roles ahead—a mother, a friend, and a hostess.

Lexi and I fully expected Laila to be the last to arrive, far after the flood of early guests, but she was one of the first, bringing with her two bottles of champagne of her own. The glow on her face let me know that she appreciated our efforts more than her repeated and profuse thanks could communicate. She breezed into the kitchen, holding a bottle in each hand, bopping along to Alexis's playlist selection, a smile bigger than I remembered seeing in a long time. A sophisticated camera was slung low around her neck. "Tab! Girl, I just . . . I just, thank you!" Laila struggled to complete her words. But I wasn't looking for her thanks, I just wanted to see her happiness. And I wanted to see her win.

"Lah!" I laughed. "Girl, put those down and go enjoy yourself. You need to figure out how you're going to ask these people for money. Right now, they think they're just here to eat and drink our alcohol." I gave her a gentle nudge on the shoulder. She handed the bottles over to a young man in a catering uniform and turned back to me. Abruptly, she wrapped her arms around me, burying her head in my shoulder. Wordlessly, she pulled me tight. I raised my arms to embrace her back.

I heard a muffled "thank you" coming from Laila that landed somewhere in the crook of my neck and felt the smile coming to my face. Just to know that I could still be there for my friend—that I hadn't disconnected from the people important to me, and that motherhood hadn't changed me into a person I didn't recognize entirely—was a warm glowing thing inside. Laila pulled herself back and gave me a grin that said everything else that "thank you" didn't, and finally turned to head out to the backyard where Alexis was zipping between tables and decorations like a human-size hummingbird.

Marc arrived after the first grouping of guests, the earliest ones, with Darrell in tow. Darrell was "that friend" for both Rob and Marc, the sure source of corruption and certainly all the bad ideas. I hadn't seen him since his summer pool party late in my pregnancy where I "beached" myself in a chair while he busied himself looking after his rotation of swimsuit models. After greeting me, Marc broke off in search of Evie as he always did. "You came alone?" I asked Darrell, not even meaning to, but more out of surprise that for perhaps the first time in a long time, I didn't see him accompanied by one or more women.

"I know better than to bring sand to a beach, Tab." Darrell gave me a sly smile and I couldn't help but roll my eyes. He was handsome enough, but I just didn't understand how, or why, he managed to entertain himself so thoroughly and consistently with the constant parade of younger women.

"I guess the *beach* is out back, then." I pointed the way for him toward the rest of the unsuspecting guests and hoped he didn't annoy anyone before they had a chance to contribute to Laila's business.

And just as Darrell walked away, I looked up to see Todd in the doorway. Todd, who I hadn't invited. For some reason, my breath caught in my throat. It wasn't lost on me that he was interested in Laila. I wondered if perhaps she'd invited him. Even though she'd made it seem like she couldn't be bothered with dating, maybe she could be bothered with the potential support for her company.

"Todd." I reached toward him for an awkward hug. Marc would call it a "booty out" embrace. One reserved for clear signaling that there was no interest or chemistry in the gesture. The tension of the exchange between Marc and Todd stuck with me from the day of Lexi's re-wedding. The last thing I wanted was a confrontation at my house on a day that was supposed to be about Laila. Todd wasn't interested in me at all, but Marc didn't know that.

"Great to see you, Tabby. Alexis invited me." He looked down with some degree of shyness that I didn't expect. Meeting my eyes again, he continued. "I guess this is my first time coming to your house. Really nice. Really, really nice place." His fidgeting made me more nervous than I would otherwise have been, even with Marc just down the hall. And I had to remind myself that I wasn't doing anything wrong, and neither was Todd. He was just a guest at a party. Even if Laila wasn't interested in a relationship, she needed all the support she could get.

"Everyone's out back," I offered with a smile. "Laila too . . ." I added at the last minute with a wink. More awkwardness from Todd as he adjusted his shirt and shifted his focus to the path into my backyard. As he walked away, I felt my body release an exhale. No sign of Marc. It was a relief to avoid getting caught in another awkward situation.

Eventually the cascade of guests slowed to a trickle. Marc emerged from the bedroom signaling a sleeping Evie who was well tended to by an incredibly gracious Andouele. I invited her to eat and mingle while I took over for a bit, but she refused, encouraging me to bring my full presence to my guests. The experience of twenty-four-hour-a-day parenting had erased so much of who I used to be. It seemed like a gift to have time apart from it.

When my mind was focused elsewhere, it was my body on alert, prepared for every need of this tiny human who was my greatest responsibility. As my maternity leave was nearing an end, when I felt the slightest bit of guilt trying to pull parts of myself back, an even deeper part of me knew that it was necessary. I'd have to increasingly find the ways to do it. Motherhood was an important development. It may have been my biggest accomplishment to date, but it wasn't my final destination.

Once all our guests, numbered just under fifty at the peak, were appropriately fed and watered with libations of their choosing, it was time for a small toast and a real explanation of why we were all gathered. While Alexis and I wanted Laila to feel like this was an event for her, we had to admit that we didn't understand enough about her business or her needs to completely take the reins of speaking about it.

Laila stood in front of all of the shower guests, invited to speak about the dream that she'd been building for herself.

"Thank you for coming," Laila started, in elegant bohemian-chic attire draping her lithe frame. Her hand held her half-full glass of champagne, which glistened in the sunlight. "I appreciate everyone coming today for what I have to admit seems pretty unusual. It's not every day that your best friends host a party for your new business at the home of a brand-new mother. So I really appreciate it. And I guess in a lot of ways, birthing a business could be like having a child.

The sleepless nights hit differently, but there are still sleepless nights, and the seemingly never-ending things to pay for, and the desire above everything to see that child thrive—because at the very beginning, you knew the potential of all that it could become.

"Everyone wants to believe their child can be the reason the world changes for the better. And I believed that when I went into local grassroots journalism. I believed that if I just told the stories of the community—highlighting the good, being honest about the bad, and realizing that there was a value in the in-between, that maybe people would discover a new beauty in themselves and in each other. And so, this is my baby. Maybe today, this is how we all change the world, starting right here, in our own backyards."

"And baby needs some new shoes!" Alexis stepped forward. I buried my face in my hand and tried to hold back laughter. Maybe there was no good way to ask people for money. "We are accepting checks, credit cards, donations, and if you're really cheap, words of encouragement, preferably written on a Tubman Twenty, just sayin'," Alexis said with her rapid-fire enthusiasm.

Laila stepped in, explaining that her business ran largely on the basis of subscriptions and advertising. She said that people could purchase the monthly or yearly subscriptions her platform offered, along with an assortment of themed merchandise. She was also part of a community crowdfunding program that allowed for investment through the purchase of shares in her growing company. We were far beyond just collecting office supplies, we were coming together on our own to support our own.

Making a survey of the crowd, I happened to catch Darrell pause his conversation with an attractive woman, squinting at his phone with his credit card in the other hand. And I saw so many others doing something similar. By the time it came to the toast, during which Alexis wasted no time in reminding people that they were there to celebrate, but more importantly to support, it seemed like nearly everyone had made some kind of effort to contribute something. And the smile on Laila's face was priceless. Focused on her, I almost didn't notice Marc sidling up next to me, until I could feel the warmth of his hand on my elbow and the heat of his breath against my ear.

"So, I just invested in your girl's platform." Marc's eyes glistened mischievously.

"Oh? Am I supposed to be impressed?" I teased back.

"You would be, if you knew how much I invested." He winked at me, sparking my curiosity and a bit more.

"Do tell, Marc Brown . . ." I felt a grin cross my face. I was enjoying the moment. As I waited for Marc to answer, he seemed jolted by something invisible. He reached into his pocket and surfaced his phone, blinking with the illumination of an incoming call.

"One sec, Tab, I gotta take this. It's my mom. Something's going on . . . Hello?" He turned abruptly, with the phone up at his ear, heading back in the direction of the house, leaving me stunned, and a little more than intrigued. If I'd known better, this was the exact time to worry.

22

MOMENTS LATER, I FOUND MARC IN THE LIVING ROOM, PACING in small steps, feverishly tapping the phone in his hand. I approached him with a smile, touching his arm, which he barely noticed in his distraction.

"An investment so big you've gotta do it twice?" I said glibly.

Marc looked up suddenly as if he'd been somewhere far away. And it was then, in just a flash, that I could see it in his eyes. They looked as if there'd been tears there, just recently wiped away. The long lashes were no distraction for the bloodshot appearance. And just as quickly, he went back to his feverish typing on his phone.

"Wha . . . what happened. Your mom?" Marc didn't look up at first. I had to jostle his arm twice to get his attention again. Finally, he paused the frenetic activity of his hands.

"It's my dad," he said flatly. And in a moment, that twinge of fear hit my core, the moment of bad news that you can't do anything about. I knew it all too well. "He's been admitted to the hospital. My mom noticed this morning, he was jaundiced. They went to the emergency room. Now he's in ICU.

Tab, I've gotta get there. I've gotta . . ." And just like that, his attention turned back to his phone.

Right then, my world started to spin askew. A house full of guests, a baby, a new mantle of motherhood, and now, a crisis. I asked Marc what I could do to help, but he didn't respond to me. Not even after I asked again. And so I simply sat down, sinking into a corner of the sofa.

As I listened to Marc's mumbling, it became clear that he was looking for a plane ticket. Any question that I'd asked was left in the air, unanswered. Meanwhile, guests were starting to trickle out of the party, some letting themselves out, others walking out with Alexis or Laila. I pretended not to see them to keep my attention on Marc as fully as I could. I had no idea how to support him in the moment other than trying to hold back my impatient need for information.

Finally, Marc looked up at me. "Tab, can you leave tomorrow? Is that too soon to bring Evie?" And just like that, my breath caught in my chest. It wasn't just the idea of a flight seemingly too soon for a newborn. It was also the timing—my test broadcast was only five days away. It was everything. And of course, all at once. There was no way I could somehow get to Florida and then have any certainty of making it back in time, especially not if Marc's father was as sick as Marc was describing. There was only one way to look at it—going to Florida meant missing my broadcast test.

"Marc, I . . . I can't," was all I could manage. And then to watch his face fall and see the disappointment register across his whole body, I knew it wasn't going to be that simple. Choices were going to have to be made, and sacrifices—by someone.

Marc sighed deeply, and I could hear the disgust in it. "Look, I have to go. My dad is in the ICU, my mom is waiting for me to confirm my travel. The earliest I can get there is tomorrow morning on an overnight flight. His eyes turned yellow this morning and the doctors don't know if he's going to make it through the next few days." Marc approached me, taking my hands and pulling me up off the sofa. "Tab," he said softly, "he hasn't met Evie yet. Please." It was that word, the *please* that pulled at everything within me. It was in his eyes, his voice, the way he grasped my hands. It was a word that said more than the others could. Coming from Marc, it was a word of deepest desperation. I had so many more questions. Did he know what he was asking of me? "Let's talk later, after everyone leaves," he said. This was the only thing more he offered before quietly slipping out of the front door, closing it behind him.

Behind me, I heard the voice of Laila, speaking thanks and approaching the door with one more departing guest, Todd.

Both of them, noticing me standing shell-shocked, stopped, pausing their conversation, each shifting their demeanor to one of concern.

"Tab, is everything all right?" Laila asked a question I didn't know how to begin to answer. All I could do was recount the facts that I knew. That Marc's dad seemed to have taken a sharp turn for the worse, and that he'd been ill with liver disease, but something about yellowed eyes landed him in the ICU.

"Jaundice with liver disease, Tabby, that's a pretty serious turn." Todd spoke up, placing his hand on my arm. "Makes sense that he's in the ICU. The next hours and possibly days are going to be critical. Marc is flying out?"

"Maybe tonight. And he wants me to come and bring Evie. He's hoping his father will be able to meet her before . . . I mean if . . ."

"That's a lot to think about," Todd replied. "A healthy baby, she might be old enough to do fine on the plane, but at the hospital, I don't think anyone would say it's a good idea to bring a baby that small into their ICU unit. Immune systems are still in development, it's a risk. Even if you do take her, you should keep it very brief—in and out."

"Tab, I'm so sorry." Laila reached in to embrace me and I let her. My head dropped against her shoulder. Here we were again, in good times and in bad. Remembering Todd's presence, I pushed myself back, taking a deep breath.

"I don't know the circumstances," Todd continued, trying to help me comprehend, "but sometimes in these situations, especially with liver disease that has been caused by an alcohol dependency, you'll find out they've been hiding their use from loved ones. But the silver lining is that there's a possibility of stabilizing the patient in the hospital, in a controlled environment." Todd adjusted his glasses after he spoke, shifting nervously, looking back and forth between me and Laila. The discussion of crisis made the awkwardness of the moment invisible. I thanked Todd in the same breath as I told him goodbye and left Laila to see him out. Making an excuse to check on Evie, I turned to head down the hallway, sucked into the vortex of an impossible decision.

23

I FOUND EVIE WITH ANDOUELE IN THE NURSERY, WHERE AN-douele had created a serene setting with just her presence and calming energy. At some point during Laila's event, she transferred there with a now awake Evie, who I last saw in her cocoon-like swaddle in the bassinet in my bedroom. I interrupted them in a moment of peaceful feeding.

The desire to protect was overwhelming in so many ways. Again, the realization that any one of my own decisions could affect the course of my daughter's life in unforeseeable ways made me feel powerless. No one had told me how the wave of new responsibility could crash upon your shoulders so forcefully that sometimes you literally stopped breathing.

Gazing in on Andouele with Evie was the calm before the storm. It was the moment that I could enjoy before the clouds of consequence started to roll in. I allowed a smile to cross my face watching them, just before Andouele noticed me. When she looked up and smiled back at me, I smiled even bigger. A smile does not always mean happiness, though. Sometimes, it's the disguise we wear when things are going well and also when everything is falling apart. Sometimes, holding that smile in place can be the heaviest thing we carry.

"Everyone gone?" A half whisper from Andouele.

"Yes, finally," I said. "Has she been . . ."

"She's been great, such a sweet, easy baby. Do you want to finish feeding her yourself?"

I imagined taking Andouele's place in the rocking chair, wondering if the usual comforts would come.

"No," I admitted. "You both look so peaceful. I'm almost jealous. I don't want to disturb."

Andouele looked as if she were about to say something more, but relaxed back into her embrace of Evie, supporting the bottle she was nursing on. I turned to head back to my bedroom—although there was nowhere to hide from the decisions to be made. Marc would want an answer and I'd have to choose between the family I created and the career I relied upon. The stakes could not have been higher.

HOURS LATER, I HEARD MARC RETURN. IT WAS HIS USUAL TIME, when he would join me for Evie's bath time, and sometimes to do late-night duty, which allowed me to sleep through most of the night. Tonight, when he arrived, Evie was napping. Although I was exhausted, I found myself still moving about through the kitchen, replacing items used by the catering team even though everything had been clean enough to wait at least a day.

"Hey." Marc's greeting was somber. When he turned the corner into the kitchen, I could see the weight of the news of his father's condition all over him. I could recognize the helplessness, and I felt for him. "Did you figure out when you can leave?" he asked, approaching me to place his hands on my shoulders. Involuntarily, I stiffened. My body was willing to speak the truths that I couldn't. I didn't want to go. And didn't think I should. I also didn't have any idea how to say that to Marc. So I said nothing. "Tabby?" he asked again.

"I'm just not sure it's a good idea, especially to take Evie now." I looked down, unable to meet his eyes. I was not expecting him to understand.

"What do you mean? A baby can travel. And . . . and what if she never gets a chance to meet her grandfather? Have you thought about that?"

What Marc didn't realize is that I'd thought about everything. As a mother. As a woman. And even as a partner. But the circumstances felt so much bigger than me.

"Of course I have. But the timing's not good. And I have to go in to work. Marc, can't we just wait . . ."

"What? Wait until it's time to go to his funeral? Is that what you're saying?" Marc's voice started to get louder, more emotional. I worried about the noise carrying to our daughter. It was our first disagreement since she'd been born and the exact kind of environment I didn't want to create for her.

"Marc, what if he gets better? It's not that I don't want to go. Just that maybe there will be another chance . . ."

"He's not getting better, Tabby. He hasn't been getting better. You know that." Marc's intensity was building. And my guilt was bubbling. It was insensitive. I knew I sounded like I didn't care, but this was a situation where I had to balance everyone's needs. I knew the cost of assuming that there'd always be one more chance. Last time I thought that, my grandmother died. "Maybe family means something different to you," Marc said sharply. "But where I come from, we don't let anything get in the way. *Nothing* comes before family, Tabby. Not work, not some promotion, not even miles to travel." He brought his hands to his head. "Damn!"

Ouch. What he said hurt. He landed a tough blow, right were I was very much still vulnerable. Still, rather than react sharply, I tried to comfort him. I wanted to soften the impact of the no I wasn't yet confident enough to say. The memory of my grandmother's death, the loss of the moment, the understanding of what it felt like not to have another chance suffocated me and left me without a voice.

"I knew you were selfish, Tabby, but *damn.* Damn!" I held my breath for a second, listening for a cry from Evie that didn't come. He was pushing it.

"Marc, how is it selfish?" I whispered. "How? I have responsibilities!"

"Tab, it's not like your back is against the wall. You have more help than my mother did. More options. How is it that you can't understand how important this is."

"I *do* understand," I pleaded into the escalating tension. "But I have to make a decision for me and Evie—"

"What about *my* decision?" Marc said. "Everything you decide, I'm just dragged along. You spend all this time not making up your mind, and this is the one thing you *can* give me a decision on?"

Those last words did it. Over the monitor, we both could hear the building cry of Evie, breaking the tension and our focus on the moment. I moved in the direction of the baby, but turned to Marc with my last point to make. The words were sizzling on my tongue.

"No one would *ever* question *you* prioritizing *your* career.

Least of all me. And when it was time for you to make what decisions were best for you, I was helpless too. How confused I was to think that this relationship was a partnership. You only care about what *you* want." Hearing a realized truth blurted from my own mouth, I smoldered inside. "I should . . . go— check on the baby." I left the kitchen quickly, tears welling in my eyes. I could hear Marc's footsteps behind me and decided to keep silent. To keep my focus on my daughter. Something inside me felt like it was breaking in half. I was going to have to give him an answer. If I couldn't figure out how to say no and make it stick, I'd have no choice but to say yes.

That night, Marc stayed. He slept in my bed, next to me, yet far away. I could feel the heat of frustration building between us. He'd been trying so hard to turn us into his definition of family. But the family I'd had didn't work. And in a different way, it seemed like his didn't either. All the while, I'd been trying to figure out what we were supposed to be and hoping we could create something new that worked for both of us.

In my room that night was my own little family, broken, breaking in its own way. It had been created by luck, good and bad, and circumstance all pulled together. But the bonds that I'd hoped for and those that Marc expected couldn't have been more different. His expectations were of a wife, a commitment that I had not made, even though it was what I thought I always wanted. Things seem so much easier when they're just words, just ideas that haven't been attached to expectations. This was the hard part that wasn't shown in pictures, posts, or loving captions to each other. We don't speak of the sacrifices and who's most often called upon to make them.

24

AND PRIOR TO HIS DEPARTURE, AT HOME, HE AND I FOUND ourselves floating at an impasse. He'd said things the night before that I'd never known he felt or thought about me— things that made me wonder even more why he'd ever planned or wanted to propose, regardless of whether or not we had a child together. He called me "selfish" and then some. He accused me of trying to keep Evie from his family and depriving her of a chance to know one side of herself. Of course, that was far from true. For the first time since she was born, I thought back to my original plan, and how somehow along the way I'd convinced myself that the journey with Marc was better. It was the conventional path, what respectable was supposed to look like.

I had planned for my on-air test broadcast as an evening anchor. Instead, the distance between me and my career goals seemed to grow. After everything Lisa did to help, we now found ourselves in similar positions—having to choose between everything we worked for and the expectations of our partners. At least Lisa had some notice, made an agreement. For me, everything I thought I was avoiding came crashing in anyway. The least I could do was to call and tell her what was going on.

"You've got to be kidding." Lisa's voice cascaded over the phone, echoing my own disappointment remarkably well.

"Lisa, I have no idea what to do," I said, holding the phone tight against my ear.

"Did you say no?"

"Can I say no? How do you say no to something like that?"

"It's simple, Tabby, just say no. If it's not what you want to do."

I paused to consider her words. "Say no, and risk . . ."

"Risk what?" Lisa said in quick reply. "Marc not liking you? His family?"

"Lisa, I feel like I'm risking everything. I mean, what if his father dies? Like . . . like . . ."

"Oh no, Tabby. You mean like your grandmother?"

I fell silent. There was so much more to say, but I couldn't say it. Regret was such a powerful teacher. Once, I'd thought that time was on my side, that a simple choice could be just that, and that the people important to me would be there on the other side of it. Granny Tab had always wanted me to chase my dreams, but somehow, in the end, she showed me the cost of ambition.

"I still replay it all the time," I said. "I wonder what would have happened if I'd made different choices. And I can't help thinking that maybe if I had been there . . ."

Lisa sighed loudly, leaving quiet between us on the phone. The more we talked about it, the more I felt the tendrils of sadness that I'd pushed down deep. *Everything happens for a reason*, people liked to tell me. But how could I say that with celebration if the reason only benefited me? And here, what if Evie never got to meet her grandfather, not ever, because of my decision?

"Lisa, if I didn't go through with it, would you be upset? After everything you did to help me, I'd just feel the worst about that. Like I'd be letting you down and wasting an incredible opportunity. And what if they really do plan on getting rid of me when I go back?"

"People told me I was crazy to quit an anchor position to go back home," Lisa said. "But I made the choice I needed to make for my family. And maybe it's a terrible decision, but it's *my* decision. The one I'm willing to live with. So let me be the last person you worry about. Do what you think is best. Do what you can live with. Everything else will work itself out."

"I hope that's true."

"It's true. I promise."

I wanted more than anything to believe her. But I'd never felt more uncertain. Stuck in a place between two equally bad decisions. Two families. Two futures. Just when I thought I'd fought hard enough to make a way forward, the ground beneath me became unsteady. Marc was asking me to jump off a cliff with him. What did this have to do with love or any of its meanings, other than sacrifice in all its forms?

25

ON THE AFTERNOON AFTER LAILA'S EVENT, WHEN MARC SENT the text message to say he'd arrived in Florida, I still hadn't made a decision. And for all the decisions I'd made before, this particular one felt the hardest. I needed to pick a future without a road map.

It wasn't easy to "just hop on a plane" with a newborn. It also wasn't uncomplicated to be a working mother who, after a far too short maternity leave, would have to return to a workplace that seemed like it was ready to replace her.

When I searched my memory for examples of other women from whom I could draw either strength or inspiration, Ms. Gretchen came to mind. She had managed to live her life without seeming to compromise herself. And in the course of it, she became an uncommon woman—two divorces, no children, and seemingly happy. But was she? If she had it to do all over again, I wondered, would she have picked the guy? One of them? Would she have had the child? I began to realize the courage required for any choice—to become a mother, or to not. To work, or to not. To marry, or to not. Every single one came at a cost you might not know whether you could pay until it was too late.

I wanted to go to her, and in my prior life, I could have. Ms. Gretchen was just a car ride away. But nothing was as simple as it used to be. With no childcare lined up, I couldn't leave Evie at home, and I had to decide whether it was safe to bring her with me.

Wanting to do nothing more than to visit Ms. Gretchen made me realize the difference that motherhood made. Or one of the differences, at least. It was like the old me had died somewhere along the way and here I was, running around like the haunt who thought she was still alive. Expecting people to see her in the same way, but she's invisible in all the ways that mattered. *Maybe motherhood has erased me*, I thought. All of a sudden, every decision, every choice, every breath prioritizes what is best for somebody else. At the bottom of that list is you.

There was a time, not so long before, that I was so clear about what I wanted. Without much hesitation, what I wanted would be what I did—the justification would be clear. *Because I wanted to*. It was the perfect "why." And the same for what I didn't want to do—it wasn't selfish, it was empowered. Now, when it came to deciding about going to Florida, at the risk of everything I'd set up for my career—for the future I'd worked, sweated, and sacrificed to build, I knew so clearly that I didn't want to go. I didn't feel like I should. But the *only* justification I could stand on was what was best for Evie. That was the only shield I could manage to hold up in the face of the fierce winds that pushed me into the direction of what others thought I should do.

Not with Ms. Gretchen, I decided.

Moments later found me shuffling around in the nursery, looking for where I last placed my baby sling. I hadn't made much use of it in the few times I'd left the house, but Lexi swore by it and Andouele had encouraged me gently to try it a few times in her postpartum visits. After flipping through a poorly organized drawer of cotton blankets and still unfolded onesies, where I'd dropped a load of laundry in an absent-minded moment of exhaustion, I found it. A neutral-colored padded contraption of fabric and clasps that looked very much like a dead octopus.

It took exactly four YouTube videos for me to arrange the floppy thing around my body, securely enough that it didn't fall off, and two more to feel comfortable enough about its security that I was willing to slide a groggy Evie inside it. Feeling the heat of her cocooned body turned my insides to melted butter. The oxytocin surge from gazing into her eyes brought me my own feeling of a warm blanket. We were fused together, as one. And in that moment, I felt so assured that we could tackle anything. In her eyes, I saw the smallest bit of my own reflection, and I was reminded that I still existed.

I could do both. I could be more. We were going to Crestmire.

AFTER I MANAGED TO UNDO THE CARRIER CONTRAPTION AND secure Evie in her car seat, I made the most careful drive on the 101 Freeway. Once we made it to Glendale and I laid eyes on Crestmire, I felt the soothing flush of relief. I pulled into the familiar parking lot and parked. While reassembling the baby sling, I had a chance to look upon the building façade that always made me feel like I was visiting a Cape Cod mansion displaced in the middle of the city. Here was still the place that I'd last felt the love of Granny Tab in the flesh. I'd come for my life lessons and comfort, and that was still here—as was Ms. Gretchen.

I passed the common area where the Crestmire residents were leisurely moving about, in the midst of their midday routines. It was just after lunchtime, which meant that several were snoozing in full-belly satisfaction.

"Come on in, honey!" Ms. Gretchen's reply to my knock at her apartment door rang loudly enough to elicit a protracted wiggling adjustment from Evie, and my own reassurance that she was in good spirits.

I opened the door to find her on her sofa, foot elevated in front of her.

"I would get up to greet ya properly, but I just finished physical therapy, and Justin wore me out!" She waved her hand in front of her face, as if a localized heat had come over her. "Come on over here quick so I can finally see my glam-child."

Ms. Gretchen had been an excellent "glam-mother" over video chats and phone calls, but there was nothing like seeing her anticipation as I approached with Evie. On my way over, I noticed the walker delicately hidden in the corner and tried to pretend like I didn't. It was the last thing I'd expect for someone who just a couple of months ago was in kitten heels on a dance floor.

"Don't mind that contraption over there, honey, that's just temporary. Justin says"—she purred his name in a way that made me blush—"that I'll be walking on my own in a month or so." Until then, I've got these. She lifted up her other leg, showing a canvas high-top sneaker with the telltale half-heart of a designer collaboration.

"What do you know about those, Ms. Gretchen? How'd you get so fancy?" I teased.

Ms. Gretchen's smile widened brightly, her blond curls jostling above her shoulders as she gave her coyest laugh. "You know I have to keep it cute," she said with a wink. I approached, leaning in to take a seat on the sofa and begin the unstrapping of Evie. Ms. Gretchen let out a soft gasp. "Oh, Tabby, she's absolutely beautiful. Even more beautiful now that I get to finally meet her in person."

I unwrapped the cloth binding us together, filling the air with sounds of Velcro and the unclipping of the carrier apparatus. Finally freeing my carefully wrapped groggy baby, I offered her to Ms. Gretchen's extended arms. "Would you like to hold her?"

Ms. Gretchen's smile was my answer, brighter than the sunlight that beamed through her open curtains, and more vibrant even, than the colorful lipstick that accentuated her thinning lips. As I handed Evie over, I only felt the slightest twinge of remorse, the faintest wish that Granny Tab could be there too, but in a sense, the three of us together like this, in this moment, she was.

Laughter, snuggles, catching-up, and one feeding pit stop later, I was deep in the fleshy comfort of Ms. Gretchen's sofa, half ready for my own nap, half reinvigorated with imagining life's possibilities in spite of the circumstances before me. I guess that feeling was overwhelming, because I was suddenly overcome with a very large and loud yawn.

"You sound exhausted, honey." Ms. Gretchen was quick to notice and acknowledge. She knew me. In person, all the things that were easy to hide across video seemed to surface in the most obvious ways.

The conflict with Marc had worn on me, but voicing it made me feel like the weight of gravity had been amplified. New motherhood, family issues, a career crisis, and the timing of my maternity leave was enough to almost make me forget that I was the one who wanted it all so badly.

"That's not even the word, Ms. Gretchen," I said languidly, shaking my head slowly.

"You know what you have, honey?"

I laughed. "A lot of problems?"

"Oh, honey, you have a lot of changes."

"Changes? That's—" I began, but Ms. Gretchen continued.

"And that's gotta feel pretty tough for you, because you know what most people are afraid of? Exactly that. Change. Which is the funniest thing—because just as sure as the sun is gonna rise, change is coming too. But people are still afraid—of the good ones and the bad ones, both—"

"But is it just changes, Ms. Gretchen? It's choices. It's—"

"But you know what they're really afraid of?" Ms. Gretchen continued as if I hadn't said a thing. "They're afraid of themselves. They think they aren't gonna make it. Can't cut it." She turned to me and took my hand. "But you, Tabby, you're more sure of yourself by now—aren't ya, honey?" Her tone sounded so sincere and concerned. Like I could let her down with my answer, so I said nothing.

After a pause, studying me again, she continued. "Did I ever tell you about how I used to love to dance? It's what made me marry my second husband. He sure did know his way around a dance floor. And he'd take my hand, even when I barely knew a thing and couldn't find the rhythm. He'd hold me tight, his arm around my back, and bring his face close

to mine. And he'd tap the beat into my palm, just like this—"
As she spoke, her slender fingers tapped a heartbeat into the
underside of my hand. *Thump . . . thump . . . thump-thump*,
the rhythm of a dance. "And I'd lean in close to him, and
feel the warmth of his cheek against mine . . ." There, she
paused and took a slow, deep breath before continuing. "And
I'd breathe in that delicious smell he had, and then—"

I paused, breathless myself, waiting for the next part,
hanging in silence, while she straddled the now and the then.

"And then, I did the most important thing. The easiest
thing by then—"

"The easiest?"

She smiled at me. Slowly, deliberately. With a patience
that could only come through the mastery of time. "I let go,"
she said. "It was easiest then to let go and enjoy the music.
The dance came on its own."

"Even though you didn't know how?"

Ms. Gretchen laughed with her whole body, her turquoise
nails rising up through the air and coming down to slap on
the knee of her still-good leg. "I didn't need to know how,
honey! That was the fun of it, to find out where I was going.
To trust that the music would take us there." She straightened
up again and faced me squarely. "If you can learn to welcome
change, dance with it, even, you'll learn the steps. You can follow any lead—you can let go with a smile and enjoy the thrill."

After a pause, her smile faded, and she continued, her
voice slightly less whimsical. "When you get to be my age, in
a place like this . . ." Ms. Gretchen looked around, gesturing
with her turquoise-tipped hand at her surroundings. "Sure,
it's nice and all. But bingo is always on Tuesday. Lunch is always at noon. You see your friends hollow and still. No more

change coming for them until we have just one more left. But no sense in waiting for that. I still want to dance, Tabby, while the music is playing for me."

I smiled at her. But it was a solemn smile, a wistful one. "But what if you don't like the music, Ms. Gretchen? The music that's playing for me isn't exactly the best for dancing."

"That's what you'll learn if you live long enough, honey. Music is music. Like a heartbeat. It won't always be consistent or melodic or even the right rhythm. But as long as it's there, there's a chance."

I wanted to believe her, but the circumstances told a different story. "Tell that to Marc," I said quietly. "He thinks I'm the worst person in the world for not wanting to come to Florida. Like there won't be other chances or a better time."

"Honey, that boy doesn't know his left foot from a tree stump. Just fumbling around wreaking havoc. Taking blame and shame he carries from one place to throw it on someone else like it's a better destination." Ms. Gretchen shook her head to mark her disapproval. "I swear, when I was teaching, the more time you spend with kids, the more you realize they never really grow up. Nobody really does. So-called adults, we're just the same kids acting out in grown-up disguises. If you look at Marc closely enough, you'll see the boy who hasn't figured out for himself what kind of man he wants to be."

"And to think, Ms. Gretchen, I could have avoided all of this if I had just stuck with my plan—"

"And then, honey, you'd have your plan, but you wouldn't have Evie. Dance the music that's playing, Tabby."

"So you're saying I should go?"

Ms. Gretchen shot straight up as if she'd been struck by a

bold of lighting. "Oh good lord no! Honey, who am I to make that kind of decision? I'm not a mother, and I'm not a wife. Nobody needs me to make decisions for anybody other than myself—and I'd be no good at it if I tried." She patted my hand again. "Don't worry, you'll make the right choice. Just remember—the dance ain't over until the music stops playing."

THAT EVENING, MARC CALLED ME FROM FLORIDA. I COULD hear it in his voice, the undercurrent of controlled anger. The frustration, the sadness. He sounded hoarse, impatient, terse.

I had gotten the basic information from him—he was staying at his parents' home in Jacksonville. His father had been admitted to the ICU at the large research hospital nearby. He'd been receiving care for his advanced liver disease up to the point that the latest crisis hit. The regular visiting hours had already ended when Marc's flight arrived, but he was going first thing in the morning.

"When my dad first got to the hospital, they didn't think he'd make it through the night." Marc's voice trembled over the phone.

I reached for the comfort of my tea mug, sitting under the recessed lights of my kitchen, perched on a stool at the island. *Do they know what's wrong?* I wanted to ask, but instead let him speak.

"Honestly, Tab, I can't believe you're still in LA."

I felt the gasp of air hit my throat and my eyes narrow slightly. I took a deep breath to steady myself and to hold in the first words that were ready to leave my lips. They wouldn't have been helpful—or nice.

"Marc, I told you I don't feel comfortable—"

"Don't I get some sort of say?" Marc interrupted sharply. "I mean, how can you just decide for my child that she'll never meet her grandfather?" His voice was rising. "I've done everything! Everything I'm supposed to do. I stepped up; I'm trying to be involved. I've offered you everything you've ever told me you wanted and everything any woman would want. You have a problem at work—you don't have to work. I make enough that if you never worked again, you wouldn't have to. But what does that get me? You're always talking about you and what you need. But when do I get to be loved, Tabby? When do I get what I need? Do you ever even think about that?"

Marc's words overwhelmed me. The accusations, the disclosures I'd never heard. All mixed in together like a tornado threatening to spiral me away somewhere I'd never recognize. "Marc!" It was all I could do just to get him to stop the flow of words, each one making it harder to breathe. Had he just asked me, *When do I get to be loved?* The words sank within me like a bundle of stones. *He didn't feel loved?* "I do love you!" I said. "I don't even know what you mean! It's just that . . . Evie is a newborn. It's too early to have her on the flight. What if your dad's condition—"

"What? Gets worse? That's why you should have left when I left, Tabby—" Marc stopped speaking abruptly. I could hear his breathing on the other end of the line. It sounded heavy. It sounded like he was pacing. We'd had arguments before, but the emotions had never been this high.

I paused again, trying to speak slowly and keep my tone even, despite how I was starting to feel. "Marc, what do you want me to do?" And instantly I regretted those words. It's not like I didn't know.

"Tabby, you're supposed to be here. Here, with me, in

Jacksonville. This is what family does. But maybe you have no idea about that."

It stung me. Like a punch, the wind knocked from my core. And then the reply that left on its own accord. "'Thafuck is that supposed to mean?" I spat the words back at him and squeezed the handle of my ceramic mug so tightly I thought it was going to break in my hand and crumble to dust.

Marc continued, the intensity building in his voice. "I'm just saying, maybe 'tight-knit' isn't something familiar. People can be *real* selfish. That's just not how we roll in my family. We stay; we stick it out—make it work. We have each others' backs no matter what—"

I couldn't figure out who he was talking about, my father or my mother. But either way, he'd poked at the wounds of my past. But *she came back!* I wanted to scream. My mother came back. But it wasn't my place or the time to defend her choices or her needs. If I'd learned anything in my short experience as a mother, I'd come to see how Jeanie Walker, the woman I'd always called Mom, was a person, caught in an impossible situation. A person with a daughter. A person who was a wife, betrayed in the worst way. A person who had needs and decisions to make that her own survival depended on. All these things I wanted to say, could have said, maybe should have, but I didn't. The rest of the words were stuck in my throat, behind the wall of tears that were ready to fall.

When the gloves come off and secrets shared become swords, words become the sharpest weapons, slicing open the wounds that haven't healed. The words that hurt the most aren't necessarily the ones that are true. The words that hurt the most are the words that you've *been afraid* are true about you. The same words you whisper to yourself in moments of self-doubt and deepest shame.

"But I see how it is in yours—" I heard him say.

"Marc, that's not—" I interrupted.

He cut me off. "Nah, I get it Tabby. I see how you are."

"You don't see me at all, Marc!" I shrieked. "You don't know me. You don't know my family. You don't even know yourself!" I launched the words back at him as a flimsy defense, rocks against a torpedo strike. As I did, I felt the first tear drop in a small puddle on the back of my hand. My insides were aching. That single tear left a trail around my thumb as it found its way down to my countertop, landing in a tiny pool below my hand.

"Tabby, I did what I needed to do to make sure I'd have nothing to regret. That I did everything I could for my family. Say what you want about me, but can you say the same about your decisions?"

And it was just then that I'd realized I'd started crying and that I would cry more and deeply because somehow, in the heat of it, he had won.

Broken and alone, I climbed into my bed that night, tears dripping to my pillow between feedings for Evie. I'd have to prepare the next day to leave on the one and only nonstop flight between Los Angeles and Jacksonville, Florida. It was an overnight flight, which was worse for the fact that with a child of Evie's age, we hadn't experienced anything close to a full night of sleep. We'd have to try managing through the time with feedings and naps on the plane.

Marc said that he would take care of the cost of travel and booking the lodging. He'd find us a place downtown, near the hospital where his father had been admitted, so that I wouldn't have to worry about commuting. These and all the other platitudes and accommodations he offered, having already succeeded in eroding my will to resist.

In the morning, I would phone the pediatrician for clearance for Evie's travel. Even though I already knew it wasn't the best idea, it likely wouldn't be forbidden. I'd have to reach out to Chris and Doug at the station and cancel the test broadcast, citing a "family emergency." Even in this harrowing moment when Marc didn't know whether his dad would make it through this phase of his illness, it still wasn't him that stood to lose his livelihood, or independence—it was only me. And sitting before a heaping plate of sacrifice, I took another bite.

Scrolling through my phone, I quickly found Lisa in my messages and opened a new text box, pausing for a moment before allowing my fingers to move across the screen illuminating the dark of my bedroom.

Please don't hate me. I've decided to go.

I didn't expect to see it, but almost immediately the text bubble appeared, signaling that Lisa was composing a reply. In moments, the words appeared.

Not to worry. Family first. I've got your back.

I let the phone drop from my hand onto the pillow, only for it to slide away from me and eventually extinguish its light. In the dark my tears continued to puddle beneath my cheek.

26

ALEXIS GAVE ME AND EVIE OUR RIDE TO THE AIRPORT. SHE HAD the car seat ready to go in the back when she picked us up, hours before any reasonable human would depart for a flight. In spite of Marc promising to buy anything that I happened to forget and picking up the very last first-class ticket for me on the direct flight to Jacksonville, I still felt as frazzled as anyone could be trying to corral the tiny universe of support for a baby into portable mode. There was the pumping equipment. There were the blankets, bottles, carrier, stroller, clothing, and other items that I'd spent months collecting and gathering in preparation to have a baby in my home. I tried my best to remember what I could in haste.

So it wasn't just as simple as getting on a plane. Marc felt like he was making it easy, but there was no easy—only slightly easier, and part of me would have loved to see him try it. "Why can't you just come?" he'd said. And how do you answer in a way that fully explains how difficult it actually is? You just say "It's hard," and even though it's true, with those words, you sound like you're whining, or weak, or simply complaining.

"Tab, I think it's good that you're going," Alexis said, hands on the steering wheel at a red light. She turned to me, "I know these aren't the best circumstances, but I have a feeling you'll be glad you went one way or another."

"Right," I replied quietly. There was nothing else to say because everything I could have said sounded selfish even as a thought. *Here's how I say goodbye to my career,* I thought. My mind echoed back Marc's words when we'd argued the night before. That I didn't have to work if I didn't want to. *Not true.* I had no plans to be dependent on him. That was never what I asked for. He said that I didn't know for sure that not getting a promotion was throwing my whole career away, that I'd put my career first once, and look what happened, did I want that to happen again? These were the lowest blows, a still-open wound of regret.

The car back in motion, Alexis spoke up again, eyes facing the road ahead. "I had to take almost a whole month off from work once to help take care of Rob's mother when she had surgery. I swear, men become complete babies when anything happens with their parents. And for whatever reason, the whole rest of the family is completely useless. Welcome to wife-life."

"But I'm *not* his wife, Alexis," I protested.

"You might as well be, Tabby. I don't know what you're holding out for. You already have a child together, and we can just imagine all the rest that comes along with that. And what if he started dating someone else? Or, what if—"

"I get it, Alexis." My tone was sharper than I intended. "Believe me, I've thought about all of this. But every time I imagine marriage with Marc, it's because of things I don't want to happen. Most of all, I don't want to wind up like my parents . . . or like his, for that matter. I'm not even sure they like each other."

"Well, I can tell you, it doesn't get easier." Alexis sighed heavily.

"Then why do it?" The words slipped from my mouth so easily, it took me a moment to realize that I actually meant them.

Alexis's mouth dropped open slightly, and closed before she said anything. Looking at her in the silence, I saw her blink once, then twice, and take in a deep breath, hands forming a tighter grip on the steering wheel.

"Tabby, you're so jaded." Alexis stole a glance at me. "Not so long ago, that was everything you wanted."

Neither one of us said much after that. Somehow, the topic changed, and then the words became less important relative to finding the terminal, avoiding the swerving of other cars in the drop-off lane, and the coordination of bags and baby, delivering me to the latest new motherhood adventure of traveling.

And in the midst of it all, the beeps and whirs and pulling, pushing, lifting, sweating, and explaining (yes, that *is* breast milk) with Evie strapped to my body, when I finally got through security and settled in to wait, I realized that Alexis never answered my question.

ON THE OTHER SIDE OF AN OVERNIGHT FLIGHT WITH A NEW-born, I appreciated having the opportunity to exit the aircraft first, but wound up getting off after nearly everyone else had deplaned. Still saddled with the feverish desperation of hope that Evie wouldn't scream her way through our entire trip and the rugged determination of a traveling solo parent, I refused to be defeated. I assembled my and Evie's carry-on belongings and eventually made my way up an unfamiliar jet bridge—the tunnel into a completely new world.

I'd never been to Jacksonville. In fact, I'd never been to much of Florida other than a trip to Miami once for a conference. The difference between the Jacksonville airport and what I remembered of Miami was that of a smaller town feel versus a much bigger one. The irony wasn't lost on me in that Jacksonville was actually much larger than Miami, both by population and by geography, but you wouldn't know that by the airport. I made it a point to research the map and the footprint, just so I'd know how far I'd have to walk from the terminal to where I'd be meeting Marc.

I walked through the concourse with a baby and a pull-along bag, hearing the din of early-morning conversations. I felt very envious of the few people passing by with coffee cups in their hands—I could smell the heady fragrance of a strong French roast, wishing for my own. It wasn't far to the baggage claim, and to his credit, Marc was easily visible as soon as I reached Arrivals. He had on a baseball cap in the unmistakable burgundy of his undergraduate alma mater. It was easy to identify the look of relief on his face, reflected in his strong and still-handsome features, even though the chill between us didn't lend itself to excitement to see him.

"Everything go okay with your flight?" he asked me right away, placing the gentlest kiss on Evie's head. She stirred a little but held on to her slumber. Marc awkwardly turned his attention to me, with a slight hesitation before jutting quickly to the right to place a light kiss on my cheek.

I nodded. "She slept most of the way," I added, sparing him the details of her first flight.

"You get any sleep?" he asked.

"Some," I lied. I was exhausted.

"I checked you in last night, to the hotel. Picked up some things. When we get there, I can watch her for a bit if you want to freshen up before we go over to the hospital. It's not far." He started guiding us toward the snaking bed of the conveyor belt. Bags from my flight started to rumble into view.

"Oh wow, bags already." I smiled, a weak attempt at a peace offering to ease the energy between us. Marc was trying extra hard to be nice. I didn't feel as motivated.

He broke into a tired but full smile in reply. "That's how we do down South, Babygirl." There appeared the flash of confidence and swagger that had attracted me to Marc in the first place. Under different circumstances, I'd have loved to see his hometown through his own eyes. He'd never given me the chance to truly know that part of him, even saving my meeting his family until it was almost time to give birth. If Evie were older, I would have made it here in a heartbeat, especially if it hadn't been during my first opportunity to lead a primetime broadcast.

INSIDE THE AIRPORT, SCENERY CAN BLEND. IN MANY WAYS, IT'S the same no matter which city you leave, or which you visit. On either side of your flight, you see the same blue pleather seats, tiled carpeting of clashing patterns, the glare of the fluorescent lighting against metal accents intended to make the place look futuristic. In the car, though, there was no question that I was in a different place. My LA-based habit of rolling down the window brought me a hot and heavy rush of moisture-laden air—the humidity of a coastal place that had a much different relationship to its neighboring water. Here in Florida, it was a warm blanket that almost smothered me. I rolled the window up quickly, checking to make sure that the cooler air flowed from the vents.

"I hope you put some extra hold in your twist-out." Marc turned to me with a quick smile before refocusing his gaze on the road ahead.

My hand went to my head, feeling the still-defined coarse dips and waves of my style, properly clumped and coiled at the ends.

"You tryin' to be cute. Florida is braids weather. But welcome to Duuu-val!" As Marc spoke, I looked at him quizzically.

"Duuu-val?" I repeated. "What's that?"

Marc laughed. "Girl, it's the name of the county. That's what we call it down here. Jacksonville. Duuu-val. That's what it is!" The name for his hometown, he seemed almost giddy, with a clear sense of pride about it. It was obvious it meant a lot to him that we were there. "I would show you around," he continued, "but I wanted to get to the hospital as soon as we could. The doctor is supposed to give an update this morning."

"Has your dad stabilized?"

"It's been up and down, but last night, the doctor seemed optimistic that he might be able to roll off some of the machines."

I felt a sliver of fear in my heart that I didn't want to acknowledge. What if I'd given up the opportunity for career security? Worse, what if I'd risked my daughter's well-being for a life-or-death circumstance that turned out to be a miscalculation? *Would I feel resentment?* It was still too early to know. Perhaps I'd come to Florida to find out exactly how far I would have to go to forgive.

"Maybe on another day I'll show you where I went to high school. It's not far from where we'll be." Marc explained that he'd gone to a school called Stanton, which was an area magnet school for Jacksonville with black history roots. It had become one of the best high schools not just in Florida, but in the entire country. He'd been an AP student and had his choice of colleges, but he went where the money pointed—Morehouse, in neighboring Georgia, on a full scholarship.

"My parents had already sacrificed so much for me," he said. "I couldn't ask them to do more. I always thought that I'd get to see my dad enjoy his retirement."

Marc said his father had been an assistant mechanic for the school district. He'd worked on the buses in the transportation fleet. It was a challenging position, stable, but not enough to sustain a family and pay for college. Marc's mother was a career administrative assistant at a local law firm.

"It was pretty rough when we lived on the Westside, but after I went to college they were able to move over to Springfield. They always talked about going all the way east to Jacksonville Beach when they fully retired," he explained as we rode along.

After about a forty-minute drive of surprisingly pleasant scenery, especially the stretch of highway that seemed to bring us across the waterway, we finally reached the hotel that Marc had arranged for us.

It was a residence-style hotel, a reminder that families could check in to places like these with no idea when they'd be able to leave. An invisible curtain of concern was draped over the energy of the place. Next to a hospital, there was no pretending that any of us were here on vacation. The room was clean and spacious, and otherwise unremarkable, except that Marc had clearly been here ahead of our arrival.

The kitchen area was stocked with bottles, and many of the familiar accessories that I'd grown accustomed to using at home. While he arranged the bags, I walked in farther with Evie, and in the bedroom, he'd installed a travel bassinet that seemed like one I'd envied online, but hesitated to buy.

"I wanted to try to make it feel like home, to make it easier on you." Marc's voice floated behind me, and I turned around to find him standing in the entryway observing me.

"This is . . ." I struggled to find words. The experience was entirely overwhelming. "Wow, Marc, I . . . didn't expect—"

"Thank you for being here. Thank you for coming. I know it wasn't an easy decision." In a moment, he'd closed the distance between us, taking my hands in his and looking into my eyes. The energy between us was hard to place. There was a shock of intensity, creating a silent crackling in the air. It was a magnetism I had no idea how to act upon. I turned away, breaking the moment, pretending to busy myself inspecting the bassinet and the remainder of the room.

"If there's anything else you need, we can go later. I was thinking you might want some time to shower and then we can head over to the hospital? My mom is probably over there already. She's been staying here too, just to be closer."

If there was one person I didn't want to be closer to, it was Yvonne Brown. But here I was, in her backyard. At some point, I'd have to face her. And maybe this was what I'd actually come to Florida to do.

27

THE HOSPITAL COMPLEX WAS MASSIVE. ABSOLUTELY ENORMOUS in an overwhelming way. It wasn't a place for a baby as small as Evie, and as I walked down the corridor, my instinct to protect her kicked in. I wrapped my arms more tightly around her, even though she was already snugly strapped to my body.

Reaching the sterile ICU wing, holding Evie felt like I was smuggling wiggly contraband into the area. There didn't seem to be any express rule against having her there, but given the surroundings and some of the glances from nurses, the presence of a newborn was an uncommon occurrence.

"He's right over here." Marc guided us to a glass-walled room, with minimal privacy from the outside. I could see an even more emaciated version of Marc's father in angled recline in the hospital bed, but seemingly alert. Marc's mother was sitting in the lone chair nearest the window. "Could you and Evie sit right there for a sec?" Marc said. He gestured to a small waiting area within view of his father's room. "I just want to see what's going on and let them know we're here."

I nodded and complied, grateful for the moment to catch my breath. Being in a hospital again brought a flood of complex memories. There was the time I rushed to see Laila. There was the trip to meet the family of Daequan Jenkins—a near casualty of an unjust attack—that earned me awards for my career, but had cost me my grandmother. And there was Evie, a surprise gift that shifted my world; she'd made me a mother.

Hospitals, like airports, somehow all managed to seem the same on the inside, but it made a world of difference why you were there. Sitting in this familiar place I'd never been, the harsh antiseptic odor of cleaning supplies and medicine swirling in my nose, surrounded by the noise of beeps and rubber soles of nurses and doctors moving about, I wondered what this trip would bring. Whose life would change? Because this time, I'd sacrificed. I'd given my career up on the altar, to cleanse my regrets, to wash away the words that, in my heart, I feared were true—selfish, heartless, ambitious. All cardinal sins for a woman and, especially, a mother.

"Tabby . . . Tabby!" Marc was soft-shouting my name and I wondered how long he'd been calling me.

"Sorry, sorry," I said, quickly gathering myself and Evie. We walked over to him and entered his father's room.

I said my polite hellos to Yvonne and a quite angular Mr. Brown. Marc's father had already been thin when I first met him, but he showed the wear of his hospital stay and whatever crisis had caused it in his drawn face. His eyes were open and focused on me, but looked dim. Then he saw Evie, and something in him shifted. He smiled, arms reaching out.

"Ahhh!" he said. "Is that my granddaughter?" His eyes lifted then, with the delight of a child.

I approached to give him a hug, not quite knowing what to do with Evie.

"Let's let him get a picture," Yvonne said. "I'll hold her for him." She reached out her arms to me.

Overriding my motherly instinct, I unstrapped Evie, disconnecting us. She immediately started to cry, which I did my best to soothe quickly. Yvonne came closer to me, cooing platitudes to Evie, successfully taking her into her arms. I held my breath, hoping that everything was okay, even though nothing about the circumstances before me brought reassurance.

Carefully, Yvonne brought a closely swaddled Evie over to her husband and gently lowered her arms to meet with his feeble ones, as he reached out, connected to tubes and wires, to hold his granddaughter. Marc fumbled for his phone, turning it several times to get the right angle.

"I can take it if you want to get in the picture," I offered, holding my hand up after hearing the first shutter sounds.

Marc looked at me, temporarily frozen. Contemplating. He knew why we were taking these pictures and so did I.

"Oh . . . okay," he said finally, approaching me to hand me the phone.

I watched him walk over to the other side of his father's bed. As Marc leaned down near him, I caught the resemblance. Even in the face of the man before me, weathered by years and circumstance, I could see who he might have been in another time. Handsome, strong, silken skin, like Marc, with a brilliant mind behind those eyes. Pulling my arms up to center the camera, Yvonne too came into view. The three of them together, holding Evie, a family. Me, on the other side of the camera, not connected; I was the photographer, the observer, not a part of this story.

Three shutter snaps in, I heard footsteps behind me. All

of us turned our attention to the doorway as a short, dark-haired woman in a white coat approached. Her straight, silky hair was pulled back into a low ponytail, but noticing the few stray strands amidst an otherwise neatly drawn style, I could tell we were not her first stop of the day. *Dr. Parekh* was written in blue monogram near her shoulder. She stepped forward and surveyed us, concern on her face.

"I'm sorry," she said. "You're only supposed to have two visitors at a time."

My breath caught in my throat. The air in the room thickened. Nobody moved or spoke, and I willed Evie to be quiet in the deepest parts of my being.

Suddenly, the doctor's demeanor softened. "I'm glad to see you're awake, Mr. Brown. Looking pretty good today." She came farther into the room.

"My son brought his daughter in from Los Angeles," Mr. Brown said weakly, but with unmistakable pride, belying the circumstances or his location.

The doctor gave an awkward smile. We all knew that this wasn't hospital policy. Plus, per common sense, Evie was too young to be in an ICU unit. But we took the chance, for a moment—for that photo.

"I . . . have an update, but I'm so sorry, there can only be two visitors per patient. Strict rules on this floor. For the safety of our patients, of course." She spoke kindly, but firmly.

"We're the family," Yvonne spoke up first. "I'm his wife, and this is our son." She didn't look in my direction.

I moved forward. "Sorry," I directed toward the doctor, without knowing which specific thing I was apologizing for. I reached Yvonne as quickly as I could and scooped Evie out of her arms, not even taking the time to replace her in the carrier. "We'll wait outside . . . downstairs . . ." I looked at Marc. "Just text me, I'll let you know where we are."

With undeniable relief, I made my way to the elevators and headed down to the lobby. Yvonne was so needlessly cruel, it was almost effortless to her. I'd traveled so far, and sacrificed so much, just to be cut out, pushed aside. I needed to get outside, to the air, to the sunshine. If I didn't, if I was pushed any further, Evie's diaper wouldn't be the only explosion of the day. I'd taken all that I could take, and soon enough, I'd be ready to make a mess of my own.

28

LAILA:

How's it going in Jacksonville?

The text from Laila came through as I was sitting on a bench, in a peaceful moment. Evie slept against my chest, and I was waiting to hear from Marc. All the possible responses to Laila's question ran through my mind. What had already happened was enough for an essay. I started to compose a reply:

Just saw Marc's dad. He seems to be better. Not sure though, will find out later.

After a moment of text bubbles, Laila's next message appeared.

Are you ok? When are you coming back?

It wasn't clear to me which question was the one that upset me the most. Outside the hospital, I was determined to hold it together. The time with Marc's family had been devastating, traumatic, hurtful even. When Marc told me once that I wouldn't like the dynamic of his family, that it could be chaotic and cruel, I had no idea what he'd been trying to spare me.

Are you ok? No, clearly. And not being okay, what did that even mean? Was someone coming to help? To save me? To make everything okay again? Who? Maybe the question was *for* me, just as much as it was *to* me. Maybe the question should be—*Are you ok, and if not, what are you going to do about it?*

Or perhaps it was most upsetting to confront the question of *when are you coming back?* Because the answer wasn't particularly important. Usually, you have some pressing reason to return—a person, or a job, or some other obligation that made a short stay make sense. Here I was caught as an invisible stranger in another world. Someone who wasn't in the picture. Someone just needed as a feeding and transportation device. I'd become a mother and day by day was making myself unnecessary in every other way. Ignoring it made it possible; seeing it now made it painful.

As many women do, instead of saying all of this, I decided on a simple and very common lie.

> I'm fine.

I typed and hit send on my reply. And then added—

> I'll be back probably in a few days. Too late for primetime anchor desk . . .

Laila typed back.

> Never too late.

That message was followed by—

> Thank you btw, finally met up with Todd. Maybe again this week. He cool.

I noted her caramel-colored thumbs up emoji at the end and smiled. Laila never told anyone anything; always held things close and let them bubble up late, slipped out over drinks or fluke. This was intentional; I just knew—it had to have been meaningful to her.

> So glad! See you soon.

I typed the words, hoping they were true.

IT WAS ANOTHER HALF HOUR BEFORE MARC APPROACHED, slightly out of breath. It was time to feed Evie, who'd become fussy, and I had gotten my fill of the heat and humidity. I was near the beach, but it was nothing like home.

Marc offered to take me back to the hotel to regroup and for the feeding time. He seemed on edge. Against every cell in my body screaming for information, I resisted the urge to ask questions until we'd made it back to the room. Marc joined us upstairs and sat in the chair across from the sofa I'd settled into.

"Everything go okay with the doctor?" Asking was like releasing the pressure in an overfilled balloon. I'd been holding on to the words so tightly, my entire body relaxed as soon as I'd set them free.

Marc turned to look at me, his expression complex, unreadable. After a pause he spoke. "Yeah, I guess. Seems like my dad is doing a lot better. Just that . . ."

"Just that what?"

He sighed heavily, his eyes lowered enough to see his lashes contrast against his face. "I'm just so disappointed in him. Tabby, I don't know what to say." He let his head drop down into his hands. His upper body was nearly folded over, drooping, defeated, and vulnerable in an almost childlike way.

Regardless of how I was feeling, his demeanor was so deflated that if I hadn't been holding Evie, my mothering instinct would have been to comfort him. My mouth opened to speak, but there were no words. And although I had so many questions, I left the space open for him to explain.

"I don't even know how to say this." Marc had finally lifted his head up to face me again and punctuated the silence with another deep breath.

"Just say it," I offered gently.

"He started drinking again," Marc blurted, his face contorted, mouth tight. The tear he'd been trying to hold in dropped down his left cheek. He sniffed and pushed it away with his fist.

"But I thought—"

"We all thought he'd stopped. When he got sick. He made it seem like he knew he couldn't keep . . . that he could stop . . ." Marc took a deep breath, another tear starting its way down. "He just hid it."

The shock of it silenced me, required more oxygen to

process. My mouth dropped open wide, covered quickly by my hand. Marc already told me his father had been a yearslong alcoholic. And that when he'd gotten sick, he'd stopped drinking. I'd never thought differently, or had reason to from the short time that I'd spent with Mr. Brown when we'd first met. Even when Todd mentioned the possibility, I dismissed it quickly. In all the time we'd dated, Marc had kept his parents from me, pushing their complexities and anything else he found ugly behind the perfectly crafted façade he'd created for his own life, far away in California. His father wasn't the only one good at hiding things.

"Marc, I'm so sorry." It was all I could offer. I was sorry for him, and all of us.

"I'm just playing everything back, you know? Every moment, like, was he drinking then? Was he lying then? To my face? I don't understand. How could this thing be so much bigger than him? He was always the strongest man I knew." Mark balled his fists against his thighs.

"It's not your fault, Marc."

"I know that," he spat back at me. "Sorry," he said, softening immediately. "It . . . It's been a long morning," he stammered.

I recoiled slightly—his tone had hurt. I was there for him, physically present, and trying to be supportive emotionally. I didn't know how to make the situation any better, so I just held Evie closer.

"I'm sorry," he repeated, standing up to make his way over to me on the sofa. This time, it was him comforting me, his hand on my arm. "It's just there's no one I look up to more than my dad. He's the person I wanted to impress, to be like. When he got sick, I always thought the silver lining was that he'd stop drinking. That we'd get that part of him back, at least for a while. And now there's not even that. There's nothing."

"Marc—" His disappointment was so palpable, deflating.

"What if I'm like him, Tabby?" Mark asked me softly, as if I might have had the ability to peer inside him for the answer, but I had none. Ms. Gretchen was right. If you look closely enough, eventually you do see the child behind the man.

I felt Evie softening her latch on her bottle and shifted our position to rearrange myself and settle her post-feeding. Marc continued to peer at me, piercing with the deep brown pool of his irises, so dark that they blended with his pupils.

"How did your mother take the news?" I asked after a long pause. Marc shifted at the change of topic and ran his hand over the top of his head.

"She took it pretty hard. Barely said a word to me coming back here. She's in her room now and said she wanted to take a nap for a bit. I told her that we'd take her to dinner tonight."

"Will she go back to the hospital today?"

"She seemed pretty upset with him. But that's between the two of them. I'm not going back today. I need a minute." Marc's face changed again, as if he remembered something. "I mean," he continued, "if you wanted to, you could head back to LA tomorrow, try to make your broadcast for work?" He reached for my arm again. "Tabby, I'm sorry I asked you to come—this is my fault."

My instinct was, again, to comfort, to soothe, to reassure. But something stopped me. It was the truth of Marc's words. It was the reality that there was no going back. Not from here. I'd made a choice, a decision—that one thing was going to matter more than another. I'd officially given up the opportunity, knowing that once I stepped on that plane, I was committed to this journey. And now, even if I could find a flight back, the travel time would leave no time to prepare. There would be no broadcast test. This decision was going to have to play out, whatever the consequence.

"Marc, it's too late," I replied. "It's too late."

29

BETRAYAL IS A STRANGE ELIXIR, AND YVONNE BROWN'S REAC-tion proved just as strange and entirely puzzling. After an hour-long nap at our hotel, she'd not only gone back to the hospital, but then headed back to their family home nearly twenty minutes away to get more personal items for Mr. Brown's release from the ICU. He was set to spend a few more days for observation in the step-down before he'd likely be discharged.

According to the doctor, as I'd learned from Marc, Mr. Brown's secret drinking caused a crisis that escalated his already degenerative liver disease into an acute life-or-death situation. The benefit of being in the hospital was the opportunity for his system to detox, not having access to alcohol of any sort, now that the underlying cause of the emergency had been discovered.

Marc insisted on taking us all to dinner, notably his mother, who he seemed particularly concerned about. It was a version of him that I wasn't used to—one that veered nearly opposite to his usually calm, cool demeanor. And I'd seen every other emotion out of him—anger, concern, happiness, even regret—but not this, this mix of fear and sadness that revealed so clearly the little boy inside of the man. Adding to this was the fact that I could not, even remotely, mistake Jacksonville for Los Angeles. I was reminded everywhere I went, if not by the air outside, then the accents, or the tall skinny trees, or the presence of so much unobscured sky. I was in the core of Marc, past the barrier of distractions that can be erected far away from home. Here, the truth of who he was had been stripped naked and left bare. It was an intimacy we'd never reached, only accessible in this place; where no amount of graduate-degree lifestyle and expensive cologne could costume his reality.

On the way to pick up his mother, Marc took us on a detour so he could show me a bit more of where he grew up. "And this is my old neighborhood . . . they call it Mid-Westside on the maps. But it's just right around Stanton, the best high school in Jacksonville," Marc said with a beam of pride.

The high school that we passed looked modern and attended to. The neighborhood that contained it was a mix of well-maintained small homes and places that had been left in disrepair, the grass mostly burned and sparse from the sun and heat. There were chain-link fences and cars scattered about, none matching the six-figure German-type that Marc drove back home.

"We lived here until I graduated," he continued. "And then my parents moved to Springfield after I left for college. They'd planned that move for years but only if I got a scholarship. If I hadn't gotten that scholarship to Morehouse, they would have stayed as long as it took to help pay for school. My dad insisted I was going to be a person who wore a suit to work. That's what he'd always say." Marc paused as he turned a corner. "But Springfield, that's closer to downtown, you'll like that. I'm gonna take you there next."

I smiled at him and turned to check the back seat, where Evie slept soundly. *Jacksonville Marc*, my mind registered. I was in the car with someone I'd had no chance to know before; the man apart from the elaborately constructed, well-polished persona that matched the Los Angeles setting. He'd become the man who wore the suit. And drove the car. And bought the nice place in the expensive area. He'd become the dreams of his parents, everything he was supposed to be. I looked down at my hands in my lap. *Except this*, I thought, my gaze lingering to my left. We were not according to plan. Evie was not according to plan. And yet, here we were; heading through an abbreviated version of the journey of Marc's life.

About twenty minutes away, the scenery changed some. The houses got bigger; the grass a bit greener, the cars newer. We'd entered the historic area of Springfield. A quick search on my phone gave me some background that I hoped to use to connect with Yvonne over dinner. I had no idea what we'd talk about, so at least I could show I was interested in more than just the unfolding drama of Mr. Brown's hospital stay.

"Zora Neale Hurston used to live here," Marc said, continuing his tour, turning masterfully through the neighborhood, as I noted the homes that we passed—the Craftsman beveled columns and Corinthian flourishes underneath the distinctive triangular arch above the front porches. Many with clean wood-slatted paneling, and some with brick accents, the character and personality seemed well-preserved. Our car finally came to a stop in front of a Craftsman bungalow in a light blue-gray color with white trim. It was recently painted and looked like a lot of the other homes in the neighborhood.

"You don't need to get out," Marc said, putting the car in park. "You can stay here with Evie, and I'll run in and get my Mom."

Not that I was going to protest, but before I could say anything, he was already out of the car, with a soft close to the door. *Still sleeping*, I was happy to note, turning to survey the back seat. Even a rental car worked its same wonders for infant slumber.

"I didn't wear anything fancy . . ." I could hear Yvonne's voice floating into the car as Marc opened the door. She had on her usual conservative attire, a yellow knit tank top with matching sweater on her arm, slacks and flat shoes. Her hair was in the same tightly curled style that could easily have been worn decades ago and was certainly neat, but far from modern.

I offered to move to the back to sit with Evie, but Yvonne refused. "Oh no, I'm gonna be just fine next to my grand-baby," she insisted. And into the back she climbed, assisted by Marc, and quickly preoccupied with tending to a sleeping Evie, who didn't really need tending, but I guess Yvonne needed something to do. I was content to take in the scenery again in relative silence. We'd have to fill up at least an hour and a half of conversation at dinner, and there was only so much chewing and swallowing to be done.

We pulled up at the restaurant that Marc selected for us: a steakhouse, nice, national, with the expected dark wood paneling, wine cubbies, and obligatory crisp white shirt–clad hostess greeting us at the door. It was much fancier than the restaurant that Marc picked in LA to take his parents for dinner, and I wondered if this choice was for me, his mother who clearly eschewed fanciness, or him.

Once seated, Yvonne commented on how over-the-top the restaurant was, and how unnecessary it was for her or for Marc to have picked it. And when we got the menus, she continued with her observations of the prices for almost everything, especially the steaks, and how we could have just gone somewhere closer to the hospital and gotten something quick. In LA, this restaurant would have been in line with a date night, or an evening out for dining, and I would have appreciated it, but not felt undeserving or that it was too much. It made me wonder whether Yvonne ever treated herself to much of anything, or if anyone had gone out of their way for her lately, or possibly ever. After the day she had, the very least she could have been afforded was a nice dinner.

I finally started to understand it as the difference between Jacksonville Marc and Los Angeles Marc. Marc himself was stuck between two worlds. There was the identity he was born with, the person in Jacksonville who only dreamed of the life he created in LA. Los Angeles Marc was another thing entirely—comfortable in places like this, frequenting them even, finding increasingly more impressive, expensive, and elaborate places to be seen and conspicuous ways to spend.

The evening started to proceed smoothly, with small talk leading into the ordering. And then, with a forkful of salad, covered thickly with the creamiest sort of dressing, Yvonne blurted, "You know, the two of you ought to think about your plans. Marc, your father and me won't be around forever." Her gaze turned from Marc to me. "I don't know what you're waiting on. Marriage"—she pointed back and forth between the two of us with her fork—"makes you family," she said, concluding her proclamation. The implication being that, sitting there, I was nothing more than Evie's food supply and transportation mechanism. That to her, without the definitions, without the pomp and circumstance and the ceremonies in place, I was nothing, no one. I had no status. I was not in the photograph.

"Ma, don't talk like that. You and Daddy are going to be around—"

Marc's mother shot him a look that silenced the end of his sentence. His words hung in the air.

"In my day, you didn't just have these loose"—Yvonne turned to look at me, with emphasis on the word *loose*— "connections," she said finally. "You have a child with someone, you marry them. Marc, *you* know that." She went on to continue her salad, crunching with satisfaction. "When I was a girl, that was the one thing I knew—that I couldn't get in trouble or I wouldn't have a future. That the decisions I made would be with me for the rest of my life. And the people I made those decisions with." She looked from me to Marc and back again. "Your father and I made sure to do things in the right order. We got married *first* and then had you . . . and—"

"Mom!" Marc called out. "Let's not do this now. It's been a long day and Tabby's come all the way from LA with Evie. Let's just have a nice dinner."

"You girls today," she said, turning to me. "You know nothing about the sacrifices we had to make. This generation thinks that everything is supposed to come so easily, to just 'work out.' Well, *somebody* has to make it work out. Somebody has to give up something—there's a cost to be paid. And none of you want to pay it."

I felt my face start to burn as if I were still sitting in the midday sun. *Oh, I know plenty*, I wanted to tell her. Thinking of all the ways that I'd made choices to support her son. What I'd given up. And even now, risking my livelihood, my independence. Losing that would be much more than just something I'd always wanted, or even worked hard for. But then, I heard her words again in my mind. This time, listening more closely, between the lines of what she'd said. It sounded like, *What do you know about love?* As if that had been the question she'd asked instead of the accusation made. And I realized that maybe I didn't know much about love at all. And that Evie, not Marc, had been my first true indoctrination.

My appetite vanished and my stomach dropped into a deeper part of my body as I thought about what I wanted to say and held back whatever less respectful words were fighting to leave my lips. For the first time, I focused on Yvonne and really studied her. She looked tired, like Diane, like my mother had looked all those nights so long ago at the kitchen table. She looked worn, faded out, her edges sanded down over the years, her form pulled downward by gravity and the circumstances I was coming to understand. The life they'd led in Jacksonville, and whatever were the ups and downs of living in a household of addiction.

And suddenly, the picture started to become clear, of Yvonne, of her behavior, even of her acerbic tone. *Like a lock and key*, Alexis had said. She told me that every mother believed somehow that her actions were out of love. For Yvonne, perhaps love looked like sacrifice. It looked like taking less every time; forgetting everything for which forgiveness was too great of an ask; forgiving because that was the thing you knew how to do—because you'd had to do it so many times.

This wasn't the life I wanted for myself. This wasn't the woman I wanted to become. And I wasn't going to continue to take the blows of her expectations.

"Ms. Yvonne," I said, "I understand your sacrifices, and I'm sorry about what happened today . . . But, it's not *my* fault." Yvonne's mouth dropped open, confusion on her face, but she didn't interrupt me. "Maybe Marc and I made mistakes on our path. But we're going to need time to figure it out. And at this point, I've sacrificed *all* I'm going to. I'm willing to go far, give up a lot, but I'm tired—*to my bones.*" My hands, balled into fists at this point, dropped on the table with a thud. I looked back and forth between Marc and his mother, the air thick with their surprise. I continued. "I let go of my fair shot at a position that I worked extremely hard for. I came here because Marc asked me to, so he'd have no regrets and so that Evie would have a chance to meet her grandfather. And after struggling *alone* through the airport with an infant, and sitting through *this* day? I'm *DONE.*" I let every letter of the word linger in my mouth, almost to a hum. In the silence at the table, I smiled at Yvonne. "And I say that with love," I added. I looked at Marc and patted his hand. "I say that with all the love in my heart."

I wasn't worried about Yvonne's reaction, or Marc's either. The time had come for me to stand up for myself. To draw the line where it belonged.

Marc seemed paralyzed, surveying his mother for any sign of response. I still had a smile on my face but was ready for battle. I meant what I said, with every fiber of my being. Yvonne looked at me and folded her arms, pulling them close into the yellow knit of her top.

"Well," she said finally. "We're certainly glad you could

make it." She then turned to Marc. "And"—she paused, adjusting her posture before continuing—"I'd really appreciate it if you could send me that picture you took . . . When I go back, I'd like to show it to Horace. It'll brighten his spirits. Th . . . Thank you."

I could hear Marc audibly exhale. The layer of tension seemed to dissipate like storm clouds after the thunder and lightning passed.

I hadn't expected the thank-you from Yvonne, but perhaps it was me who needed to thank her. She'd helped me make a very important decision.

30

AFTER WE'D MADE IT BACK TO THE HOTEL, HAVING DROPPED Marc's mother at the hospital for her third round of visiting with her husband, exhaustion hit me in a wave. I'd managed to feed Evie and put her down for what I hoped would be a longer sleep and then flopped down on the sofa.

To my surprise, Marc sat down next to me, slipped off my shoes, and picked up my feet, placing them in his lap. They'd been slightly swollen and throbbing, and I was grateful for the heat of his hands, wrapped around the sensitive parts of the inside of my foot sole. He twisted, gently, and stretched the skin there, rubbing the length of the top of my foot and up my leg, so softly it tickled. I wanted to tell him to stop, that I was too tired to reciprocate or even enjoy it properly, but I said nothing, instead closing my eyes and letting a deep sigh bring my body further into calm.

I will not become like Yvonne, I silently repeated to myself. My life, my terms.

"I'm sorry about dinner . . . my mom, all that," Marc said quietly. He too seemed to be exhausted, and unspooling. The tightly wound exterior that he wore in LA was no match for the circumstances, or for his hometown.

"I'm sorry about that too," I replied, meaning mainly that I, not him, had to sit through it. "Everyone's under a lot of stress."

"But it's more than that. My mom had no right to say we aren't family. You came all the way . . . you gave up—"

"My chance at work?"

"Yeah, that," Marc said quietly. His hands finally let my feet go, and he gently placed them back on the ground and then turned to face me. "I just spent so much time looking at my parents and thinking, *This is it*, you know? *This*, this love, this partnership, this longevity. And I never noticed how it wore on my mom, or thought about what she'd given up, or even *how* it worked. Just that it had for so long."

I had more to say, but was too tired, so drowsily nodded and let Marc continue.

"My parents knew each other from high school and got married. My mom even managed to go to college and graduate, first in her family with a four-year degree. And the doctors told them too that they couldn't have children, but here I came, my mother called me her 'miracle baby.'" Marc paused, seeming to be briefly caught up in what he was recalling. "My dad's family was so poor," he continued, "they pulled the kids out of high school to work, so he was lucky to get through vocational school.

"My mother was as prim and proper as you could imagine, so I'm sure you could guess her family couldn't stand it when she started hanging around with my dad. They thought he wasn't good enough for her. And he always wanted to give her more. When he couldn't, he started drinking. I watched it, watched him change. Bad day at work—drink. Get in an argument with my mom—drink. Bills start piling up—there's always some money for a bottle, so drink." He looked at me as if I'd say something, but I held the space for him, open with my silence and attention.

"I said I would never get married, Tabby, not until I'd made it financially. I never wanted to be in that same position—not like that. So powerless that all I could do was—"

"Drink?" I offered.

"Yeah."

"Marc, why do you want it now?"

He studied me, looking at me quizzically, as if perhaps he'd expected me to know the answer. "I didn't at first, because I didn't know what else love could be. Love as obligations, what you give up; not what you get. But then, I saw you as a mother, how fearless you became. How hard you fought and pushed. But most of all, I saw how you loved Evie—the care and the sacrifice. I knew then that it was there in you, and if you could love me like that, accept me like that . . . and maybe that's what hurt so badly when you didn't come to Jacksonville."

"But, Marc, I *did* come to Jacksonville . . ."

"Why, though? What made you change your mind?"

Maybe it was the fatigue. Too tired to hold it back, I spoke the truth that many women live, but never say. "I decided to put your needs before mine," I mumbled drowsily. "You said I was *selfish*. And I wanted to prove you wrong. I'm not selfish, Marc."

"Tabby, I'm sorry for what I said."

"Um-hmm," I mumbled, eyes half closed. Marc moved closer to me.

"I mean it, I *am* sorry."

I opened my eyes, locked with his.

"I'm sorry," he said again, closer to me this time. "I'm—"
And then, it was me that bridged the space between us. I
kissed him.

The warmth started at my mouth. His met mine willingly.
Damp heat, and soft slicked lips, the familiar pressure of his
against mine. We pressed together quickly, like the pages of
a book just finished, the satisfaction of knowing what happened, of what will happen flowing quickly through my chest,
my arms, my fingertips.

My breath quickened. More of me awakened. His hand
brushed against my nipples, lightly enough to stiffen them.
They weren't ready for him, but were sensitive enough to signal my body for pleasure. I moistened. Before that point, I
could have stopped, but now, I didn't want to. I couldn't.

"Tell me what you want." His voice so low, its gravelly
purr reached me and heightened my anticipation.

"We have to be quiet . . . the ba—" Marc pressed his lips
to mine again, kissing me deeply, massaging me with the
gentle strength of his tongue, giving me shivers as its tip ca-
ressed the space between my teeth and upper lip.

"What do *you* want?" he asked again, slower this time,
with emphasis.

And this was how something inside of me broke, a wall
I'd erected, disconnecting me from the core of myself, what
I hadn't felt. It was there—still there, a longing. Desire, and
a wish to be desired. Finally, reconnected to my body. In this
moment, it was mine again.

"What—" The kiss was on my lips again, moist, hot, the
presence of Marc's face so close to mine, the smell of him

intensified—the warm citrus, wood, and sweet spice—made me catch my breath, sharply, audibly.

"Mmmm . . ." I still couldn't speak. Just the soft noises that meant to say "more," and "yes," found their way forward.

"—do—" he said. He was so handsome, his long lashes touching his flawless deep-brown cheek. The texture of his hair, the shiny waves and curls and the tapered touch of the barber's expert lines, so perfectly accentuating his features. I took him in, breathing more heavily now, faster.

"—you want, Tabby—tell me," he commanded.

"Everything," I whispered back, finally.

"Everything. . . ." He repeated, kissing my neck, lingering for a beat longer to chase it with the tip of his tongue.

"Everything . . ." He used the word at every part of my body he touched. With his mouth, his hands, working his way down my body. Unbuttoning my jeans, his hands at the sides of my hips, his fingers hooked into the waistband. I could feel his fingertips as they looped into the top of my panty line, dragging the soft fabric downward with the rest of my clothing. His kisses covered every revealed place, lower, then lower again, placing heat and pressure in neglected areas until finally his mouth covered me, delicately at first, and as I moistened further, he deepened himself into me step by step, little by little.

And then, quietly, gripping his arms, my fingertips buried in his shoulder blades, right there on the sofa, I became mine again, reconnected to myself, expanded and engulfed, a whole being fully indulged in the pleasure that was my own.

It was the perfect kiss goodbye.

31

MAYBE MARC WAS SOMEONE I JUST KNEW HOW TO FORGIVE. I could forgive him, but I did not want a relationship that depended so much on such a habit. That's what my next days in Jacksonville assured me. Yvonne Brown had learned over the years to forgive Mr. Brown. Just like Granny Tab had learned how to forgive, and even my mother in her own way.

I started thinking about love too. I wasn't romanticizing how you could fall into it all at once, or after a single passionate night. I was contemplating the love that was more than a feeling, that at some point demands a trade-off. A love that endures in spite of shifting circumstances. I was learning the lessons of love when it becomes a decision—the difficulty of swimming against the current, rather than going with the flow. The love that required not just a person you know, but a person you know how to forgive. I could love Marc Brown, and still not marry him. Of this, I was sure.

On the day I left Jacksonville, Mr. Brown was being discharged from the hospital. Still on maternity leave and having already missed the opportunity for the primetime anchor test slot, I had decided to stay the week. Marc showed me more of his hometown and introduced me to a smattering of local friends and family. And still, nothing taught me more about him than that first day we spent in the shadow of his father's betrayal. Sometimes wounds needed to be reopened to heal. Mr. Brown put himself in a predicament that ultimately might have bought him more time and another opportunity to right his wrongs with more than an apology after the fact. Certainly, there would be more for Yvonne Brown to forgive.

On my arrival back in LA, Laila picked me and Evie up at the airport. Marc had decided to stay another week to help his mother, and I couldn't miss Lisa's farewell broadcast. Beyond that, I had just a week and a half left in my maternity leave, which I'd have to use to figure out how to add work back into my new life as a mother. Without question, there'd be another day that brought me and Evie back to Jacksonville, but our time there had served me well. Loose ends in Los Angeles beckoned us back home.

"Girl, I didn't think you were coming back!" Laila proceeded to hammer questions at me, one after another, as we wound through the cloverleaf exit path via the maze of airport traffic lanes.

I answered the questions in rapid succession. "His house was nice—his parents live in a historic area near downtown—no, we didn't stay there, a hotel near the hospital . . . he didn't have a girlfriend in high school, just a friend he took to prom—yes, she was cute, kinda plain . . . Yvonne was, well, the same—Yvonne."

"So, relationship? You with him or nah?"

"It's a nah for me," I said. To that Laila's eyebrow raised.

"I've heard that before, Tab. You're done? Or you're done, done?"

"Just the relationship part. That's done, done."

"Did something happen in Jacksonville? Something you're not saying?" Laila probed. "What, did you meet some of his relatives and say, oh hell no, not this family reunion?" I laughed. But I had met someone in Jacksonville.

"I just finally saw the real Marc, and you know what? He's not going to be how my story ends, Lah. I want more."

"That's what I'm talking 'bout!" Laila growled at me, slapping the steering wheel. "That's what I'm talking 'bout, girl!" She turned to me, beaming.

"What about you and Todd? 'He cool' sounded like your developments are *much* more interesting than mine," I teased.

Laila gave me a closed-mouth coy look. "Girl, now you know. Don't try to play me. We were talking about you!" She made a playful poke to my shoulder, which forced a chuckle from my throat. "But, let's just say a door has been opened . . ." Laila couldn't hide the smile.

"Well," I replied. "Depending on what he knocked with, I can imagine what door that was—" Laila laughed and I joined her.

"Like I said, he cool, real cool. We'll see. I'm still in my bag. Focused . . . on growing my business." Laila turned to face me, with a knowing look. "Girl, you're a better one than me. I would have taken my chances and done the broadcast."

"It's too late now," I mused, half to myself, half to her. "It's going to be a whole new world for me at KVTV after Lisa leaves. I have no idea what's on the other side of my maternity leave. No idea."

"You can always join me in the tech space—my little online world of community reporting," Laila offered. "I'm going to be thanking you and Alexis forever for jump-starting me with that event. I'm over halfway to my crowdfunding goal. It's not too late to add a partner," she teased.

"A partner in business, or a partner in life?" I shot back with a wink.

"Maybe both," Laila said, after a pause. "I am glad I gave Todd a chance. He's nice, really consistent. Plus, he has a lot of patience for what my life is like right now. He's busy too."

"I admire you so much, girl, if I had the courage to step out there, I would, but I have a mortgage and a baby, so I'll be on the W-2 plan for a minute."

"Nothing wrong with that, Tab," Laila said, pulling us into my driveway. "Just don't do what I did at the newspaper and lose sight of your value. You have options. Don't let them forget it."

She reached for my hand and held it. We sat like that for a second, in the car, in my driveway, simply basking in friendship and the warmth of the sun shining on our faces.

"Coming in for a bit?"

She shifted awkwardly. "Girl, I can't. I'm going to help you unload and then . . . I'm supposed to be meeting Todd for dinner."

"Oooh, come through Todd!" I ribbed. We'd come a long way, and for the first time in a long time, I felt good about where we were both headed.

32

A WEEK LATER, I FOUND MYSELF TRYING ON WORK CLOTHES
again, looking for anything nice in my closet that also fit. For the
first time, I noticed that I had a surprising number of clothes
items that didn't contain elastic around the waist parts—the
previous version of my body hadn't required it. Motherhood
looked nothing like the "snap-back" photos posted on social
media. There was no snap. There were slow changes, so slow
that I'd started to feel like I'd sacrificed my old self entirely.
And maybe that was okay. This new me had new strengths
that needed more room, and some stretch in the waistband.

Finally, I settled on a blended ensemble of a forgiving tan
shift dress and my favorite red cardigan that always brought
me a little extra bit of confidence, courtesy of Ms. Gretchen.

I still hadn't found a regular babysitter, so Alexis and Andouele were my fill-ins, even though Andouele was far too
expensive as a babysitter to make regular practice of it. Today,
she would come for a couple of hours so that I could join the
rest of the KVTV team for Lisa's farewell. And somewhere
along the way of making preparations to leave Evie for a bit,

the realization started to grow roots that very soon, this would be every day.

On the drive over, buckled into the driver's seat, hands gripping the steering wheel, the gnawing feeling of unease started to spread thorough my body like an ice-cold drink. Lisa had truly tried to help me before she left, passed me the ball, and I didn't take the shot. She'd been an unexpected ally, a friend and a needed support, even when I had no idea what I was up against. She had the power to stand up to Chris Perkins and the fearlessness to go toe-to-toe with Doug. I wasn't Lisa and I also wasn't Laila, who had enough courage to make her own way, riding out the journey even through the challenging times.

Knowing that I was going to have to find my way on my own was both the thrill and the threat that accompanied me through the doors of KVTV. The familiar industrial carpet, the pocked acoustic tiling in the ceiling greeted me. I walked deeper into the buzz of the staff gearing up for the prime-time broadcast. Lisa's last. I made my way to her office, the grand, spacious light-filled showplace that had hosted my meltdowns and the conversations that had brought us closer. This day, boxes were scattered around, the formerly immaculate wall decorations were strewn about the floor, decamped from the bare picture hangers still dotted around the room.

Lisa was standing at the window, looking out over the view, observing the LA bustle. The diminishing sunlight cast a glow through the highlights in her hair, making them almost fiery white against the glossy golden blond of her signature color. She looked taller to me in her heels, but perhaps that was because I still wasn't used to walking around her office in flats. We were both in our own transitions, finding our way forward into something new.

I knocked on the doorframe.

Lisa turned around, slightly startled, and then broke into a wide, white-toothed smile. "Tabby!" She approached me quickly, dropping the cup she was holding next to a box on her otherwise nearly empty desk. "Come on in!" she added, gesturing to the chairs in her seating area.

"I know you're probably gathering your thoughts . . . for this evening. I just wanted to pop in to see you. And to say thanks . . . and I'm sorry, again."

"Sorry for what?" Lisa looked genuinely confused for a fleeting moment. She maneuvered to the chair farther from me and her smile returned. "Tabby, you look great, by the way—loving the red!" Before sitting down, she held out her arms for a hug, waving her fingertips in a gesture to bring me closer. I came to meet her and wrapped my arms around her slender frame.

"I just still feel so bad that I missed the broadcast," I said, retreating from our embrace toward the open seat. "You went out of your way for me and I—"

"You did what you had to do for your family. Let's just say I know a little something about that." Lisa gave me a wink.

"Thanks, Lisa," I said with a sigh. "And maybe I'll never get another chance, but I just couldn't face regret like the last time. To never know whether I made the right decision, or not, no matter what happened in my career or how many people told me it was okay. It hasn't been."

"I understand," Lisa said as we both sat down. "Just make the decision you can live with, the one that gives you the most peace. The rest, you have to believe will work itself out—that you'll get another shot. Tabby, you're incredibly talented, opportunities will come, you just have to trust that." She smiled and reached out to touch my leg. "It's not bye forever, Tabby, just bye for now." Then she stood up. "Where will you be watching? The control room, or down on the floor?"

"I'll be on the floor, watching right behind the camera."

"Good," she said. "That's very good." And then she shifted to pull a compact out of her handbag, and a tube of her so-perfectly coordinated lipstick. Typical Lisa, she first checked her teeth, and then did her touch up. Flawless as usual. Still holding the compact, she looked up at me. "See you down there?"

I stood up, smoothing the dress and straightening my sweater.

"Yes, see you down there." The rest of my words stayed stuck behind the building lump in my throat as I realized I was leaving Lisa's office for the last time. I glanced back at her, my hand on the door, before I pulled it closed behind me.

33

REACHING THE STUDIO FLOOR FOR THE FIRST TIME IN MONTHS, I felt incredibly awkward, like returning home after a long time away only to find that your parents turned your bedroom into a space for guests. Perhaps I had outgrown KVTV news, or perhaps it never held a space for me in the first place.

A very small group of colleagues had collected in the corner of the broadcast set, behind the cameras. In front of us, at the desk facing the cameras, Lisa and her co-anchor engaged in the usual banter, with a palpable undercurrent of anxiety. The reality of Lisa's last broadcast grew in the air around us like an achingly slow crescendo. I watched the countdown to on air, the last makeup and teeth checks in the studio monitor, and suddenly became aware of a presence behind me. It was Chris Perkins, who gave me a nod, but signaled that he was all eyes and attention on Lisa. It was her time.

"Since this is the last broadcast," Lisa began, eyes direct, looking into the camera, "my last broadcast at KVTV, I'd like to thank you for the years that this city has welcomed me with open arms, made this a home for me. And as I take my leave to spend time with my family, I'd like to acknowledge the work of women, especially those of us working the so-called second shift, the one inside the home, for the sacrifices it takes, for the vacation time that doesn't accrue, and the paycheck that never comes. I have the privilege of making a decision to return to my home, to take on the role of caregiver with the support of a loving partner and sustained by a long-term career.

"And as I consider this opportunity, this coveted seat that I've held, I've realized that we don't often get the chance to be ourselves, to speak for ourselves. I've had the great honor to work alongside some of the most passionate and fearless colleagues that anyone could ask for. People who have reminded me above all to be true to myself. And in the news, that's uncommon. If you want to know who inspires me, who makes me think of what I still have left to accomplish, then you must hear from Tabitha Walker—"

Hearing my name, I let out a sharp gasp that seemed like it was in synchronicity with several others around me. I didn't dare steal a glance behind me at Chris.

Lisa was still talking, even though it started to sound like I was underwater, hearing the echoes above me.

"Even though Tabby is on maternity leave," Lisa said to the camera, "I asked her to be here today, which will be my last at the KVTV anchor desk, not for an interview, but to take my place in this broadcast. Tabby—" Lisa motioned for me behind the camera. For a second, my body refused to move. Lisa kept motioning until I moved toward her, breaking all the rules of broadcast. Every single rule. They could pull the plug at any moment, but I kept walking, willing my feet to move forward. A producer swept to my side, placing a mic kit in my hand.

"Here, quickly, put this on," she whispered, as we then both fumbled to get the clip of the tiny microphone on the top of my cardigan, and to drape the wire behind me. There was no place to attach the transmitter to my dress, so I just held it behind my back and kept moving forward.

Finally, I managed to turn around and look at Chris— glowering, red in the face, and arms folded. But I didn't freeze. I didn't stop or hesitate, I just kept moving. Lisa kept talking, nestled in her seat until I arrived at the end of the anchor desk, still off-camera. Then she stood up, arms out-reached to me. "Tabby, this is your chair." Lisa pulled out her seat and turned it in my direction. We were in uncharted territory for a primetime broadcast.

It was unconventional, irreverent, reckless even. But now was the moment to do it. The ships were burning. The port aflame. But I wasn't afraid, not anymore. I stepped up to the platform and placed my hand on the chair she'd turned out for me.

"You win, I win," Lisa whispered in my ear as she walked by me, squeezing my elbow as she passed. The weight of the moment overwhelmed me, but my years in live television had conditioned me beyond my reflexes. We were on the air, we were live, and there wasn't a second to waste. I was already miked. Swiftly I took the seat and braced for anything to hap-pen, quickly locating the teleprompter in front of me. If I had any chance of stopping them from doing an emergency push to commercial, I'd have to think quickly and I'd have to speak. Everyone on set was stunned speechless. So I took my shot.

"Wow," I said to the camera, acknowledging the circum-stances and the likely shock of the audience I was address-ing. "It would be beyond an understatement to say this was unexpected. But it's an honor to be able to pay tribute to our departing colleague, Lisa Sinclair. I'm Tabitha Walker, joining you at the desk in the middle of my maternity leave. I think I can speak for the entire KVTV family in saying that we are going to miss the force of nature that is Lisa Sinclair. But as we know, it's not bye forever, it's just bye for now. We love you, Lisa, and thank you . . . for everything." In the time that I spoke, the other anchor seemed to have a moment to regroup. If the red light stayed on and the prompter scrolled, we could still do the broadcast. I knew him from the station well enough; if only the prompter would continue, perhaps he would also. Then out of the corner of my eye I saw the producer next to the camera. She was rolling her hands around each other, the signal to keep going.

A bewildered Dan seemed to steady himself and found his words. "We are certainly going to miss Lisa, and she has never failed to surprise . . . and delight us with her gifts. A big welcome to KVTV's weekend anchor, Tabitha Walker, who is sitting in for our departing Lisa Sinclair. . . . Our lead story this evening is rising home prices in the Southland area—is now the time to sell?"

As I listened to Dan cue up the first story of the evening, I shot a glance at Lisa. She'd moved back behind the camera, and was standing next to Chris. For me, there wasn't anything left to do but my best, and that's exactly what I did.

34

AFTER THE BROADCAST, I STAYED ONLY BRIEFLY FOR THE TOAST and celebration. While I was there, colleagues congratulated me and Chris noticeably avoided me. It wasn't a question of could I perform the primetime anchor position, it was always a question of what would happen after. Only this time, in comparison to the last, Lisa had found a way to use her departure as a means to absorb the consequences. I understood why she didn't tell me; she couldn't. But she'd allowed me to innocently take my second chance. As long as Chris didn't suspect me of being in on it, I'd be judged by ratings and ratings alone. A mistake is only a mistake if it doesn't pay off.

"Thanks for not leaving me hanging," Lisa managed to say to me. "I know it was a crazy thing to do, but, Tabby, you deserve this spot. I couldn't leave without at least trying."

"Nothing like thinking that you might get fired, and then turning around and doing the thing that would *make sure* you get fired," I joked nervously.

"You're not going to get fired," Lisa said. "I already spoke to Chris. He was pissed, but understands that you had nothing to do with the moment." She smiled mischievously. "I'm a loose cannon, Tabby, a woman without a job! Unhinged and untethered," she laughed. "You, my friend, are a consummate professional with a *very, very* promising career. Let the ratings speak for you—viewers love unscripted moments." She winked at me.

"Lisa, there are some things maybe you could get away with, but that list is a lot shorter for me," I said, taking her hand. "Still, maybe it's a chance to try something new. To take a shot."

"Shoot your shot," Lisa teased.

"Oh, I shot my shot all right . . . ready, aim, fired!" I said, laughing, but only half-joking.

MARC CAME OVER THAT EVENING FOR EVIE'S BATH TIME. AFTER we got her settled and down for sleep, we had a chance to talk. He hadn't seen the broadcast or heard the news, so when I said "I think I might be getting fired," he was completely shocked.

"Because you went to Jacksonville?" he said, springing into upright position on the sofa.

"Not quite, Marc. Maybe indirectly, but no."

Marc looked at me with wide eyes. "So what happened?"

"Lisa brought me up to do her last broadcast for her."

"Wait, while they were on-air?"

I nodded my head yes. Marc's eyes widened even further.

"And they didn't go to commercial?"

"Nope."

"So, what now?'

"Well, the broadcast went pretty well, actually. If it hadn't been so unorthodox, it would have been almost the perfect broadcast test."

"Is this your way of saying all is forgiven? You want to get married now?" Marc gave a feeble laugh.

"That's not what I'm saying, Marc," I said, and then hesitated before the next words, which seemed to flow from me so naturally now. I said them, because finally I was sure. "Actually, I *don't* want to get married." As I spoke, I could hear almost the exact same words in Marc's voice echoing in my memory. It was what he said to me so many years ago. And now I could finally understand why he said it.

Marc took a sharp breath in. I braced for what was to come. To my surprise, he just sat there, lips pulled into a tight line. His face wore a look of resignation. "I figured as much," he said finally. "After the way my mother treated you . . . and some of the things I said."

I went over to sit next to him. "It's not just that, Marc," I said softly. "I have some things of my own I need to work on . . . on my own."

"Then what's your plan, Tab?" Marc turned to look at me as I got up from the sofa.

"Alexa, play nineties R&B," I said loudly into the air. Moments later, the sounds of heavy liquid bass and the harmonies of Jodeci filled the room.

"We're going to wake up Evie," Marc hissed, pointing in the direction of the bedroom.

I brought my finger up to my own lips to quiet him. "I closed the door. She'll be fine," I offered. After all, I wasn't so worried about the perfect bedtime, or the neat order of everything, not anymore. I was perfectly in the moment, come what may.

"Marc, ask me to dance."

"What?" Marc looked at me confused.

"Ask me . . . to dance," I repeated, slowly and deliberately.

"Like now? You want to dance now?"

"Yes, while the music's playing."

Marc's face relaxed, and an understanding crossed his expression. "Tabby Walker," he teased, extending his hand to me, "will you dance with me?"

I felt the wide smile break out on my face, and studied him for a pause. Handsome Marc, Jacksonville Marc, Los Angeles Marc, Evie's father, and my ex-boyfriend Marc. As I bridged the space between us, walking forward to take his hand, I saw him clearly perhaps for the very first time.

"Why yes, I will, Marc Brown. This song is my jam."

EPILOGUE

IT TOOK CHRIS TWO FULL DAYS TO REACH OUT TO ME AFTER Lisa's rogue final broadcast. The ratings were in, and he wanted to speak before I was due back at work the following week. His message was stern, brief, and to the point. I couldn't read much into it, and I noticed that Doug Reynolds wasn't part of the communication.

We agreed to do a video call to save me the trip back into the office, which I figured couldn't be good. I still asked Alexis to come over to watch Evie for a few so that I could focus on the call without distraction.

I adjusted my computer several times, settling it finally on my kitchen island, with a backdrop into my living room. The sunlight hit perfectly for the camera. I hoped he wouldn't notice my repeat of the red cardigan he'd last seen me in. I made it a point to place it over a subtle white sleeveless silk top, which I hoped would remain stain-free long enough to make its appearance in front of him.

When I logged in to the meeting, on the screen in front of me was Chris, in his usual gray office. I tried to imagine on what stack of paper he chose to place the laptop. He looked a little less pasty, less tense, but still his frenetic energy translated even through the virtual meeting room.

"Tabby," he said. "Thanks for taking the time to meet today."

I returned the greeting, waiting nervously for what he'd say next, and where the conversation would head.

"As I said, I wanted to talk to you about . . . your performance a few days ago. I'm absolutely sure you know that we cannot support or condone the continued unsanctioned segments. It's not how the news works. That's for a different format—"

"Chris," I interrupted, slightly panicked. "I had nothing to do with Lisa's decision. I'm sure she told—"

"She told me, yes," Chris said, and continued. "And as I was saying, we just don't think the news is the right place for your ideas."

Right then, my mouth dropped open and after a sharp inhale, I stopped breathing. The screen in front of me started to blur and I had to blink to regain my composure. I *would not* cry.

"But, but what about the ratings?" I asked, after quickly recovering. "My segments have been top rated. I mean, what happened with the broadcast?" Visions of Scott Stone laughing came to mind. I could only imagine his glee in finding out I was fired. But I wouldn't be. Not without a fight. "Chris," I said forcefully, "you were the one who told me to fight for my perspective. That it was my responsibility to make my voice heard. And with no support from you. Now you want to penalize me for it?"

"I wouldn't call it penalize, Tabby. Far from it," Chris said, a look of confusion crossing his face.

"But you're letting me go," I said. Could they even do that? Wasn't it still my maternity leave? I guess technically what I did was insubordination. They had the right.

"Letting you go?" Chris said, looking puzzled. He started to speak, but a new square appeared on the screen, connecting to audio. It was Doug Reynolds. "Ah, here's Doug. He got pulled into something last minute, and I thought he wouldn't be able to join."

Doug Reynolds? I thought. *To fire me? Who's joining next? HR?*

"There she is!" Doug bellowed. His backdrop seemed to be another part of his expansive executive floor office.

"Doug, I was just telling Tabby our thinking. That the news wasn't the right fit."

"Ah yes, perfect. And so, Tabby, what do you say?"

"Doug," Chris said quickly. "We didn't get there yet."

"Get where?" I asked, now completely confused. I looked from Doug to Chris, from Chris to Doug.

"Tabby," Chris said, "we'd like you to start your own show."

My own show? I thought. Inside, my mind was screaming. *My own show?!*

"Yes, on KVTV," Doug added. "Our Sunday mornings are dragging. Your broadcast ratings were off the charts, across almost all demographics. Impromptu, our viewers love it. We need you to bring that same energy to this new platform. Your stories, your perspectives. Viewers want to hear from you."

I was speechless.

"So," Chris said, "we wanted to run this idea by you, to see if you're game to try something very new when you return. You'll have a chance to transition from your anchor slot, but we'd start ramping up right away to build your team. There's a lot to do to set up a show."

"So, it'd be my *own* show?" I managed to finally say.

"*The Tabby Walker Show*," Doug said excitedly. "Or whatever you want to call it."

Say yes, silly! My mind screamed at me. *Easiest yes of your life.* And it was. I could hear the music playing.

"Yes!" I said. "Yes, absolutely, yes."

The call with Chris and Doug wrapped and I was left in a state of stupor to slowly close the top of my laptop. I sat in stunned silence for a few minutes while my body and mind reconnected and the fog of excitement cleared. *Not fired*, my mind reminded me. My own show. My own show. My own show!

I threw my head back. "Aleeeeexxxxxiiiiisss!" I shouted at the top of my lungs. I wanted the sound to ring full and loud, though my entire house—the pure unbridled joy even worth a screaming baby. "Allleeeeexxxiiiss!" I called again.

I heard her footsteps scrambling toward me. She had Evie in her arms, who was to my surprise, seeming to enjoy the ruckus.

"Tab! What? Are you all right?" Alexis looked genuinely startled. My face squeezed so hard into a smile that my cheeks hurt.

"We did it! We did it! Girl, we did it!" I stomped my bare feet beneath me, slapping hard against the wood below in a dance of victory, and headed over to Alexis with my arms extended to her. She only had one hand free, but that was enough.

"We did it?" Her voice was a higher pitch than usual, and I could hear the excitement building. "You got it?"

"My own show, Lex, they're giving me my own show!" I squealed, and Alexis followed suit.

And together, with Evie, we bounced, up and down, up and down, my hand holding hers, just like when we were girls, squealing with delight.

ON A SUNNY SUNDAY, THE LAST BEFORE THE END OF MY MATER-nity leave, I sat outside with Alexis and Laila as we gathered to celebrate a major milestone—Laila had met the crowdfunding goal for her company, sparked by our "business shower," but really supported by the audience of readers she'd been cultivating since she started her entrepreneurial journey. We were celebrating that, and the unbelievable fact that I had my own show upcoming on KVTV.

"Come through community!" Laila lifted her champagne glass into the air, sloshing a bit that dripped down the side.

"Cheers to that!" I added, reaching for my own glass.

"Cheers to you, Tabby! And *The Tabby Walker Show*!" Alexis said excitedly.

"I mean, Tabby, I don't know how you did it, but epic, epic masterclass in bossing up," Laila added.

I beamed, inside and out. "Let's toast," I said. "I haven't had champagne in over a year. I'm ready to drink." I raised my glass, aiming for Laila's.

"Wait!" Alexis said quickly. "We all have to make sure our eyes meet."

Laila and I both gave her the corner eye glance and then looked back to each other.

"I'm serious!" Alexis screeched defensively. "I learned it from a client. If you don't meet eyes, it's seven years bad sex."

"Oh?" Laila and I both responded simultaneously.

"Well, do I need to pour myself another glass, or does it count if we didn't drink yet?" Laila asked.

"I'm not sure," Alexis replied.

"But do we want to take chances?" I offered, looking back and forth from one to the other.

"No!" we all managed to say in unison, with Laila shaking her head for emphasis and then leaning over to pour the contents of her glass on the grass patch closest to her seat.

"Laila, you'll kill the grass!" Alexis scolded. "I'm taking mine inside to pour it down the sink. Do we have more champagne?"

"Of course there's more champagne, Lex!" I called back.

Moments later, I heard the pop of a cork, followed shortly by Alexis returning to the doorway, a full glass in one hand and an open champagne bottle in the other, covered to the neck in condensation.

"Here we are! No bad sex!" Alexis proclaimed. "Oh, Tabby," Alexis held the champagne bottle at an angle as she filled my glass. "Did I tell you that Ms. Gretchen finally reached out to me about that house up the street? You think she's really serious about buying it?"

"I wouldn't put anything past Ms. Gretchen." I said, pausing the glass before my lips, remembering the rules of the toast. "She said she'd outgrown Crestmire and was ready for change."

"I guess there's no such thing as too old," Laila added.

"No such thing as too old, and no such thing as too late," I said wistfully.

"And there's no such thing as having too big of a vision for your life!" Alexis held up her glass and put down the bottle after the ring of bubbles had neared the rim of Laila's champagne flute.

"Then, to life!" I proclaimed, lifting my glass to my friends.

"To success!" Laila added, excitedly, but stopping short of touching mine. She widened her eyes to look at me and then at Alexis. "Am I doing it right?"

"Girl, it's not that extreme," Alexis giggled. "We just have to meet eyes." She looked casually from me to Laila and back again.

"I had to make sure, because nobody has time for all that—"

"To love!" Alexis cut her off, nearing her glass to mine.

"To love!" was echoed by me, and I heard Laila say it as well, just before the satisfactory clink of our glasses coming together, our eyes wide and open, connected to mark the past and the present, and all that awaited us in the future.

LATER THAT EVENING, I LEANED AT THE DOOR OF MY BEDROOM, observing a sleeping Evie, tucked into her bassinet. As I reached for the light, I whispered to her my last words of the night, what I'd learned from my mistakes.

"If at first you don't succeed, Ladybug, do the hard thing. Try, *always* try again."

ACKNOWLEDGMENTS

GRATITUDE IS TRULY THE MOST DELICIOUS CELEBRATION FOR the end of a journey.

Thank you to everyone who has helped along every crook of the path that brought this Black Girl's story to the world.

Thank you to each and every reader of this book and of this series. From the very moment that the first Black Girls book became a thought in my mind, it was you who motivated me to make it the best that it could be. That motivation powered me through classes, outlines, drafts, rewrites, edits, and braving reviews. Declaring a series at the end of the first book, *Black Girls Must Die Exhausted*, was an incredible challenge that, at first, I had no idea how to meet. Honestly, I was afraid that I couldn't do it and wouldn't be able to figure out how. But you stayed with me. You kept asking, *What happens next?* You never let up. And so I knew I couldn't let you down. I fought the doubt and all the obstacles, determined that I'd at least do my best to make each book somehow better than the one that came before it. This book, the finale, *Black Girls Must Have It All*, I wanted to be the payoff for everything that came before it—every word you read, every character you met, every new reader you brought into the fold of our worldwide community. I hope that you found this book deserving of your incredible support, encouragement, and trust.

Flowers, applause, appreciation, and utmost thanks to the amazingly supportive team at Harper Perennial. To my incredible editor, Sarah Reid, I thank you. We're a dynamic duo and it was a true honor craft this story with you. What no one (thankfully) will know is the true nature of that first draft of *Black Girls Must Have It All* I sent to you with the note, "I'm so sorry that you have to read this." But with your expert care, encouragement, and talented eye, look at what it became. When I was exhausted, you truly showed me the magic of editing and made me believe that this book could have it all. Because of you, now it does.

Doug Jones and Amy Baker, you are the best cheerleaders and I know there will be so much more to celebrate. Thank you to Heather Drucker, Megan Looney, Karintha Parker, Lisa Erickson, and each person past and present who in so many ways has been part of this book, and the exhaustive process of bringing it to readers so beautifully—Robin Bilardello, your epic covers! To each of the outstanding teams that have been not just a part of this book, but also this series, from sales, to copyediting to proofreading to distribution— thank you all so very, very much!

And thank you to the booksellers, retailers, and librarians who have continually supported me, this book, and the entire Black Girls series. Thank you for taking a chance on me, and I hope to always deliver something that will bring a smile of delight to your customers and community.

Thank you to my agent, Lucinda Halpern and the wonderful team at Lucinda Literary. You continue to believe and chase the impossible with me and I am forever grateful. Thank you also to Joe Veltre and the team at Gersh. You're making my film and television dreams come true, one deal at a time!

Also a thank you to Ashley Bernardi, Samantha McIntyre, and the team at Nardi Media, as well as Dawn Hardy, The Literary Lobbyist, for all of your early belief, hard work, and tremendous support all along this unlikely adventure.

Thank you to my friends and family for your support and encouragement in so many ways. Writing this book in particular was one of the most difficult things I've ever done. I wanted so badly for it to be great. And pursing greatness makes you dig deep and face the unknown. Thank you for making sure that I was never alone in the dark. Mom, you're always my most willing first reader; and Dad, always first in line to buy a copy. Danielle (and JP), thanks for being a sisterfriend and for teaching me everything I needed to know about being the best mother to a newborn. Bernice, my co-counsel and trusted reader with every book, just like the first, thank you. Kerry Ann, you very generously helped me create my forever forward editing ritual of something sweet—right on time! And last but not least thank you Jeff, for holding my hand and still letting me type. For changing the forecast when it looked like rain. I love you all.

And finally, thank you so very much to my ever-growing family in the literary world. It has been a tremendous pleasure to meet so many illustrious and unbelievably talented people in just a single lifetime. The generosity of spirit that I've encountered is contagious, and I commit to pass it forward. It's truly a privilege to do art with you.

ABOUT THE AUTHOR

JAYNE ALLEN IS THE PEN NAME OF JAUNIQUE SEALEY, A GRADU-
ate of Duke University and Harvard Law School. Drawing
from her unique experiences as an attorney and entrepreneur, she crafts transcultural stories that touch upon contemporary women's issues. She is the author of *Black Girls
Must Die Exhausted*, her first novel, which she calls "the epi-
taph of my thirties," and *Black Girls Must Be Magic*. A proud
native of Detroit, she lives in Los Angeles.

DON'T MISS THE FIRST TWO BOOKS IN JAYNE ALLEN'S CAPTIVATING TRILOGY

"Masterfully written and pitch perfect, *Black Girls Must Be Magic* is, simply, magic."
—GOOD MORNING AMERICA

"Smart, sophisticated. . . . Allen seamlessly blends sharp social commentary with a heartwarming story of friendship between irresistibly complex characters."
—EMILY HENRY,
New York Times bestselling author of *Beach Read*